Families and Friendships

Margaret Thornton was born in Blackpool and has lived there all her life. She is a qualified teacher but has retired in order to concentrate on her writing. She has two children and five grandchildren.

D0993982

Also by Margaret Thornton

Northern Lives

One Week in August
Love and Marriage
Pastures New

Yorkshire Sagas

Cast the First Stone
Families and Friendships
Old Friends, New Friends

MARGARET THORNTON

Families and Friendships

CANELO

First published in Great Britain in 2013 by Severn House Publishers Ltd

This edition published in the United Kingdom in 2021 by

Canelo
Unit 9, 5th Floor
Cargo Works, 1–2 Hatfields
London, SE1 9PG
United Kingdom

A CIP catalogue record for this book is available from the British Library.

Print ISBN 978 1 80032 720 7
Ebook ISBN 978 1 80032 390 2

Look for more great books at www.canelo.co

Printed and bound in Great Britain by Clays Ltd, Elcograf S.p.A.

1

One

Nearly all the pews were occupied on that Sunday morning in late February. All the members of the usual congregation were there, plus others who came less regularly, all of them eager to see the christening of baby Stella; Stella Jane Norwood, now nine weeks old, the daughter of the Reverend Simon Norwood, the rector of St Peters, Aberthwaite, and his wife, Fiona.

As Simon had reminded them all, the more correct name of the service was Holy Baptism, which involved more than the giving of a name to the child. It was a way of welcoming the baby into the family of the church, to become a member of the Christian community. Some families preferred a private ceremony, just a few friends and family members on a Sunday afternoon, and Simon was always ready to go along with their wishes. It was becoming more usual now, though, for the baptism to be an integral part of the morning worship. And that, of course, was what Simon and Fiona wanted for their own baby girl.

Simon had asked his friend from college days, the Reverend Timothy Marsden, to officiate at the baptism; he had also conducted their marriage service in the summer of 1965, almost two years ago. Simon wanted to share in the promises to care for the child's spiritual welfare along with his wife and the godparents and, indeed, all the members of the congregation who were invited to take part in the responses.

Simon turned his head to smile at his wife during the singing of the first hymn, 'Praise My Soul the King of Heaven'. She was not in her usual place in the choir stalls this morning – she was a soprano in the church choir – but there at his side. Just as he was not in his rector's stall but a part of the congregation along with his family and friends. His heart swelled with love for Fiona as it always did when he looked at her, more so than ever now as his eyes travelled to their precious baby girl in her arms.

His wife was smartly and fashionably dressed – as always – in a cherry red coat with a black velvet collar. The length of women's skirts was short, and getting shorter, as the sixties went on, but Fiona had kept within the bounds of propriety with her knee-length coat. She knew she was constantly watched by the eagle eyes of some of the more elderly, faintly disapproving, members of the congregation; the women of course, certainly not the men. A black pillbox hat was perched on top of her golden hair, cut short now in an elfin style, and black knee-high boots in patent leather completed her ensemble.

She smiled back at Simon as their eyes, simultaneously, lighted on their baby girl, now sleeping peacefully. Fiona would soon hand the baby over to Joan, one of the friends she had chosen to be a godmother. Joan would be the one to say the child's name, Stella Jane, as she handed her to the minister for the blessing. Her friend, Diane, would have the honour of carrying the baby out of the church at the end of the service. So that it would all be fair, Fiona thought to herself.

Diane was one of her oldest friends, from as long ago as their schooldays, although they had lost touch for a while.

Joan Tweedale was a much newer friend, a woman who had been very kind to her when she had married Simon and become a very inexperienced wife to the rector. It was Joan who had made the beautiful shawl that was wrapped around baby Stella. It was fitting, therefore, that she should be the first of the godmothers to hold the child. It was an exquisite shawl, crocheted in fine white wool in an intricate design of cobwebby lace. Fiona guessed her friend must have started working on it as soon as she had heard the news, last spring, of the forthcoming baby. Fiona had long admired Joan's talent for knitting, sewing, crocheting – all kinds of handiwork – and she had spent many happy times in Joan's handicraft shop on the High Street, choosing wool for her own, far more humble, attempts at knitting.

It was a lovely, memorable service. Stella only whimpered a little as the vicar made the sign of the cross on her forehead, opening her eyes in surprise at the sudden wetness on her head. She stared uncertainly at the strange person she had not seen before, then focused more surely at her mother standing by his side. Fiona was convinced that Stella, now two months old, was beginning to recognize both her and Simon, and she was sure that the baby gave a half-smile now as she looked at her.

When the godparents and parents and all the people present there had made the relevant promises to care for the spiritual well-being of the child, Timothy walked down the central aisle with the baby in his arms, with Fiona at the side of him. He was introducing baby Stella to the church folk – as Simon always did when he conducted a baptism – and making her a part of the congregation.

Fiona saw only happy faces smiling at both her and the baby. There were whispers of, 'Oh, isn't she lovely?',

'What a beautiful baby!', and 'God bless her!', and a few of the older ladies were wiping away a stray tear. She noticed that even Mrs Bayliss and Miss Thorpe, the two women who had been the most critical of her not that long ago, were now smiling along with the others.

When the service ended the little family, along with the Reverend Timothy, stood at the door bidding farewell to everyone. It seemed to Fiona that the criticism surrounding her several months ago was now a thing of the past. Even Ethel Bayliss, the wife of the church warden and a bigwig of the Mothers' Union, who had been her severest critic, smiled at the baby. 'She's beautiful,' she said. 'You must both be very proud of her.'

Ethel's henchman – or woman – Mabel Thorpe, a spinster of the parish, smiled and cooed at the child, adding, 'Yes, really beautiful, just like her mother.' Well, that was a turn up for the book! thought Fiona, smiling at the woman who had once tried to cause trouble for her. Babies, of course, usually brought out the best in people.

It was quite a small gathering at the rectory for the obligatory christening party. Fiona had wondered whether they should make more of an occasion of it by holding a get-together in the church hall for everyone who wished to attend, as the church folk had done to welcome her and Simon back from their honeymoon. But Simon had demurred, saying that it was just a family occasion. His parents were there, having stayed the night at the rectory after travelling from their home near Bradford the previous day. Simon's sister, Christine, and her husband, Tom, had set off from their farm in the far north of Yorkshire very early that morning, as had Diane and Andy and their children, whose home was in Leeds. Simon's friend, Timothy, and his wife, Susan, also lived in Leeds where Timothy was a vicar at a church in the suburbs. They would need to travel back soon after the luncheon party so that he could take the evening service at his own church.

Joan Tweedale and her husband, Henry, completed the company. Henry, who was the organist and choir master, and who, like his wife, had been a good friend to Simon and Fiona, had been asked to be the godfather to Stella.

Fiona, with the help of her mother-in-law, had prepared the buffet lunch – sandwiches, sausage rolls, cakes and trifle – early that morning, leaving the food covered in cling film to be all ready on their return from church. It was a happy gathering, and baby Stella slept peacefully after she had been fed and duly handed round from one person to another to be fussed and told time and again that she was a lovely little girl.

'And so good, isn't she?' said Diane in some surprise. 'Does she never cry?'

Simon laughed. 'You should hear her at six o'clock in the morning! We don't need an alarm clock, that's for sure.'

'At least she's sleeping through the night now,' said Fiona. 'And that's good, I believe, at only two months. I must admit I didn't like that two o'clock feed, and Simon couldn't help. He used to roll over and go back to sleep.'

'Never mind; he'll be able to help when she's on a bottle,' said Simon's mother. 'You must make sure he does his share, Fiona.'

'I've no complaints on that score,' replied Fiona. 'He's a dab hand at changing a nappy, aren't you, darling?'

'I am now,' Simon said, laughing, 'but it took me a while to get the hang of it.'

He was proving to be a wonderful father, and baby Stella had brought them even closer together as a couple, if that were possible. The previous year had been a traumatic one, but they had weathered the surprises and the storms which, looking back on them, had turned out to be minor ones.

Fiona would never have believed how much difference a tiny baby could make to the running of a household. Everything seemed to revolve around feeding times – every four hours at first – but Stella was sleeping through the night now, though waking early. Fiona knew she would not be able to carry on feeding her for much longer because her milk supply was dwindling, but that was not a topic for general discussion. As Simon's mother, Freda, had said, he would soon be able to help with the bottle feeds. She knew he would do that willingly, and she, Fiona, would be able to return to the tasks she had undertaken in the parish, to relieve Simon. She had, of course – although rather regrettably – resigned from her post at the local library. She was now a full-time mother and housewife and, at the age of thirty-two, she knew that it was time for her to enjoy the new experience.

Henry Tweedale lifted his glass of golden sherry to toast the baby's health and happiness and God's richest blessings, and then three of the womenfolk – Joan, Freda and Christine – offered to tackle the washing-up.

Fiona had been looking forward to a chat with her old friend, Diane. She saw her only every few months and there was always a lot of catching up to do.

'Goodness me! Seeing your little one has made me feel quite broody again,' said Diane as they settled down together on the window seat overlooking the rectory garden.

It was a dismal outlook on a cold February afternoon, but clumps of snowdrops were braving the winter and early shoots of daffodils and crocuses were already peeping through the soil between the bare branches of the rose bushes. Over the privet hedge the fourteenth-century church of St Peter, with its squat grey tower, was visible. Tall elm trees formed a background, and in the distance were the snow-capped hills rising from the North Yorkshire dale.

'Do you mean it?' asked Fiona in reply to her friend's remark. 'What does Andy say about that?'

'Oh, I haven't said anything to him,' smiled Diane. 'Actually, I've only just thought of it. Stella's such a cutey, isn't she? To be honest I think it's too late for us to start again. I've settled down to my teaching job, now that our two are almost secondary school age. I just felt myself reminiscing, that's all. I must remind myself that babies are jolly hard work. I seem to remember being relieved when they had both started school.'

'Stella is a good baby,' said Fiona. 'I know I'm very lucky, and Simon is such a devoted daddy. Sometimes I find it hard to believe that it's all turned out so well for me. I'm so happy Diane.' The joy shone in her eyes as she smiled at her friend.

'And it's no more than you deserve,' said Diane, taking hold of her hand for a moment. 'After all that you went through...' Fiona's face turned thoughtful for a moment, and she nodded a trifle sadly as she remembered the awful time that Diane was referring to.

'I still think about her, sometimes, you know,' she said quietly. 'Not so often now, not since I married Simon. But when Stella was born it brought it all back, just for a little while. But I knew it was all for the best at the time, though it nearly broke my heart, parting with her.'

Fiona was thinking of the baby girl she had given birth to in 1952 when she was seventeen years old, the baby she had been forced to give up for adoption. Diane had not known about it at the time because Fiona had been sent away to a home for unmarried mothers in Northumberland as soon as her parents had learnt of her pregnancy. They had then moved to another part of Leeds so that Fiona would not be near her former friends when she returned home. Consequently Fiona and Diane had lost touch for a few years, until Fiona's parents had been killed in a coach crash and Diane had sought her out again. Finding one another, though, they had discovered that their friendship was as firm as ever, and so it had continued. It was not until 1965, however, that Fiona had met and married Simon.

'You never knew what had happened to the baby?' asked Diane gently.

'No... it all happened very quickly after she was born. She was whisked away after I had held her for a little while... She was beautiful; dark-haired, not fair like me and like Stella is.'

'Yes... of course she would be,' replied Diane quietly.

'Do you know, Simon asked me, soon after Stella was born, if I'd like to try and find her again, that first baby? But I said no. I must admit that I've thought about it sometimes, over the years, but I know I can't do it. She may not even know she was adopted. Parents don't always tell them, although I think they're advised to do so nowadays. Even if she does know it could prove very unsettling. She is probably very happy with her adoptive parents. I've hoped and prayed so much that she is. I think

Simon suggested it because of Greg arriving so suddenly on the scene.'

'Yes, that must have been a tremendous shock,' said Diane, 'for all of you. How did Simon's family take it?'

'Very well,' said Fiona. 'Greg's a lovely young man, he really is. You can't help but like him. He comes to see us every few weeks.'

'I wondered if he might be here today,' said Diane. 'I'd like to meet him sometime.'

'I'm sure you will,' said Fiona. 'But Greg said himself that it wouldn't be fitting for him to be here today. He bought a lovely silver bracelet for Stella, though. Of course, he's her half-brother, isn't he?'

It had certainly been a shock when Gregory Challinor, aged twenty-two, had arrived in Aberthwaite the previous spring, looking for his real father, the Reverend Simon Norwood. Whilst Simon had been in the RAF during the Second World War, serving as a navigator in an aircrew, he had become friendly with a young woman called Yvonne who was in the WAAF. Gregory had been the result of that relationship, although Simon had been unaware of his existence, even of his conception, until the young man had appeared, firstly at the church – to get a first look at his father – and then on the doorstep of the rectory.

'There was never any doubt then in Simon's mind that he might be an impostor?' asked Diane.

'Oh no, not at all. Greg's the image of Simon. He has a look of his mother as well, of course.'

'Yes, you've actually met her now, haven't you?'

'Yes; Greg brought her here for a day, just before Christmas.'

'Wasn't it all rather embarrassing?' asked Diane.

'No, not really. I think Yvonne felt a bit uneasy at first, meeting Simon again after so long. And so did I, to be honest, meeting her. But Yvonne's a very likeable person, and she's so sensible and matter-of-fact. I should imagine she was always a very practical young woman. She disappeared off the scene, you know, when she discovered she was pregnant. It wasn't a "one night stand" sort of thing. She and Simon were getting very fond of one another, but she must have thought it was best to do what she did. The war was at its height, and, from what I gather, she thought it wouldn't be fair on Simon. She knew he was a decent young man and he would have stood by her. But he didn't get the chance.'

'It all worked out well for her, though, didn't it?'

'Yes; she married a man who was a doctor, rather older than herself. They had two more children, but he always regarded Gregory as his son, and Greg still refers to him as his father, which is only right. He died a few years ago, and that was when Greg found out the truth and decided to find Simon. Fortunately they get on like a house on fire, Simon and Greg. They're more like brothers or friends, really, rather than father and son. And Yvonne's friendly with a man she works with now... so all has ended happily.'

'It's strange, isn't it, that the same thing should have happened to you and to Simon? That Stella is... well, she's really the second child for both of you, isn't she?'

'Yes... and you could say that Greg turning up when he did was very fortunate for me. Excellent timing as it happened, because Simon's story took the heat off me for a while. Well, for good, I should say. The folk in the congregation seem to have accepted me as I am now, warts and all! Simon told them all about Greg turning up and who he was, which I thought was very brave of him. But he wanted them to know the truth before the gossip-mongers started up again, like they did with me.'

'They all seem to be very supportive of you and Simon, from what I could see of them this morning,' said Diane. 'I'm sure you have lots of friends in the congregation as well as Joan, don't you? She's rather older than us, I gather?'

'Yes, Joan and Henry are in their late forties. Joan has been a real friend to me. She was the one who stepped in and read the riot act, so to speak, when the gossip started about me. It soon stopped, I'm glad to say. And as I've told you, Greg arriving when he did gave them something else to talk about!'

Certain members of the church, mainly the older women, who should have known better, had tried to start a smear campaign, ostracizing Fiona for a while when it was discovered that the baby she was expecting was not her first child. But Simon's revelation, coming hard on the heels of the first one, had rather taken the wind out of their sails. Simon was very quickly forgiven for his misdemeanour. He had always been a popular rector ever since he had come to the parish some seven or eight years previously.

'You're happy here, in Aberthwaite, aren't you?' said Diane. 'You must have found it a great change from the grime and smoke of Leeds. We've noticed the difference in the air. It's so fresh and clean, and the people all seem very friendly.'

'Yes, so they are, on the whole. It's mainly a farming community, and a market town, of course, that has developed over the years. There's a market twice a week in the town square, and it's a real gathering of the clans. I enjoy going there to do most of my shopping. But you're always regarded as an outsider if you weren't born and bred here. I got to know a lot of people, though, when I worked in the library.'

'And now you're the rector's wife!' said Diane. 'Goodness! Who'd have thought it? D'you remember the Reverend Cruikshank? Your Simon's a far cry from him, isn't he?'

'I should certainly hope so!' Fiona gave a mock shudder, remembering the strait-laced and judgemental vicar at the church they had attended in Leeds. 'Don't remind me!... D'you still go to St Luke's?' she asked.

'Yes, but it's very different now. Old Cruikshank left years ago, and the new vicar is much easier to get on with. He's more like your Simon. He really tries to understand everyone. There are none of those 'holier than thou' cliques like we used to have. We had some good times, though, didn't we, despite old Cruikshank?'

'Yes... so we did.' Fiona was thoughtful for a moment before saying, a trifle hesitantly, 'Do you still hear from Dave?'

'We still get a Christmas card from them every year,' replied Diane. 'And Andy gets an occasional letter. Very occasional! Blokes aren't much good at letter writing, are they? But yes... we keep in touch. That doesn't worry you, does it?'

'No, why should it? Dave and Andy were good friends, weren't they? Just like you and me. And he's far enough away. Philadelphia, isn't it?'

'Yes, that's right. They came over here two years ago, Dave and Patsy and the two children, and they called to see us. Patsy's a very nice girl — well, woman, I suppose I should say now. She's a real Yankee Doodle, of course; very friendly and bubbly. Dave said he still misses Yorkshire. I don't suppose he would have gone over there except for his parents emigrating. And he managed to get a job there when he left university; he's an industrial chemist. But I think you know all that, don't you?'

'Yes, I remember. I'm glad he's happy. Does he… did he ever ask about me?'

'Yes… He was very concerned when you disappeared off the scene; we all were. So I let him know when you and I met up again. I thought it was only right. He doesn't know about… well, about the baby. There would be no point. As far as he knows you were ill, and then you had a sort of breakdown and went to relatives up north to recuperate.'

'And that's more or less the truth of it,' said Fiona, 'apart from one small detail! But as you say, it's best if he never knows about it.' She sighed. 'He was a nice lad, though, wasn't he?'

And somewhere, possibly not too far away, there was a girl of fourteen – nearly fifteen – with the same dark hair and, maybe, the same winning smile.

Two

Debbie Hargreaves had known from an early age that she was adopted. The word Vera had used, however, was 'chosen'. When the little girl was four years old, just before she started school, Vera decided she should tell her the truth in case she might hear about it from someone else. It was more or less common knowledge in their neighbourhood that Vera and Stanley Hargreaves had been married for several years, longing for a child that never appeared, before they decided to adopt a baby girl. Not that Vera really thought any of her friends would be so indiscreet as to say anything to Debbie, but it was better to be safe than sorry.

Vera told her one night after she had read her a bedtime story – the one about the gingerbread man was the current favourite – that she had a true story to tell her. The child listened attentively, her brown eyes wide with curiosity, as Vera told her how she and Daddy had gone to a big house in the country to choose a baby girl.

'We had waited a long time, you see, Debbie,' she said, 'and we'd asked God to send us a baby of our own but… well, it didn't happen.'

'Why not?' asked the little girl. 'Why didn't God do what you wanted? Our teacher told us at Sunday school that if you want something very badly, and you asked God about it, then he'll answer you.'

'But God sometimes says no,' replied Vera. 'He doesn't always say yes, because he knows what's best for us, you see. And I think he wanted us to be your mummy and daddy.' It was a very simplistic way of putting it. Vera wasn't altogether sure that she believed it, but it seemed to satisfy the child. Debbie nodded seriously as though she understood. Vera thought at times that she was wise beyond her years.

'Anyway, Daddy and I went to this big house,' she continued. 'Your grandad took us in his car because it was quite a long way. And we went into a room where there were some cots with babies in them, very tiny babies.'

'And one of them was me!' said Debbie excitedly. 'Was it, Mummy?'

'Yes, it was. The other two babies were boys. But Daddy and I thought we'd like a little girl. And there you were, fast asleep. And on the pillow at the side of you was a little pink teddy bear.'

'Rosie!' cried Debbie. 'It was Rosie, wasn't it?' She pointed to the teddy bear that sat on a shelf with her collection of toys: a floppy-eared rabbit, a panda, and a baby doll. Her constant companion, a rather shabby bear called Joey was in the bed beside her where he always was at night. But Debbie had always seemed to understand that the little pink bear was a bit special, not really to be played with but given her own place on the shelf where she wouldn't get too dirty. Vera had told her that the little bear had been given to her when she was born, a sort of christening present, and that she must take great care of it.

Now Vera told her what she believed to be true. 'You see, darling, the lady whose baby you were at first couldn't keep you. She wasn't able to look after you, and so she decided that you should go to another mummy and daddy who would be able to look after you much better. And I think that the little teddy that you call Rosie was a special present from her, because I'm sure she really loved you very much.'

'But you're my mummy and daddy now, aren't you?' asked the child.

'Yes, of course we are. And we love you very much.'

'And what happened to the lady?' Debbie always wanted to know the ins and outs of everything. 'Didn't she want to see me again?'

'I'm sure she thought about you a lot,' said Vera, 'but she knew you'd be happy with us and that we'd take good care of you. She must have been very sad to lose you, but I'm sure she's happy again now. Maybe she has another little boy or girl now. But we've got you, haven't we? You were a very special baby, and now you're our own special little girl.'

'I think that's a very nice story, Mummy,' said Debbie, in a matter-of-fact way. 'And I hope the lady is happy now.'

Vera's eyes misted over a little as she kissed Debbie's cheek and tucked her up in bed. 'Goodnight, darling,' she said. 'Sleep tight, and God bless.'

'Goodnight, Mummy,' she answered.

Vera was sure in her mind that Debbie would not worry about what she had been told. She was a very practical little miss sometimes. She had never been a clinging sort of child or one who cried very readily. She was affectionate and lovable to a degree, but Vera guessed she might not be over sentimental when she grew up. Already she was developing a mind of her own. Vera's mother said she was a 'right little madam'.

She was well-loved, though, by all of them: by Vera and Stanley, Vera's parents, and her brother and sister and their families. She had brought a lot of joy into their lives.

Stanley and Vera's home, since 1950, had been in the little town of Whitesands Bay, on the Northumberland coast, not far from the city of Newcastle. The skyline of Northumberland was dominated by the symbols of the coal, iron and steel, and shipbuilding industries – the winding gear, slag heaps and the tall factory chimneys – that had made the region an important centre of the industrial revolution. But the landscape was predominantly rural, and within sight of the collieries with their rows of miners' houses there was green pastureland and pleasant farms and villages. Parts of the coastline were beautiful, with long sandy beaches and rocky cliffs around which the seaside resorts had developed. Whitesands Bay was such a one; a pleasant place to live, the nearest colliery being several miles away.

Many of the lads who had attended school with Stanley had become coal miners, or had gone to work in industry or at the docks. But Stanley's parents, Bill and Dora, had not wanted their son to go down the mine. Bill was a miner and suffered every so often with bronchitis, until he died in his early sixties with emphysema, soon after the end of the Second World War.

Bill and Dora had been blessed with only the one child, Stanley, and they had been anxious to do the very best they could for him. They lived in a mining village in a two-up, two-down cottage in a row that opened on to the street. At the rear, however, there was a small piece of land, communal to the row of cottages, and Bill loved to work on his plot when he was not too weary after his shift at the colliery. He grew vegetables – potatoes, carrots, cabbages, onions, lettuces – as much as the small plot would allow; and even managed to grow flowers in tubs – marigolds, Sweet Williams and night-scented stock – grown from seeds. Stanley enjoyed helping his father in what they liked to call their garden, although it was hardly worthy of the name. It was soon clear that Stanley had a natural bent for working with the soil, and his parents agreed that when he left school he should, ideally, work in the open air instead of down the mine.

Stanley and his father sometimes cycled out into the surrounding countryside on a Sunday afternoon, on a pair of rusty ramshackle old bicycles. There was hardly any traffic on the roads, especially on the country lanes, and they looked forward to their brief excursions into the green and pleasant farmlands, not all that far from the soot and grime of their own cobblestoned street.

There was one farm they passed that was more of an arable farm, concentrating on growing crops rather than rearing livestock. They kept a pig, and hens and a cockerel. Some of the hens were fattened for sale at Christmas time, and they also sold their own new-laid eggs. Bill and Stanley sometimes called at the farmhouse and bought a half-dozen eggs, and so they got to know the farmer and his wife quite well.

The land was cultivated for the growing of potatoes, sugar beet, Brussels sprouts and other kinds of vegetables in their season. There was also a small orchard with apple and pear trees, and greenhouses where they grew tomatoes and cucumbers and flowers for sale, mainly chrysanthemums and dahlias. The farmer, Alec Pritchard, employed only a few full-time workers, but several more on a temporary basis when help was needed with the potato harvest or for picking the Brussels sprouts for the

Christmas market. But some were permanent; and so it happened, fortuitously, that when Stanley was fourteen years old and ready to leave school, a vacancy occurred at the farm. One of the farm hands was getting married and moving away from the area. Alec had known Stanley for a couple of years and realized how much he loved the land and the open air. When he offered him a job at the farm Stanley and his parents were overjoyed at the turn of events.

He started his employment at the farm in 1929, and continued working there for eleven years until, in 1940, he was called up for war service. By this time he had married Vera, the girl he had been courting since their schooldays. He did not serve overseas, neither at the start of the war, which culminated in the evacuation from Dunkirk, or later in the D–Day landings. He spent his time at a camp in the north of England, not far from his home, by which time he had been promoted to the rank of sergeant. In some ways he felt cheated, always conscious that he could not say, in honesty, that he had 'done his bit'. All the same, he hoped he had done a worthwhile job in charge of the supply depot, and he was delighted to resume his married life with Vera. They were hoping that very soon they might be blessed with a child.

In 1950, when they had been married for fourteen years, they both knew that they were ready for a change of scene. They had managed to scrape enough money together soon after their marriage to buy – or at least to secure a mortgage – on a little cottage not far from the mining village where they had been brought up. It was quite near to the farm where Stanley was still employed. He was by now the second–in–command there, virtually Alec's right-hand man. Vera's earnings as a shop assistant –

she had worked in the general store in the village for many years – had helped with their finances. They had always been thrifty, and they felt it was time for them to make a move. And maybe, in a new environment, the child that they both longed for might appear at last.

Vera fancied a complete change. As a child she had loved the little town, Whitesands Bay, where her parents had taken her and her brother and sister for occasional visits, and she knew she would love to live there, and bring up the child they hoped to have in the clean fresh air of the seaside. Stanley was willing to go along with her idea, provided he could find a job there. He was experienced only in working on the land, and having worked in the open air for so long would not want to have an indoor job.

Luck was with them. Stanley applied for, and was offered a job in the parks department of the seaside town, helping to tend the flower beds and rock gardens that were a feature of the promenade, and the colourful displays at the roundabouts in the town. There was also a small park on the outskirts, at the very end of the promenade. They found a house that suited them and which they could afford; a two-bedroomed terraced house with a small paved area at the front, but with enough land at the rear to be cultivated as a garden, and even enough room for a small greenhouse.

And so it was there, in the May of 1952, where they brought their newly adopted baby daughter. They christened her Deborah Mary – the Mary after Vera's mother – but she was always known as Debbie.

Three

Debbie had been born in Burnside House, a home where unmarried girls could stay for a few months before the birth of their babies, the children usually being given up for adoption. It was quite a pleasant place, all things considered; a large house in its own grounds in the Northumbrian countryside, midway between Newcastle upon Tyne and the market town of Hexham. It had once belonged to a wealthy family, then had been taken over by the nearby Methodist churches.

Vera and Stanley Hargreaves had been friendly with one of the auxiliary helpers there, a young woman named Claire Wagstaff. She was a near neighbour of theirs in the village where they had spent the first years of their married life, and they still kept in touch when they moved to Whitesands Bay which was not all that far away. When the longed for baby did not arrive and they had decided that they would like to adopt a child they approached Claire to see if it was possible for her to help them. She agreed that she would do what she could, and would put in a good word for them. The adoption was carried out legally through an accredited society; but it helped that Claire, with the agreement of the superintendent of the home, had recommended the couple as being an ideal choice for parents.

Claire, only thirty years old at the time, was nearer in age to the girls at the home than were some of the staff members. She sympathized with them and tried to understand their problems, although the nurses and helpers were warned not to get too friendly with the girls, especially with any one more than the others. Claire had, however, formed an affinity with Fiona Dalton who arrived at the home in the January of 1952. She understood that Fiona had been staying with an aunt and uncle for a while. Her parents, finding out about her pregnancy, had been shocked and ashamed of her and could not wait to banish her to relations in the far north of England, as far away from Leeds as possible. Fiona was such a nice girl, friendly and polite and so pretty. She often confided in Claire, who knew she would be heartbroken at parting from her baby. The girl had desperately longed to keep her daughter once she had set eyes on her, but with such intransigent parents it had been out of the question.

And so the baby girl was adopted by Vera and Stanley. Fiona had asked Claire if she knew where the baby would be going. She had answered evasively, but as truthfully as she could, that they were not allowed to say, not to anyone, especially not to the mother of the child, but that it was 'for the best'. And she did assure Fiona that the baby would have a very good, loving home. Neither did Claire ever tell her friends, Vera and Stanley, the name or the whereabouts of the girl who had given birth to Debbie, except to say that she was a lovely girl who had been well – albeit strictly – brought up.

Sometimes, however, there was a happy ending when the girl, usually at the eleventh hour, was allowed to keep her baby. That was what had happened to Ginny, the girl who had been Fiona's particular friend when they were in Burnside House. Ginny's parents were adamant that she should not marry Arthur Gregson, the father of her baby. Ginny, the eldest child of a large family, was one of the chief breadwinners in the household, and it was expected that she would go back to her job as a shop assistant and carry on helping with the family finances. Besides, it wasn't as if Arthur was her boyfriend and they had been courting. He was just a friend of long-standing who lived nearby; they had gone out, just the two of them, for a drink one night, and things had gone too far. Arthur, though, decided he wanted to do right by Ginny, and he was more than a little fond of her; they had been close friends for ages. Ginny didn't need much persuading to marry him, and he managed to wear down the resistance of her parents. Ginny's baby, a big healthy boy with his mother's ginger hair was born in April, 1952, just a month before Fiona gave birth to her little girl.

Claire Wagstaff and Ginny still saw one another occasionally as both families lived in the Tyneside area. So it was that Claire heard news of Fiona from time to time. She had been pleased to hear that she had got married, eventually, to a clergyman. And when she and Ginny met by chance one day, when they were both shopping in Newcastle, she was delighted to hear about Fiona's baby. The two women went to have a coffee together to catch up on the news.

'How lovely!' said Claire. 'And what a pretty name, Stella Jane. I'm really pleased for her. I still remember how distressed she was when she had to part with her baby. I felt sorry for her, going back to those sanctimonious parents of hers. I'm glad she managed to escape from them eventually.'

'Actually, they were both killed in a coach crash a few years later,' said Ginny. 'Fiona wrote to tell me. She was upset, of course, as she would be. I suppose they thought they were doing the right thing in making her give up the baby. That's what my parents wanted me to do until Arthur managed to get round them. But they think the world of Ryan now, and of Carl and Sharon.'

'You were lucky,' said Claire, 'that things worked out so well for you. Just as they have for Fiona, eventually. Do give her my love, won't you, when you write?'

'Yes, of course I will. Fiona went to live with her gran, you know, when her parents died. I rather think she was closer to her grandmother than to her parents. She looked after the old lady until she died. She lived till she was ninety, so that was why Fiona was rather older when she got married. She moved up to Aberthwaite for a complete change of scene, and then, of course, she met Simon. He's lovely, is Simon! Real dishy! I was quite amazed when we met him at the wedding. Not a bit like you imagine a vicar would be. So handsome...'

Claire laughed. 'Tall, dark and handsome, eh?'

'No, medium height, and brownish hair, I suppose,' replied Ginny. 'Certainly handsome, though, and a really nice friendly sort of chap. I'm looking forward to seeing baby Stella. Arthur says he'll take me soon; I'll get me mam to look after the kids. Fiona says Stella has fair hair, like she has. I 'spect she's a beautiful baby. Fiona was a real pretty girl, wasn't she? Well she still is, of course.'

'Her first baby was dark-haired,' said Claire thoughtfully. 'I suppose she must have taken after the father.'

'Yes, maybe she did,' said Ginny. 'I'd been left for a month when Fiona's baby was born. So I never saw her. I wonder what became of her?'

Claire shook her head as though she had no idea. 'She'll be in a good home, you can be sure of that,' she replied. 'We try to do the best that we can for all the babies.'

Claire Wagstaff knew how to keep mum. There was hardly anyone who knew that she had helped Vera and Stanley Hargreaves with the adoption of the baby they had called Deborah. And she would not dream of telling Ginny that she still saw the fifteen-year-old girl, who had been Fiona's dark-haired baby, from time to time. Ginny and Arthur lived in South Shields, and Whitesands Bay, where the Hargreaves family lived, was only a few miles away. It was possible that some day their paths might cross, but Claire knew she must keep her own counsel.

'Do you still work at Burnside House?' Ginny asked.

'Yes, I'm still there,' Claire said, smiling. 'Seventeen years I've been there, but I only do part-time. Our two are both married; I'm going to be a grandma soon! But I'd miss it now if I gave up, and it helps with the budget. What about you, Ginny? Do you work – go out to work, I mean?'

'Yes, I do. I'm a dinner lady, at the junior school where our Carl and Sharon are. Ryan's at grammar school now. You know, that new place they built, Kelder Bank, not all that far from where you work. He's in the fourth year now. Time flies, doesn't it? He'll be taking his O levels next year, or whatever they call 'em.'

'Oh, that's good,' replied Claire. 'I've heard good reports of Kelder Bank. He should do well there.'

Kelder Bank was a new grammar school, a co-ed one, that had been built a few years ago to take the children from the villages and small towns round about. Buses were laid on to ferry them to and fro. Claire knew about it because Debbie Hargreaves went there. She, too, was in the fourth year, as was Ginny's son, Ryan. Fiona's and Ginny's babies had been born within a month of each other. So it was hardly surprising that they should be pupils at the same school. All the same, Claire's heart had missed a beat on hearing that the two fifteen-year-olds might be acquainted. But she knew that she must not breathe a word about her discovery. It might well be that Fiona was still curious about what had happened to her baby, or that Debbie might want to find her birth mother – she knew that she was adopted – but they would certainly not find out from her. On the other hand it might be that Fiona had decided to move on with her life and not look back. She certainly seemed to be happy now, from what Ginny had said, with her husband and her new baby girl. And Claire knew that Debbie had a good home with Vera and Stanley. She could not have been adopted by a more devoted and loving couple. Claire hoped she was still as happy with them as she had been when she was a tiny girl. She knew that although she had played a part in the adoption, feeling at the time that it was the right thing to do, her involvement in the matter was now at an end.

–

Debbie had proved to be a good baby. Her parents suffered comparatively few sleepless nights, although Vera, who had waited so long for her own little child, felt that there was nothing she would not do for her. She had been such a precious gift to both of them.

As she grew into a toddler, then a little girl, there were very few problems with her. She had a sunny disposition, smiling readily at people she knew, and also at those who, at first, were strangers to her; she was by no means a timid child. But her sunny smile could turn just as quickly to a frown and sometimes a few crocodile tears if something displeased her, like the sun disappearing for a while behind a dark cloud. She certainly had a will of her own, a stubborn streak that Vera and Stanley knew they must try to curb.

She settled down well at her infant school, just a few minutes' walk from where they lived. She was a bright and intelligent child. She learnt to read very quickly, and her early teachers admitted that she was well ahead of many of her peer group. They did not put too much emphasis upon this, however. The policy of the infant school was to encourage all the children, the less able just as much as the cleverer ones, and not to indulge in too much competition between them. Debbie's parents, Vera more so than Stanley, had told her that she was a special little girl because she had been chosen by them, and Debbie was quick to inform her school friends about her 'specialness'.

'I'm special, because my mummy and daddy chose me to be their very own little girl,' she would say to anyone who would listen, including her first teacher, Miss Peterson. The young teacher warned Vera and Stanley that Debbie's tendency to boast should, perhaps, be gently curbed? She also pointed out herself to Debbie that all little boys and girls were special to their parents, so maybe she should say no more about it? Debbie was fond of Miss Peterson and looked up to her in the way that most children revered their first teacher; and so for a while she kept quiet.

When she was six years old, though, and had moved into a different class, she couldn't resist telling her tale to the children on her table, ones that she thought might not know about her. One of the boys did not want to know.

'There's nowt special about you, Debbie Hargreaves,' he retorted. 'You were adopted. That's what me mam told me. Your mam and dad couldn't have a baby of their own, so they had to have you. 'Cause your real mam didn't want you. And they're not your real mam and dad neither, not like mine are. So there!'

Debbie didn't reply to him. She retreated into a haughty silence because she didn't really know what to say. But she lost no time in telling her mother when she got home.

'Mummy, there's an awful boy in my class. He's called Gavin Ramsbottom, and he said I wasn't special, like you said I was. He said that you and Daddy 'dopted me, and that you had to have me 'cause my own mummy didn't want me. I don't like him, Mummy, and I shan't ever talk to him again. Anyway, he's got a silly name, hasn't he? The other kids laugh at it sometimes, an' he gets real mad. And it serves him right. But I am special, aren't I, Mummy? You did choose me when I was a baby, didn't you? And you are my real mummy and daddy, aren't you?'

'Of course we are, darling,' said Vera. 'I told you all about it a long time ago, didn't I? I told you how we went to that big house and chose you. The proper grown-up word is adoption. You were adopted, love, like that boy, Gavin, said. But he didn't need to be so rude to you. He doesn't understand all about it, you see.' Vera didn't know who this Gavin Ramsbottom was, but it was no secret in the neighbourhood where they lived that Debbie was an adopted child.

'Now, listen darling,' Vera continued. 'You mustn't keep telling everybody how special you are. Just stop it right now, because it isn't nice to show off, is it? And it isn't nice to laugh at people's names either, is it? Or about what they look like, or… or anything. Just try to be friends with all the boys and girls in your class, and don't show off any more. Do you understand, Debbie?'

Debbie said that she did, and they didn't mention the matter again.

–

Whitesands Bay was a pleasant place in which to grow up, away from the grime and the squalor that still existed in some of the towns and villages in the Tyneside area. It had grown from a small fishing village into a lively seaside resort frequented by the people from the immediate area for day trips, and by visitors from further afield for longer stays. There were long stretches of sandy beach, hotels and boarding houses, an amusement park with rides and sideshows, and facilities for those who wanted to play golf or tennis. Boats could be hired for a trip along the coast and around the small island close to the north end of the bay, with its lighthouse and rocky cliffs. The sea was safe for bathing, and anglers fished from the short pier.

Nearby Tynemouth was an interesting place to visit, to watch the busy river life and the shipyards, and to see the trawler fleets setting off or returning from their trips. Stanley sometimes remarked that there was no need for them to take holidays away from home as they had all that they needed on their doorstep. But Debbie knew that he was only joking because he enjoyed their holidays as much as she and her mother did. They usually went away for a week each year, to Whitby or Scarborough, and once to the Butlin's holiday camp at Filey.

As Debbie grew older she became less boastful. She was a sensible child and came to realize that she would make friends rather than enemies if she refrained from showing off and always insisting that she knew best. She learnt to curb her tongue, although her parents knew that she had a streak of self-will that might be harder to restrain when she became a teenager.

She progressed from the infant to the junior school, where there was more of a sense of competition between the pupils than there had been in the infant department. She maintained her place on the 'top table', and was usually the top of the class or very near to it in the twice yearly tests. Vera was secretly pleased when she did not always come first. It was good for her to realize that she was not 'the only pebble on the beach' as Stanley used to remark to her, jokingly.

In the way of most little girls she found a 'best friend'. Shirley Crompton lived in the same street, so the two of them walked to and from school together, and attended Sunday school and the Brownie pack. Apart from the odd falling out they got on well together. Vera was pleased about the friendship because the family was what she considered a respectable one. Mr Crompton was an electrician, well known in the area for his competent work and reasonable charges. Vera made it her business to meet Madge Crompton and the two women formed a casual friendship, drinking coffee at one another's houses and taking the occasional trip into town. Madge was about the same age as Vera, rather older than some of the other mothers, and she had two older children who attended the grammar school, Kelder Bank.

'I do hope our Shirley passes the eleven-plus,' Madge remarked to Vera one day as they sat in Madge's house enjoying their 'elevenses'. 'I want her to go to Kelder Bank, like our Graham and Alison. They're doing very well there. There's not much doubt about your Debbie passing, is there? Shirley's always telling me how Debbie came top in the spelling test, and she's good at sums, isn't she? Our Shirley struggles a bit with numbers, same as me. Her dad now, he's a wizard at adding up, with bills an' all that.'

'Yes, I suppose Debbie's bright enough,' replied Vera. 'Well, I know she's very clever actually, but Stan and I have learnt not to praise her too highly all the time. It doesn't do. We don't want her to get big-headed, although we'll be as pleased as Punch, of course, if she gets to the grammar school. Stan and I didn't get there… Anyway, your Shirley knows how to put our Debbie in her place, doesn't she? I've had a laugh to myself sometimes. She's met her match with Shirley alright!'

'They get on well though, don't they?' said Madge. 'It'll be nice if they can both go to the same school.'

Fortunately both women got their wish. When the results were announced in the spring of 1963, both Debbie and Shirley had passed the exam and would start at Kelder Bank School in the following September.

–

Learning came easily to Debbie, although she did not have quite such an easy ride at the new school. There were pupils there from all over the surrounding area, not just from Whitesands Bay, and she was not always the leading light in the monthly tests or the end of term exams. Vera and Stanley had high hopes for her that she would eventually go on to the sixth form and possibly on to college or university.

It had been apparent, though, from an early age, that Debbie's chief interest, like that of her father, was in

31

outdoor pursuits rather than book learning, especially in gardening. She did her homework, quickly, because she had to do it, and she enjoyed reading books, but she was never happier than when she was digging and planting, her hands covered in soil. Stanley had encouraged her from being a tiny girl, not knowing whether she would take to it or not. She had her own little plot in the back garden and her own space in the greenhouse. Stanley taught her how to nurture the seeds and then to plant the seedlings, when they were large enough, in the garden. As she grew older she spent her pocket money on packets of seeds from Woolworth's, brightly illustrated with pictures of marigolds, nasturtiums, candytuft, Virginia stock and Sweet Williams.

'You've got green fingers, Debbie,' Stanley told her when she was seven years old.

'No, I haven't, Daddy,' she replied, carefully inspecting her hands. 'They're pink, the same as everybody else's. When they're not mucky,' she added, wiping her soil covered hands on her working dungarees.

Stanley laughed. 'No, green fingers means that you've got a knack for it, for making things grow. And you don't mind getting your hands messy neither, like some fussy little girls do.'

'And I'm not frightened of worms neither,' she replied. 'They do a good job in the soil, don't they, Daddy?'

Her parents wondered if the phase would pass, as children's interests tended to do. But it didn't. Her favourite subject when she progressed to the grammar school was biology. She enjoyed dissecting frogs and worms, and viewing insects through a microscope, laughing at her friends who were squeamish.

It was Stanley who found her a Saturday job when she was fifteen at a garden centre on the outskirts of the town. It was owned by a friend of one of his work colleagues. Debbie was now in the fourth year at Kelder Bank, already studying the subjects she would take at O level when she was sixteen. Her parents agreed that it would be ideal for her as she was so interested in horticulture, and Debbie was delighted that she would be earning some money of her own. Also, it was an easy cycle ride away from her home.

She started there in the early summer of 1967, working only Saturdays at first and the occasional Sunday. When she was asked if she would like to work there for her summer holiday, for the whole month of August she was thrilled at the idea.

What Vera and Stanley did not know was that she had met someone there who made the prospect even more appealing.

Four

Fiona had never been happier than she was at this present time. She had a wonderful husband and an adorable baby girl. Stella was a happy and contented child and a few months after her birth Fiona was able to return to helping Simon with some of his work in the parish.

He had always insisted, however, from the time of their marriage that he did not want his wife to be regarded as what he termed an unpaid curate, which was the lot of many clergy wives. Fiona was a person in her own right – at that time she had worked as a librarian in the Aberthwaite branch – and, therefore, could not be at the beck and call of the parishioners. She had, however, of her own volition, taught a class of girls in the Sunday school, sung in the church choir, and had formed a 'Young Wives and Friends' group which met once a fortnight on a Tuesday evening in the rectory lounge.

She also lent a hand when required with the catering at church functions. Mrs Ethel Bayliss, who was in charge of all the catering arrangements and a bigwig in the Mothers' Union to boot, had resented Fiona at first, considering her to be a most unsuitable rector's wife; and she it was who had tried to cause trouble when it was discovered that the child that Fiona was expecting was not her first one. Mrs Bayliss now, though, was all sweetness and light compared with how she had acted in the past. Babies, it seemed, sometimes brought about a change in even the most difficult of folk, and now Fiona was made welcome in the kitchen.

'Wonders never cease!' she remarked to Simon, following the spring 'bring and buy' sale where she, Fiona, had been in charge of the book stall (with baby Stella sleeping peacefully in the nearby pram) and then had helped with the washing-up afterwards. 'Ethel treated me like her best friend, would you believe?'

'Yes, I suppose I might believe it,' replied Simon, a trifle unsurely. 'There's a good side to everyone, but sometimes it's a bit difficult to find it. Ethel has been more affable just lately. I dare say she regrets all the trouble she caused, or tried to cause. Most people prefer to make their own judgements, rather than listen to Ethel Bayliss. I shall still be wary of her, though. As I've mentioned before, I'm going to apply for a curate. The congregation has increased recently, and I'm hoping that the powers that be might consider that we're in line for one. But you can be sure that whoever we get there will be something wrong with him,' he laughed.

'Now, we don't know that, do we, Simon? He might turn out to be exactly Ethel's cup of tea. Like you were when you came here. She never found any fault with you, did she, until I came on the scene?'

'Oh, I don't know about that. We'd had our moments, Ethel and me, long before you arrived. She didn't like being ousted from her position of enrolling member of the MU, when Millicent took over.'

'Well, she's back at the helm now, alright,' said Fiona. 'I could never have done that job, not in a thousand years!'

'Of course you could,' replied Simon. 'I'm realizing more and more what a competent person you are, as well as being my lovely adorable wife.' He teasingly kissed the tip of her nose. 'But I agree that, under the circumstances, you're far better taking a lead with the younger women rather than the – what shall I say? – more mature women of the parish. Your Young Wives group is going from strength to strength, isn't it?'

'Yes, I believe it is,' agreed Fiona. 'We've had a few new members since the Riverside housing estate was built. We wondered if they might come once, and then decide it wasn't to their liking. But they seem to be enjoying the things we do, and they're staying the course, so far.'

'It's the same with the new families we've acquired from the estate. We've had a couple of weddings from there and three christenings, and that funeral last week, although that's not something to rejoice about. The families living there seem to be mainly the younger age group, so the funerals may be few and far between. It's quite likely, though, that a lot of the families will be the sort of folk who come to church only three times in their lives.'

'When they're born, when they get married and when they die,' added Fiona. 'And maybe at Christmas and Easter, and Harvest Festival, of course. We mustn't forget that.'

'Don't let's be cynical, though,' said Simon. 'I've always believed that the main thing is to make people welcome, whether they come to church every week, or only once in a while. And if they feel that they're made welcome they're far more likely to come again.'

'Yes; that was one of the first things I noticed when I started coming to St Peter's,' said Fiona. 'I was made so welcome… well, by most people, anyway. Apart from the fact that I was falling in love with the rector,' she added with a laugh. 'I felt that they were pleased to see me, and there was none of that "holier than thou" attitude, like there was at that church I went to in Leeds. The feeling that you're found wanting, instead of being accepted as you are. But I mustn't get started on that again. It's all water under the bridge, as they say. The thing is, Simon, you run a happy ship here with contented passengers, if you know what I mean.'

'And with you as my first mate, how can I go wrong?' he smiled. 'You're such an encouragement to me, darling, in all that I'm trying to do. And you've livened up the place no end, starting up the Young Wives group and bringing in the new families. That's all down to you, you know... I don't often mention her, but Millicent – God rest her soul – didn't have the same appeal as you have, especially to the younger women... to say nothing of the men! And that's what we need. New blood in the church, or else it will stagnate. There are so many other distractions now to lure people away from Sunday worship.'

'Yes, television for one thing,' said Fiona. 'Attendances drop at evening service, don't they, when there's a good play on the TV? Or *Sunday Night at the London Palladium*,' she added smiling.

'Yes. How can I compete with Bruce Forsyth?' laughed Simon. 'We've still got our stalwarts though who come rain or shine. The Sunday school attendances are dropping, too, despite the few new families we've got. I think that more families getting cars has a lot to do with it. I was talking to the superintendent, and we agreed that it might be time to think about changing afternoon Sunday school to a morning one.'

'So that families are free to go out in their cars on Sunday afternoon?' queried Fiona. 'Is that what you mean?'

'Yes, I suppose so. I know it seems like pandering to them, but we've got to move with the times. Better to change our routine than risk losing them altogether. I know it might cause a few problems at first. The Sunday school teachers would have to miss the morning service – well, part of it anyway. The idea would be for the children to stay in for the first part of the service, and then go out when it's time for the sermon.'

Fiona laughed. 'The teachers might be quite relieved… Only joking!' she added, as Simon gave her a mock-disapproving look. 'You know that I think you preach a great sermon, and so do all the people I talk to. They like your touch of humour and the way you keep abreast of the times.'

'That's good to know. But they're not likely to tell you that they think I'm hopeless, are they? All the same…' he sighed, 'I must admit I feel rather jaded at times when I'm preaching twice a day, apart from the times when we have a visiting preacher. That's another reason why I've decided to apply for a curate. Never mind, I'll soldier on and trust that somebody turns up.'

'Like Mr Micawber,' remarked Fiona.

'Quite so! But maybe the boss up there…' he pointed heavenwards, 'might listen and lend a hand.' He smiled. 'I must be seen to believe in what I tell others, mustn't I? To practise what I preach, as they say.'

'You always do, Simon,' said his wife seriously. 'No one could say otherwise.'

Fiona knew that Simon's trust in the God he served was strong and absolute. And since meeting him, then falling in love with him and marrying him, Fiona's faith, too, had become stronger. Her reliance on God had lapsed, and she had not attended church for several years, following the trauma of her first baby's birth. It had been a long time before she had plucked up the courage to tell Simon all the details of her past life. But it was all out in the open now, and it had made them even stronger as a couple.

Fiona had known from the start that Simon had been married previously to a woman called Millicent. She had wondered at first how she, Fiona, would fare in comparison with her. Not so much in Simon's eyes – she had come to realize, gradually, that it had not been an ideally happy marriage – but rather in the eyes of the older members of the congregation, especially the women of the Mothers' Union. Millicent had been the enrolling member for the group, which was the prerogative of the rector's – or vicar's – wife. As such she had ousted the formidable Ethel Bayliss from the post, and, apparently, this had caused some contention at first. Later, though, it seemed that Millicent could do no wrong; especially since she had died, suddenly, of a severe attack of flu, a couple of years before Simon had met his new wife.

Fiona had suffered by comparison with the older, far more sensible and sober Millicent. She had been deemed young and frivolous, and far too glamorous and fashionable for the wife of a clergyman. But she had proved to her critics that she had what it required, and more besides, to be an admirable rector's wife.

Simon's first marriage had been childless. Fiona had known how much he wanted a family, and they had both been thrilled when she became pregnant. It was not until then that Fiona had been forced to tell Simon about her first pregnancy and the birth of a baby daughter. Someone she had known in the home for unmarried mothers had seen her at the clinic, and so the news had leaked out to the folk of the parish. Simon had been a wonderful support to her at that time. She had realized then that she should never have had any fears about telling him.

It had seemed like a coincidence too great to be believed when, quite early in Fiona's pregnancy, Simon had opened the rectory door to a strange young man. Strange inasmuch as he was someone whom Simon didn't know, although in his appearance he was far from strange, in fact there seemed to be something familiar about him. Simon had recalled then that the young man had been in church the previous day, at both the morning and evening services, but had disappeared quickly without a word.

Simon was soon to realize why the young man looked familiar. It was as though he was seeing himself when young, although this man was dark-haired whereas Simon was fairish; and there was, inevitably, a look of someone else about him, someone that Simon had once known quite well. He had introduced himself, rather hesitantly and embarrassedly at first, as Simon's son – a son of whom, until that moment, he had no knowledge. There was no doubt in Simon's mind that he was speaking the truth. The story he told confirmed it all.

Simon had served in the Second World War as a navigator in an aircrew, planning routes to strategic sites in Germany and taking part in countless bombing raids. When the war was at its height he had met a young WAAF called Yvonne Stevenson. They had not intended their friendship to become too serious – Yvonne already had a boyfriend in the navy – but as the war raged around them they sought comfort with one another and the inevitable happened. Simon had suffered the loss of his skipper, the pilot of the aircrew who had died when the plane burst into flames on arriving back at the airfield, the rest of the crew having managed to escape.

Then Simon had been injured himself, although not too badly, during a further raid, and had been granted a period of leave. He knew by then that he was falling in love with Yvonne and intended to make his feelings clear to her. When he returned to the camp, however, he found that she had been posted to another airfield, and that was the last he saw of her.

And then, twenty-three years later, there was Gregory Challinor, a fine young man whom anyone would be pleased to call their son.

—

Greg, as he was always called had been shocked, and somewhat dismayed at first, when his mother had told him, soon after his father's death, that Keith Challinor was not, in fact, his real father. He and his younger brother and sister had always been treated in exactly the same way and there were very few people who knew the truth.

Yvonne had discovered that Simon was now a clergyman, the rector of a parish in Aberthwaite, North Yorkshire. It had taken a good deal of courage and heart searching for Greg — he had loved his father, Keith, so much — but eventually his curiosity had got the better of him and he had sought out the Reverend Simon Norwood.

It was a decision that he had never regretted. He and Simon had quickly formed a bond and their liking for one another had soon become affection. They were more like friends, though, or elder and younger brother, and Greg, by mutual agreement, always called his new-found father Simon.

Greg visited Aberthwaite every couple of months for a long weekend. He and Simon would walk on the fells surrounding the little town on the Saturday, maybe have a drink at a local pub in the evening, and then Greg attended the morning service as he usually did at his home in Manchester. He grew fond of Fiona, Simon's attractive young wife, too.

'Cor! She's quite something!' he had remarked to his few friends who knew his story, when he had first met her. 'What a smasher, eh? I didn't say that to Mum, although I think there might be a plan for them to meet quite soon. Fiona's a lovely lady, so kind and thoughtful, and she makes me really welcome.'

He watched baby Stella grow, too, from an adorable baby to a cute little toddler with her mother's golden hair and the silvery grey eyes of her father.

When he visited them in the June of 1968 Stella was eighteen months old, walking very ably and beginning to talk. He was pleased when the little girl recognized him, calling out 'Greg!' and smiling delightedly.

'Good to see you again, Greg,' said Simon, shaking his hand, then giving him a bear hug. Fiona kissed his cheek, telling him he was very welcome.

'Me, me!' cried Stella, opening her arms for Greg to lift her up.

'My goodness! You're a ton weight,' he exclaimed. 'What a big girl you are, Stella.'

'Don't wear nappies now,' said Stella, and they all laughed.

'Only at night,' added Fiona, 'but I don't think Greg wants to know about that. Yes, she's growing up fast.'

'And you're looking well, Fiona,' said Greg, putting the little girl down. 'Positively blooming.'

'There's a reason for that,' said Fiona, smiling at him and then at her husband. 'Stella's going to have a little baby brother... or sister, of course.'

'That's great news,' said Greg. 'Congratulations! So... when will it be?'

'December,' said Fiona. 'The same month as Stella's birthday. It's early days yet, so I've only told a few people. My friend, Joan, knows, and Simon's family. And my friend, Ginny, from Tyneside. She was the very first to know, apart from Simon. They came to see us a little while ago, and she guessed... as close friends do. Time enough for the gossip-mongers in the parish to find out,' she said, laughing. 'But I'm sure they'll be very pleased.'

'I have some news as well,' said Greg. 'Nothing as exciting as yours, but come outside and look at my new means of transport.'

'You've bought a car!' said Simon. 'Well, good for you. And learnt to drive as well, presumably?'

'Come and see,' said Greg with great pride. They had been standing in the hallway, and now they all trooped out into the front garden, There on the path was a little red mini car, all gleaming with newness, with a bright red petrol tank.

'Wizard! That's a smashing little job,' exclaimed Simon, reverting to his old RAF slang. 'When did you get that?'

'About a month ago,' said Greg.

'Brand new, is it?'

'Almost. Just one careful owner. And I passed my test, first time! I had several lessons before I bought the car. I'm getting quite proficient now.'

'Yes, they're great little cars,' said Simon. 'Not suitable for a family, of course, but ideal for a first car. I've often admired them.' The mini had become amazingly popular since it had been brought out a few years earlier, very handy for nipping around the town, and was within the budget of most people. 'You drive to work now, do you?'

'Yes, of course. I'm there in no time compared with the bus. But I'll have a bit further to travel before long. That's another piece of news. I'm moving into a flat of my own...'

He had arrived early on Friday evening, travelling from Manchester when he had finished work for the weekend. After Stella had been bathed and put to bed and they had enjoyed their evening meal, Greg told Simon and Fiona all his news.

'I've put a deposit down on a flat,' he said. 'Just a small one, but it's self-contained. One bedroom, a living room, bathroom and kitchen. It's a few miles from the city centre, on the way to Oldham. Possibly a bit further to travel, but I've got the car now.' At the moment Greg lived with his mother and younger brother and sister in Didsbury, a rather affluent district of Manchester where his father, Keith, had practised as a doctor.

'You've done very well for yourself,' observed Simon. 'I'm sure your mother must be very proud of you. It'll be a wrench for her, though, won't it, you leaving home, with your brother and sister both being away?' Greg's brother, Graham, was in his first year at Leeds University, and his sister, Grace, was due to finish her teacher training at Bingley College this summer.

'Mum'll be OK,' said Greg, smiling. 'I've told you before; she's a survivor. Actually, we rather think she'll be getting married soon. We're just waiting for her to tell us.

And we all like Brian very much so we'll be very pleased for her.'

'What about your flat then, Greg?' asked Simon. 'Are you buying it, dare I ask? Or renting?'

'I'm buying it!' said Greg, with a beaming smile. 'Well, with a mortgage, of course. But Dad left us all quite a tidy sum, so I've been able to put down a good deposit. And I've had a rise as well. The firm's on the up and up, I'm pleased to say.' Greg was a junior partner in a firm of solicitors in Manchester, where he had worked since leaving university three years previously.

'I shall look forward to entertaining you all when I've settled in,' he told them. 'Sorry I can't put you up, but I've got to start small, then maybe I'll progress to buying a house, some day.'

'You've done very well as it is,' Fiona told him. 'And what about... she's called Helen, isn't she?'

'Oh, I'm afraid Helen's history now,' said Greg, a trifle regretfully. 'It was good while it lasted, but we decided to call it a day. It was mutual and we parted on good terms. So... I'm footloose and fancy free at the moment.'

Fiona thought to herself that he would probably not stay that way for long. He was a personable young man with his father's – his real father's – winning ways; the same warm smile and thoughtful grey eyes. He was pleasantly handsome, too, which, coupled with his friendliness – albeit with a touch of modesty – would be bound to attract many a young woman.

'Simon and I are really pleased you came and found us,' she told him later, whilst Simon was having a long telephone conversation with a member of the church council, which often happened of an evening. 'Of course I've told you this before, haven't I?'

'The same goes for me,' replied Greg. 'You've become my second family. And I'm really pleased about your news, Fiona... You'll be wanting a boy this time, maybe?'

'Perhaps; I might...' she replied. 'One of each, it would be nice. But I don't really mind. You do know, don't you,' she added, 'that Stella was not my first child? I'm sure Simon will have mentioned it. I did say to him that he should tell you.'

'Yes, and so he did,' said Greg. 'A strange coincidence, wasn't it, the same thing happening to both you and Simon? It must have been a very traumatic time for you, having your baby, then losing her?'

'Yes, it was. It took a while for me to forget. Well, I've never really forgotten, of course, but it doesn't hurt any more.'

'And have you never been tempted to find out what happened to your little girl?' he asked.

'I was tempted at first, but not now. I still think about her sometimes. I'm sure to, I suppose, but not as much as I used to do.'

'There's always the chance that she might want to find out, like I did,' said Greg. 'That is if she knows she was adopted. She might decide to look for you. Have you thought about that?'

'Sometimes,' replied Fiona. 'It's a possibility. At the moment, though, I'm very contented. Amazingly happy, in fact...' She didn't really want anything to come along and disturb her comfortable and settled way of life.

Five

'Of course you can't leave school, Debbie,' said Vera, for the umpteenth time. 'Your teachers all say how well you're doing. You've taken — how many O levels is it? Eight? — and you'll no doubt pass them all...'

'It's nine, actually,' said Debbie, in the offhand manner that was starting to irritate her mother so much.

'Well, nine then,' snapped Vera. 'That's even better, isn't it? And it makes what you want to do even sillier. Leave school, indeed! Now, I don't want to hear any more about it. Neither does your dad... do you, Stanley?'

Stanley Hargreaves, from behind his newspaper, gave an audible sigh. 'No, Debbie. Your mum's right. We think you should make the most of the chance you've got to go into the sixth form. You're a clever lass, and we don't want you to waste all this... well, all this book learning and so on.'

'Yes, your daddy and me, we never had the chances you've got, to do all this schooling. We had to leave school when we were fourteen and get a job, like it or not.'

'Tell me the old, old story...' muttered Debbie under her breath, but Vera heard her.

'And don't be so cheeky, young lady! I don't know what's happening to you just lately. You never used to be like this.'

'Yes, just you watch what you're saying, pet,' said Stanley, a little more tolerantly. In a way he could understand how his daughter felt. All this sixth form business, then college or university was very strange to him. After all, Debbie was sixteen, and, as Vera said, they had been working for two years when they were that age. But things were different now, he supposed, and he was doing his best to support his wife in what she wanted for their precious daughter.

'And don't forget,' he added, 'your mum's going out to work now, so that we can have a few extras, and you never go short of anything.'

'Nobody asked her to,' retorted Debbie. 'She's doing it because she wants to, aren't you, Mum? And that's what I want to do; go out to work instead of going into the boring old sixth form. I've already got a job, and Mr Hill says I can work there full time in September if I want to. And I do want to. You know how good I am with plants, Dad. You've been telling me ever since I was a little girl that I've got green fingers – like you have. I thought you would understand. It's what I enjoy doing, more than anything.'

'And we don't want to stop you from doing it, Debbie,' said her mother. 'You could still carry on working at Sunnyhill, like you're doing now, at weekends and in the holidays, if you went back to school.'

Debbie had been helping out at the Sunnyhill garden centre on the outskirts of Whitesands Bay for almost a year now. Vera and Stanley had once called in to see her there, much to Debbie's annoyance. But Mr Hill, the owner, had made them very welcome and had given them glowing reports of how keen and helpful she was, and how she had an aptitude for the work in the garden and in the greenhouses. She would willingly do the more menial tasks, too, such as making the tea and running errands, which, as the junior member of staff, she was expected to do. Vera could have told him that it was more than she did at home, but she kept quiet.

Debbie, however, had not been pleased. 'Don't come in again,' she said to her parents. 'You made me feel a fool, checking up on me like that, as though I'm a little girl. It wasn't as if you really wanted to buy anything.'

'Yes, we did,' said Stanley. 'I bought some fertilizer for the tomatoes, and a new pair of shears. And I had a real good chat with Charlie Hill, all about greenfly and pest control. He's a real nice chap, and very knowledgeable. He gave me a good discount, too.'

'Yes, he is very nice,' agreed Debbie. 'But you know just as much as he does, Dad, about gardening and everything. You've been working in gardens longer than he has.'

'Aye, well; he's had the brass to set himself up in business, hasn't he? And jolly good luck to him. Your mum and me, we just wanted to see how you were getting on, that's all. But we won't come again if you don't want us to.'

'OK, then,' said Debbie, feeling relieved. 'Actually, Mr Hill says you can have a discount anytime you want to buy anything. If you tell me what you want I can bring it home for you.'

Vera had guessed that it might not be entirely the work that was the attraction at the garden centre. When she and Stanley had called there Debbie had been in one of the greenhouses, watering the tomato plants whilst deep in conversation with a blonde, tousle-haired lad. He looked a little older than Debbie, but Vera had summed him up straight away as a nice respectable sort of young man. That they liked one another was obvious from their smiling glances and laughter.

When Debbie had seen her parents she had almost dropped the watering can and the look on her face spoke volumes. 'Mum! Dad! What are you doing here?' she cried out.

The lad walked away with a smile saying, 'I'll leave you to your visitors, Debbie. See you later.'

'Mr Hill told us where to find you,' said her father. 'Sorry, love. We didn't think you'd mind us coming to have a look at you.'

'Yes, sorry if we're interrupting your work,' added her mother with a sly smile.

'It's not that...' Debbie shrugged. 'You just gave me a shock, that's all. I wasn't expecting you.'

'Yes, we can see that,' said Vera. 'He seems a nice lad,' she added nonchalantly, nodding towards the retreating figure at the end of the greenhouse. 'Who is he?'

'That's Kevin,' replied Debbie, a trifle grumpily. 'Kevin Hill. He's Mr Hill's son, actually.'

'Oh well, that's good,' said Vera. 'I'm glad you've got some friends here.'

That had been back in April. Now it was July, and Vera and Stanley had not gone to see Debbie again at her work, feeling it was better not to vex her unnecessarily. She was difficult to cope with as it was. They had, however, learnt a little more about Kevin Hill.

It was soon after their visit to the garden centre that Debbie had asked – she had, in fact, asked, rather than just telling them – if it was alright if she went to the pictures that night with Kevin. It was Saturday and she had been working all day. Because she had been polite and asked them nicely, they had agreed, and had not quizzed her overmuch. After all, she was sixteen; quite old enough to have a first boyfriend, they supposed. And he was the owner's son…

The two of them had gone out together a few times since then. Kevin had called at their house to pick her up and bring her home, and they found him to be a very courteous and pleasant sort of lad. Debbie had moaned a bit when Vera had said she must concentrate on her school work, with her O levels coming up very soon, and must always be in by half past ten.

But now the O levels were over, and they were all anxiously awaiting the results. School would finish in a week's time for the summer holiday. Debbie was getting more obstreperous with every day that passed, being more insolent than ever and defying the ten thirty deadline now that the exams had ended. Moreover she was adamant about this business of leaving school, and Vera and Stanley were wondering if it was all because of Kevin Hill. He seemed a nice enough lad, but was he, in fact, encouraging Debbie in her bid for freedom?

–

Debbie had been happy at Kelder Bank for the first four years, at least as happy as you could ever be at school. It was common practice to pretend that you disliked school, even though you might consider it to be really not too bad. She was able to cope quite easily with the work in most subjects. She did not find it hard to study or to do her homework. She did well in the end of term exams, although she was not 'top dog' as she had been at the junior school.

It was during her time in the fifth form, when they were studying like mad for their O levels that Debbie began to feel restless. She had started working at the weekends at Sunnyhill the two days in the week to which she looked forward immensely. Her school work had started to take second place, which worried her parents very much, especially her mother. Mum seemed to be continually on her back these days.

'Have you finished your homework, Debbie? You have? Well, you've been very quick about it, I must say!'

Or, 'When are you going to tidy your bedroom, Debbie? It's a disgrace! And you used to be so tidy. I could write my name in the dust on your mirror. And please remember to put your dirty clothes in the linen basket. Don't leave them all over the floor...'

Or, 'Half past ten, and not a minute later. You've got school tomorrow, and you know what you're like at getting up in a morning...'

That was after she had started going out with Kevin Hill. Seeing Kevin at weekends was, of course, one of the main reasons that she looked forward so much to Saturdays and Sundays. She had liked Kevin as soon as she met him, and dared to believe that he liked her as well. When he had first asked her to go to the pictures with him she had been over the moon with excitement. Nor had it been just an isolated occasion.

After their first visit to the cinema to see *Georgie Girl* they went on to see rather more daring films such as *Alfie* and *The Graduate*. Films that Debbie was not sure her mother would approve of; Mum was getting very stuffy and critical these days.

At least her parents seemed to like Kevin. The fact that he was the son of the boss was a point in his favour. Kevin called for her and took her home again when they had been out for the evening, kissing her goodnight at the gate. Discreetly at first, but then, as they grew friendlier, they lingered a little while longer in a secluded shop doorway or alleyway.

Whitesands Bay was not exactly a swinging sort of town, compared with many in what was being called the 'Swinging Sixties'. Liverpool seemed to be the place to be now. How Debbie would have loved to visit the Cavern where the famous Beatles had played. But it was out of the question up there in the wilds of Northumberland. There were not only the Beatles, but Cilla Black, the Searchers, and Gerry and the Pacemakers. Elsewhere there were the Rolling Stones, the Who, the Kinks, and the very amusing Herman's Hermits.

Debbie and her friends had to be content with listening to their records. She had a Dansette record player and saved up for the records of her favourite bands, the Beatles being the one she liked best of all.

No, Whitesands Bay could not compare with Liverpool or London, but a few discos had sprung up in the town, where records were played by disc jockeys, as opposed to the music of live bands. Debbie would have loved to dance the night away, like many of the local teenagers were able to do, those who did not have to get up for school the next morning. For work, maybe, where they would, no doubt, turn up bleary-eyed, which would be frowned on at school.

Kevin was a sensible lad, conscious that Debbie was two years younger than he was; and so he steered her away from pubs, or from the pills that could be bought – within the law – for not very much money at some discos and clubs.

Sometimes, during the summer, they just walked on the promenade or along the pier, stopping for a coffee or a milkshake at a coffee bar. Kevin also lived in Whitesands Bay, and he made sure that she stuck to her parents' deadline of ten thirty. When she told him that it had been extended to eleven thirty he believed her, not knowing anything about the rumpus it had caused at home. However, once her exams had finished Vera and Stanley, somewhat reluctantly, gave in to her demands. They liked Kevin and trusted him with their daughter.

He had not yet been invited to their home for 'Sunday tea' or some such occasion, which was a sign that the lad was the accepted boyfriend. Kevin, however, was quite content with the status quo. He liked Debbie as much as any girl he had known so far and was happy for things to carry on just as they were.

As for Debbie, she believed she was in love with Kevin. She knew he was her first boyfriend and all that, as her mother kept reminding her. 'You're only sixteen, Debbie, too young to be getting serious with a boy, especially while you're still at school…' and so on and so on. She didn't really know how seriously Kevin felt about her. He had not said he loved her or anything like that, but she had her hopes and dreams.

He was so different from the lads she knew at school. Older, of course, and more knowledgeable about all sorts of things. He, too, had attended Kelder Bank School, although Debbie had not known him then with him being a couple of years ahead of her. He had left when he was sixteen to work with his father and, as he was the only son, the business would no doubt be his one day. But that was a long time ahead, of course.

He had more money to splash around than the lads at school. He didn't own a car of his own, not yet, but he was saving up for one. On occasions he borrowed his father's Morris Oxford. On rare occasions that was; Mr Hill guarded his car like the crown jewels, but Debbie felt like a princess when they drove along the promenade of Whitesands Bay.

He was good-looking, in a funny sort of way with blondish hair that always looked untidy no matter what he did to it. He had strong features, with a rather longish nose, and a merry smile that showed a little gap in his front teeth. Debbie couldn't help boasting about him at school, because he was older and took her to places that the lads at school couldn't afford.

Some of the girls had boyfriends, mainly lads in the same form at Kelder Bank. Her best friend, Shirley Crompton, had been 'going out' with Ryan Gregson, a lad in their form, for a few months. At least that was what Shirley called it, although Debbie guessed that they didn't often go out anywhere. They just hung about together at school, at break times and dinner time. One problem was that he didn't live in Whitesands Bay as Shirley did, but in South Shields, several miles away, so they didn't meet all that often away from school. Shirley sometimes went to watch him play football on a Saturday. He was the goalie in the school team, being a tall, well-built lad, far more muscular than many of his peer group, and he had bright ginger hair.

Debbie had the feeling that he didn't like her very much, and so she decided that she wasn't too keen on him either.

'Your friend Debbie, she's a real little bossy boots, isn't she?' he had remarked to Shirley. 'And always showing off about something or other. I can't understand why you're so friendly with her. I must say, you hold your own with her though, don't you? She needs taking down a peg or two.'

'She's alright,' Shirley would reply. 'I like her. I've been friends with her ever since we were in the infant school, and we went to Brownies and Sunday school together as well. And our mums are friends. Yes, I know she shows off a bit. I must admit I'm sick of hearing about this marvellous Kevin. I've met him and he's quite nice and friendly; but I think she's doing most of the running, to be honest. I hope she doesn't get hurt.'

'Serve her right,' muttered Ryan.

'Oh, don't be like that, Ryan,' said Shirley. 'I feel a bit sorry for her, actually. She was forever boasting when she was in the junior school that she was special. She was adopted, you see, and her mother had told her she was a very special little girl.'

'Oh, I didn't realize that,' said Ryan.

'Well, no; she doesn't talk about it now, although I think it's pretty common knowledge round about where we live. Her parents are rather older; I should imagine they're turned fifty now. They're both very nice. I know Debbie gets cross because she thinks her mum's always on at her, but I don't suppose she's any worse than mine. I sometimes wonder, though, how she really feels about being adopted. I wonder how I would feel, if it were me…'

Six

It was when Debbie started at Kelder Bank School at the age of eleven that she began to think more about the fact that she was adopted. Near to the school, not much more than a mile away, there was a big house called Burnside House. She had discovered it was the place where girls went to stay if they were expecting a baby and were not married. Her mother had not told her very much about the 'facts of life', except about periods, and how it was nature's way of making sure you were ready for the time when you might have a baby. She had known, of course, that babies grew inside your tummy, but she had been somewhat confused about how it got there in the first place. And Mum didn't tell her about that; neither did she ask. The knowledge came to her gradually though, through confidential chats with her girlfriends, and by keeping her eyes and her ears open.

When she was twelve she asked her mother, 'Mum, you know that big house near to our school? Burnside House, it's called. Well, was that where I was born? You used to tell me that you went to a big house in the country because you wanted a baby girl. So... was that where you went?'

'Yes, that's right, Debbie,' her mother had replied. 'Burnside House, that's where we went, your daddy and me. I haven't set eyes on the place from that day to this.

It's sort of "off the beaten track", as they say, and so we've never needed to go past it. Why did you ask, Debbie, after all this time?'

'Oh, some girls at school were talking about that place. Linda knows somebody who's gone to stay there. And I said to Shirley, I bet that's where I was born.'

Her mother nodded, looking a little anxious, Debbie thought. 'Don't worry your head about it, pet,' she said.

'I'm not,' said Debbie. 'I just wondered, that's all.'

Then, a year or so later, she asked again. 'Mum, Mrs Wagstaff works at Burnside House, doesn't she?' Claire Wagstaff was a friend of her parents. Not a very close friend; not close enough, for instance, for Debbie to call her Aunty Claire, a courtesy title she had always used for some of her mother's closest friends. But she called at their house every now and again. Debbie found her very nice and friendly, and she had always shown an interest in her, Debbie, asking her about how she was going on at school and all that sort of thing. But it was only recently that the penny had dropped, so to speak, and she had discovered Claire's place of work.

'Yes, she does work there,' her mother replied, in answer to her question. Then, as she had said before, 'Why do you want to know, Debbie?'

'Because I've only just realized, that's why? Has she worked there for a long time?'

'Er... yes; for quite a few years.'

'So was she there when I was a baby?' Debbie persisted. 'When I was born, I mean. Is that how you got to know her?'

'Oh for goodness' sake! Questions, questions!' said her mother. 'Listen – I'll tell you about it, then perhaps you'll let it drop, will you? We knew Claire long before you were

58

born. She was a neighbour of ours when we lived in the village, before we moved here to Whitesands Bay. I told you how your daddy and I wanted a baby, and it didn't happen, so we decided to adopt a little girl. We knew that Claire worked at Burnside House, and we'd kept in touch with her after we moved, and so we asked her if she could perhaps help us, just a little bit. She put in a good word for us with the adoption society; it was very kind of her. And so... we adopted you, didn't we? Now, are you satisfied, Miss Nosy Parker?'

'Yes...' Debbie nodded thoughtfully. 'So Claire knew the lady; the lady whose baby I was?'

'Well, of course she did,' said her mother. 'That's obvious, isn't it? But I told you, didn't I, that she couldn't keep you? I know she loved you, but she had to let you go.'

'She was an unmarried mother then, wasn't she?' said Debbie. 'That's why girls go there, isn't it? Because they're having babies and they're not married?'

Her mother looked startled; no doubt, thought Debbie, because she had found out so much about having babies without it being talked about at home. She answered a bit sharply.

'Yes, she was having a baby and she wasn't married. That's what happens to girls, Deborah, when they don't think about what they're doing. Now, we're not going to say any more about it, alright?'

Debbie nodded. Mum never called her Deborah unless she was cross or upset about something. She hadn't meant to vex her mother. She was just curious about... well, everything.

'It's all right, love,' her mother said then, a little more gently. 'I don't mind you asking questions, and I suppose you're bound to think about it sometimes. Your daddy and I decided to be honest with you – about you being adopted – right from the start. You're still happy about it, aren't you, Debbie? You know how much we love you.'

'Of course I'm happy, Mum,' said Debbie. She smiled at her mother, then, on an impulse, kissed her cheek, something she didn't often do spontaneously.

'That's OK then,' said her mum, giving her a hug. 'Your daddy and me, we don't want you to worry about anything.'

Vera had had quite a shock when Debbie started asking questions, although she had guessed that she might do so as she got older. She seemed happy enough at first with the answers she had been given. Nothing more was said on the subject for ages, whilst Debbie continued contentedly enough at school. She seemed to enjoy her lessons, and did her homework without any trouble. She worked away at her own little plot in the garden and helped her father with his gardening as well. Shirley Crompton was still her best friend, at school and Sunday school, and in the Guides now, to which they had progressed from the Brownies.

Vera had thought it was a good idea when Stanley managed to get her a weekend job at the Sunnyhill garden centre. She clearly enjoyed it very much. It meant that she couldn't go to church now, on a Sunday morning, or to the teenage class on a Sunday afternoon. But that didn't worry Vera overmuch. She and Stanley didn't always go themselves, but they had tried to bring Debbie up in what they believed was the right way, and they trusted her to be a good, responsible girl.

It was inevitable, too, that she should eventually have a boyfriend. And Kevin Hill was a decent, well-brought-up sort of lad from a very respectable family, or so he seemed.

But there was no doubt that Debbie was becoming more difficult as the weeks and months went by. Vera worried about it, but Stanley rather less so. 'Teenagers all go through this stage,' he said, trying to console his wife. 'I've talked to the fellows at work, and they say their kids are all the same.'

'But she seems to be growing away from us,' said Vera. 'I know she was never a very clinging sort of child, but I feel sometimes that she can't be bothered with us at all. I do wonder, Stanley, if it's because she was adopted; whether she's thinking about... well, about finding her real mother.'

'You're her real mother,' Stanley replied. 'Don't be silly, Vera.'

'Yes, I know that, Stanley, and I've always tried to assure Debbie that we're her real parents now. But you know what I mean. She hasn't said anything, not since that time a couple of years ago when she was asking about Claire and all that. But she can be so difficult at times – well, a lot of the time now – and she's secretive, as well, as though there's something on her mind.'

'She'd be just the same if she were our own flesh and blood,' Stanley replied. 'You take it from me. It's just a phase she's going through. And I like young Kevin. She could have done a lot worse, I can tell you. Some of the young trainee lasses we're getting at work now – drinking, smoking, swearing, and goodness knows what else! I wouldn't be happy if she was friendly with one of them. I don't think Kevin's likely to lead her astray.'

'I do wonder, though, if he's encouraging her in this business of wanting to leave school. He left when he was sixteen, didn't he? And we had such high hopes for her, Stanley.'

'Aye, well maybe we're wrong to try and push her into something she doesn't want. I'd far rather she was happy, Vera pet. And you can see yourself that she's best at anything to do with gardening and growing things. Maybe Kevin's encouraged her in that way, and happen she could take it further. You can go to college for all sorts of things now, you know; agriculture, farming, gardening and all that.'

'Yes, maybe that might appeal to her,' said Vera thoughtfully. 'I've not heard her mention it, though. She just seems set on leaving school and working full time. Anyway, let's wait and see what sort of results she gets with these O levels.'

'Yes, that's all we can do at the moment,' said Stanley. 'Now, for goodness' sake, stop worrying!'

–

Debbie had asked questions about her birth mother and Burnside House, not because she was unhappy at home, but because she was just curious. She had always had an inquiring mind, wanting to know the ins and outs of everything. And once she knew she was satisfied then, for a while.

She knew she was lucky. She had a lovely mum and dad, and she knew she loved them very much, deep down. But she didn't tell them so, nor was she often openly affectionate with them. They were always there, steady and reliable… if a little bit old-fashioned. They were several years older than the parents of many of her friends.

She suspected she might even be what some people called 'spoilt', because she was an only child; indulged, that was, with regard to material things, but not with regard to behaviour. Her mum and dad would not stand for any nonsense, as they put it. She had to do as she was told and abide by what they said.

She never went short of anything and got most things that she asked for, within reason. And since her mother had started working part-time at a newly opened fancy goods shop on the road leading to Whitesands Bay, there had been rather more money to spend on a few luxuries, such as a fridge, a larger television set, and an automatic washing machine.

Debbie had a very nice bedroom, which was the envy of some of her friends who had to share with their sisters. It had been decorated – by her father – in the colours she had chosen; pale yellow, with one wall papered with a design of bold yellow and orange flowers; orange curtains to match and an orange candlewick bedspread. She had contemporary G-plan furniture, her record player and a shelf for her books, progressing from Enid Blyton and Noel Streatfield to Edna O'Brien, Kingsley Amis and Alan Sillitoe as she got older. Although she was always happier grubbing about in the garden, rather than sitting reading a book.

Her mother had allowed her to buy a minidress, and a miniskirt and tight sweater, although at school the skirts were regulation knee-length, sometimes rolled over a couple of times at the waistband, if they thought they could get away with it. Mum had also let her have her dark curly hair cut short, though she had needed a lot of persuading. 'Oh dear, Debbie! You'll lose all your lovely curls,' she had said. But even Mum had to admit it looked nice, styled with a fringe and back combed in what was called a 'bouffant' fashion.

Debbie was fifteen when she met Kevin Hill, and it was then that she began to realize that there was a life outside of home and school, exams and Guides and all that. Working at the garden centre and mixing with people who were older than herself gave her a taste for the wider world. It was then, also, that she started to think about how she had come to be in the world in the first place.

What about her mother? She knew that 'birth mother' was the correct term, as opposed to her adoptive mother. She had never thought of Vera like that, though – she was just Mum – until quite recently.

What about the girl – she must only have been a girl at the time – who had given birth to her? What had she been like? A wild, disobedient sort of girl who had 'got into trouble', as her mother would say? Or... had she been led astray and not known what she was doing?

And what about the lad – or man, maybe – her real father? Was he very young too, as she assumed her birth mother had been? Had he disappeared from the scene, or had the two of them got married later? The thoughts and images went round and round in her head, but she didn't tell anyone how she was feeling, not at first. Not even Shirley, her best friend, and certainly not her mum and dad. Neither did she tell Kevin, when she first met him, about her being adopted.

It was after she had known him a while and they started going out together that she had started to rebel against the strictures imposed by her mother: getting home by ten thirty, tidying her bedroom, not wearing too much lipstick because it looked common. And, above all, about studying hard at school – hadn't she always done so? – so that she could get good results in her O levels and go into the sixth form and then to university. What a complete waste of time that would be when she could go out to work and earn some money.

'I'm fed up with my mum nagging at me all the time,' she complained to Kevin as they walked along the prom one evening. It was just a few weeks before the exams. 'I'm working hard at school, like I always do, but she never shuts up about it. About going into the sixth form, and I've told her I don't want to. I want to leave school and work at Sunnyhill. Your dad said he'd take me on permanently, if that's what I want.'

'He suggested it, Debbie,' Kevin replied carefully, 'because he knows how you enjoy the work and what a hard worker you are. Not like some of the lazy louts we've had from time to time.' They stopped walking and leant against the railings, looking out at the sea that was fully in, lapping against the sea wall.

Kevin was not sure that his father had meant it seriously. He recalled that what he had actually said was something like, 'You're a grand little worker, Debbie. I'd like to employ you full time; I would that! But I know you've a long way to go with your studies. Don't forget about us though, will you, when you go off to college or wherever?'

'You're a bright girl,' Kevin told her now. 'You could do much more than work in a garden centre. You're far cleverer than me. That's why I left school when I was sixteen. I didn't want to carry on – my O levels were only so-so – and Mum and Dad said it would be best if I started work and learnt more about the business. Dad hopes I'll take it over some day.'

'Oh, don't you start!' snapped Debbie, rather put out. 'You're as bad as my mum. Dad's not so bad, actually. I think he understands how I feel…' It was then that she told him.

'I was adopted, you know. Vera and Stanley, they're not my real parents. I've always known about it and never minded. But just lately, since Mum's been getting on at me, I've started wondering…' She had never put her thoughts into words before. 'Wondering what it would have been like with my real mother.'

'Gosh! I never knew that, Debbie,' said Kevin. 'You look rather like your mum, actually – the same dark hair, and the way you speak and… well, you're just like her.'

'I suppose that's 'cause I've always been with her,' said Debbie. 'You pick up accents and speech patterns and all that.'

'I think your parents are great,' said Kevin. 'You've been lucky, haven't you, to get such a nice mum and dad?'

'You don't have to live with them,' muttered Debbie. 'No, like I said, Dad's OK most of the time. It's Mum…'

'But all mothers worry about their children, Debbie, especially about daughters. I remember my parents being the same with our Jennifer. I think she was glad to get married and move away. They're OK with me, though. Perhaps it's different with boys. But I suppose you can't help wondering… You don't mean that you would do something about it, do you? You wouldn't try to find your birth mother?'

'I don't know,' said Debbie. 'I've thought of it, I must admit, but I'm not sure how to go about it.'

'Then forget it,' said Kevin. 'You might be making a big mistake. And just think how your parents would feel; they'd be very upset, I'm sure. Just try to think how lucky you are.'

Debbie answered as though she had not heard his last remarks. 'I do know something,' she said. 'I was born in Burnside House; you know, that place for unmarried mothers, not far from our school. And I know a lady who works there, Claire Wagstaff she's called. She had quite a lot to do with my adoption. So I've got some facts, if I ever wanted to take it further.'

'Forget it,' said Kevin again. 'Count your blessings, Debbie.' He sounded as though he were her uncle or something! Kevin was so sensible and unadventurous at times. Then he leaned towards her and kissed her lovingly on the lips. 'Come on, let's go and have a coffee at Katy's Kitchen. I must make sure you're home by half past ten!'

She pulled a face at him, but the memory of that kiss lingered. She really did like him a lot.

Seven

'My mum's still nagging me about staying on at school,' Debbie complained to her friend, Shirley the following day. They had just finished their lunch and were sitting on the grass near to the tennis court, idly watching a couple of girls who were more energetically inclined having a friendly match. Shirley and Debbie enjoyed tennis, but were content just now to bask in the warmth of the midday sun. It was mid-May and unseasonably warm for the time of the year.

'She knows jolly well I want to leave and start working full time,' she went on. 'What's the point of sixth form and college and all that, when there's a job waiting for me?'

'But you could still carry on working there,' said Shirley, just as Debbie's mother had said. 'Don't you realize how lucky you are? You're dead brainy; you know very well you'll get good grades in everything. Not like me. I'll be lucky if I can scrape through with half a dozen passes. But I'm still going on to the sixth form, that's if I do alright. And not just because my parents want me to. I'm looking forward to it.'

'You can't be! Haven't you had enough of school? Oh, I see… I expect Ryan's going into the sixth, isn't he? That's why, isn't it?'

'No, it's not that at all,' retorted Shirley. 'He hasn't decided yet. Anyway what about you and Kevin. He's the big attraction at the garden centre, isn't he? Not the job.'

'No he isn't!' It was Debbie's turn now to be indignant, although she knew that what her friend had said was true in part. 'I love working there, and Mr Hill has asked me if I'd like to work there permanently.'

'You're so clever, though,' said Shirley, a trifle enviously. 'Everybody says so. You'd get into uni as easy as anything. I do wish you'd change your mind, Debbie. It'll be a lot more fun in the sixth form. You can just study the subjects you really want and drop the rest. Just think – no more maths or Latin! I know you'd probably do the science things, and I'd do the arts, but we'd still be together a lot of the time.'

Debbie might have been slightly tempted, but she wasn't going to admit it. 'I was telling Kevin last night,' she said now, 'about me being adopted. He didn't know, but then he wouldn't, would he?' She admitted then to Shirley, as she had to Kevin, 'I've started thinking about my real mother lately; my birth mother, I mean. It's weird, Shirl. I keep wondering what she's like, and where she lives and everything. I never used to bother, but I suppose it's because Mum's been getting on my nerves lately.'

Shirley looked shocked. 'You don't mean... you wouldn't try to find her, would you?'

Debbie wasn't sure that she meant what she said next, but she was fed up of people telling her what she should or should not do. 'I might,' she said. 'Yes... I think I might. I already know where I was born. I asked my mum and she had to tell me. It was in that place near here, Burnside House, where unmarried girls go. And I know the woman who had a lot to do with it, Claire Wagstaff. So it might be quite easy.'

'No; I don't think it would,' said Shirley. She shook her head emphatically. 'She probably lives miles and miles away. She might not even be in this country any more. Anyway, I don't think you should, Debbie. It might all go wrong, and your mum and dad would be ever so upset. They're so nice, your mum and dad.'

'What's up with you?' said Debbie. 'I haven't said I will; I just said I might. So keep your hair on... I might even think about going into the sixth form, who knows?' She gave her friend a playful push. 'Come on, don't get all stroppy with me.' In the distance they could hear a bell ringing. 'Gosh, it's half past one! Time we weren't here. Come on, Shirl...' They hurried along the path to the back door of the school.

Shirley was quiet and thoughtful. She had a lot on her mind, because she knew something that Debbie didn't know. But she had been sworn to secrecy.

–

It had been few weeks previously that Ginny Gregson had told her son, Ryan, that they were going away for the weekend. 'Just your dad and me,' she said. 'So we were wondering if you would look after Carl and Sharon for us? You're quite old enough to be left now, and I know you're sensible. I'll leave some food in the fridge and there are lots of tins in the cupboard, so you won't have much to do. Cook some sausages and beef burgers, and there's beans and spaghetti. And don't let them stay up till all hours; you know what they're like...'

70

'OK, Mum, OK,' Ryan answered, laughing. 'Don't fuss. 'Course I'll look after them. It'll be great, the house to ourselves and nobody nagging at us.'

'Less of your cheek!' said Ginny. She knew he was only joking with her. She got on with him remarkably well compared with the trouble that some mothers experienced with teenage sons, and daughters, of course. He was a sensible lad – quite grown-up, in some ways, for sixteen – and his time in the Scouts had made him well able to cook simple meals and look after himself. And Carl and Sharon, aged twelve and ten, were good kids, not much trouble.

'You could ask Shirley to come round, if you like,' Ginny told him, 'if her mother will let her.' She guessed Ryan would ask her anyway, so it was as well to show him that she didn't mind. 'For Saturday tea, perhaps, so long as you make sure she catches the bus back alright. I know I can trust you, can't I, Ryan?'

'Of course you can, Mum,' smiled Ryan. 'We're only friends, Shirley and me. There's no need to worry.'

Ginny liked Shirley Crompton. She was a quiet, friendly sort of girl, and she was from a very nice family, according to Ryan. She could see why Ryan liked her too. She was pretty with short blonde hair, blue eyes and a trim figure. She had no doubt that she could trust Ryan, or else she would not dream of leaving him on his own.

'Where are you going anyway?' he asked.

'Oh… sorry; I should have said. We're going to see my friend, Fiona. She's married to a vicar, and they live in Aberthwaite in North Yorkshire. They've got a little girl, Stella; she's about sixteen months old, and we still haven't seen her. We keep saying we'll go, but we've only just got round to it. Don't you remember? We went to their wedding, about three years ago. You all stayed with your gran and grandad.'

'Yes… I think I remember,' said Ryan. 'How did you meet her, Mum? I mean, with her living in Yorkshire?'

'Oh, I've known Fiona for ages,' replied Ginny. 'Even before you were born. In fact we were expecting our babies at the same time…' She stopped suddenly, aware of what she had just said. She had a habit of doing that, wittering on without really thinking about what she was saying.

Ryan noticed, of course. 'I thought you said she got married three years ago, and her baby girl's not two yet. Was she married before then?'

'No… no, she wasn't,' said Ginny. 'Girls aren't always married when they have babies. I assume you know that?' she added with a smile. 'I suppose I might as well tell you. Fiona and me, we were in Burnside House at the same time, waiting for our babies to be born. Yes, I know it's a home for unmarried mothers, but I wasn't married at first, you see, when I was expecting you.'

Ryan grinned. 'Yes, I think I already knew that, Mum,' he said. 'I knew the dates didn't tally. But it's no big deal, is it? You had to get married; so what?'

'No…' Ginny sighed. 'It's no big deal, as you say. But when I found out I was expecting a baby – you, of course – my parents weren't too happy about it. I know attitudes are changing now; not all that much, but it's not as bad as it was. Back then, though, it was looked on as something dreadful if a girl was pregnant and not married. I was the oldest of five, as you know, and my mam and dad were relying on my wages to help out with the bills and money for food and all that.'

'Didn't Grandad have a good job?' asked Ryan. Ginny's father had been a coal miner and had retired a few years earlier. 'It doesn't seem very fair to me that they were relying on you. What do you mean? Did they want you to give me up... to be adopted?'

'Well, I suppose they did at first,' Ginny admitted. 'I remember we always seemed to be hard up. And they didn't want me to marry Arthur – your dad – because we weren't really courting. He was just the lad next door, and we were good friends rather than anything else. I know it sounds awful, but we went to the pub one night and had too much to drink and... well, you know what happened!'

'But you did get married, Mum. And you and Dad, you seem to get on really well together. I know you might argue now and again, but everybody does. Gran and Grandad changed their minds then?'

'Oh, your dad can be very persuasive,' said Ginny. 'He begged me to marry him – I didn't need much coaxing – and then he went to work on my parents. And my gran put in her two pennorth; you don't remember her, but she was a real tough old girl, and she thought what they were doing was wrong. So it all worked out OK in the end.'

'Yes, I'm real glad it did, Mum,' said Ryan, sounding rather perplexed. 'I might have been brought up by somebody else. That's a dreadful thought.'

'So it is,' Ginny agreed. 'It wasn't what I wanted at all, but I couldn't do anything about it. I was only seventeen, and I knew how annoyed my parents were. Arthur was twenty, though, and he managed to convince them that he loved me, and that he had a good job and could look after me. And so he has, Ryan. I think your gran and grandad felt guilty afterwards when they saw how happy we were together. And they doted on you, and our Carl and Sharon. They never mention it, of course, how close we came to losing you.'

Ryan nodded thoughtfully. 'Yes, there's no doubt who my parents are, is there, Mum? I've got your red hair and blue eyes.'

'And your dad's build...' Ryan was almost six foot now, like his father, with a sturdy muscular body. '... and his roguish grin.' Ginny smiled reminiscently. 'I couldn't resist it, could I? And his common sense, too, I hope,' she went on, 'and his perseverance. Your dad could have gone a lot further if he hadn't had to leave school at fifteen, like we all did if we didn't get to the grammar school.'

'He's done well though, hasn't he, working at the docks?' said Ryan. Arthur had started as a docker, and was now a foreman in charge of one of the warehouses.

'Yes, so he has; but we want more than that for you. That's why we were so pleased when you passed to go to the grammar school. And Carl will be going there soon. Your gran and grandad were so proud of you; the first one in the family to go there. And your nan and grandpa Gregson, too, of course.'

'So... all's well that ends well, as they say,' Ryan commented. 'And it could all have been so very different. Actually... there's a girl in my form who was adopted,' he continued. 'She's Shirley's friend. Shirley was telling me about it not long ago. Debbie's always known though, and she told Shirley that she was born in Burnside House. That's quite a coincidence, isn't it, Mum? Perhaps she was there at the same time as you; Debbie's mother, I mean.'

Ginny was instantly alert. 'She must have been, mustn't she, if the girl's in your form? You say she's called Debbie? How old is she? When's her birthday?'

74

'Don't know,' Ryan replied. 'I'm not all that bothered about her. I don't like her all that much, to be honest. No, hang on… her birthday's in May, not long off, because I remember Shirley seeing a card she liked, and she bought it for her.'

'What does she look like?' asked Ginny, her curiosity growing by the minute. She must have known this girl's mother. It might even be… Goodness! Supposing it was…?

'She's got dark hair. She's quite pretty, I suppose. Why…? Oh crikey! You don't think she might be the daughter of this Fiona, do you?'

'She could be,' said Ginny. 'In fact, who else could she be? Fiona's baby was born in May, a month after I left, so I never saw her. But I know she had dark hair. Fiona told me.'

'Hey, wait a minute,' said Ryan. 'I've got that form photo we had taken in September. I'll go and get it.' He went upstairs, returning a few moments later with the said photograph. They had had individual ones taken at the same time, and the one of Ryan was displayed on the sideboard; the other one was in his bedroom.

'That's Debbie,' he said, 'on the front row next to Shirley. She's had her hair cut now, and she looks a bit different, but it's a good likeness.'

Ginny looked at the photo and gave a gasp. 'Yes… oh my God!' She didn't often swear or blaspheme, and she pulled herself up at once. 'I mean… good gracious me, yes! She's the image of Fiona. She had blonde hair, though, like Shirley has. Fiona was a real pretty girl. And this girl's just like her. The same smile, and the way she's holding her head on one side, just like her… mother. Oh goodness; what am I going to do?'

'I think you'll have to keep mum about it... Mum!' replied Ryan. 'Best to say nothing at all, eh? Your friend, Fiona, she's married to a vicar?'

'Yes, and they're very happy, from what she says, she and Simon. I was really glad about it. Fiona deserves to be happy after all she went through.'

'Then it would be best not to put the cat among the pigeons, wouldn't it? She may not even have told her husband about the first baby.'

'Oh, I'm sure she would, knowing Fiona. She was a very honest and straightforward girl. She wouldn't be likely to keep any secrets from him. Anyway, there was a skeleton in his own cupboard that only came to light quite recently. Simon had a son that he didn't know anything about until he arrived on their doorstep last year.'

'Wow! I bet that was a shock. And him a vicar too. I wonder what the folk at his church think about it?'

'He's a called a rector, actually; it's a country parish,' said Ginny. 'Apparently they know all about it and don't think any the worse about Simon. He's very popular there. It happened during the war, when he was part of a bomber crew, and he met this girl who was a WAAF. It's rather a long story... It's Fiona that I'm concerned about now. I shall have to try to act normally when I see her and not even hint at what I know. I'm sure she's put it all behind her now, and she won't want any more complications in her life. I know she was very upset at the time, when she had to give up the baby. I'd left by then, but she wrote and told me how awful it was.'

'Her boyfriend couldn't marry her then, like you and Dad?'

'No... he was a lad in the sixth form, like she was. He didn't even know about it. Her parents were far worse than mine. They practically disowned her, they were so ashamed, and they sent her up to Northumberland, as far away as possible, to an aunt and uncle. Fiona was such a clever girl. Some of the other girls thought she was a bit snooty because she'd been to a grammar school and the rest of us hadn't. But she wasn't stuck up at all; she was really nice, and so kind and thoughtful. We've kept in touch ever since. You say you're not very keen on this Debbie? It sounds as though she's not got her mother's nice nature.'

'Oh, she's alright, I suppose. A bit of a show-off, but Shirley seems to get on well enough with her.'

Ginny nodded thoughtfully. 'I suppose it would be asking too much of you to make you promise not to tell Shirley about this?'

'I won't if you don't want me to, Mum...'

'No, I expect you'll tell her anyway. But I certainly don't want it to get to Debbie's ears that we know who her real mother is. At least we're assuming we do, but it seems pretty certain to me. Now I come to think about it, Claire Wagstaff was rather cagey when I asked her if she had any idea where Fiona's baby might have gone.'

'Who's Claire Wagstaff?'

'She was one of the helpers at Burnside House. I see her from time to time when I'm out shopping. She was quite friendly with Fiona and me, although they weren't really supposed to get too friendly with the inmates.'

Ryan laughed. 'You make it sound like being in prison, Mum.'

'It wasn't too bad,' Ginny smiled. 'It was better for me, of course, when I knew I would be able to keep you. But I like to think I made it a bit more bearable for Fiona, and I knew that Claire did her best to cheer us up. It's unusual, you know, for babies to be placed with adoptive parents who live so near. Does Debbie live in Whitesands Bay, same as Shirley?'

'Yes, quite near to where Shirley lives. Debbie's father works for the council there; he's a gardener.'

'I wouldn't be surprised if Claire had something to do with that adoption,' Ginny said thoughtfully. 'Like I said, she seemed a little bit ill at ease when we were talking about it. I thought at the time that she knew more than she was letting on. Oh dear, Ryan! You've certainly given me a shock! We must be very careful not to open a whole can of worms...'

Eight

Ginny and Arthur were looking forward to their weekend in Aberthwaite. They set off early on the Saturday morning in their ten-year-old Hillman. It was all that Arthur could afford at the moment, but he kept it in good repair and spent many hours washing and polishing it until it gleamed. It had proved invaluable with three children to be ferried around to various events; but it was good now to have the car, and two whole days, to themselves.

Their home was in South Shields. After their marriage they had lived with Arthur's parents for a while in a street of terraced houses near to the docks. Following that they had rented a house in the same district, then, when Arthur was promoted they had managed to scrape enough money together to secure a mortgage on a house some distance away from the quays and warehouses of the industrial part of the town. They were only five minutes' walk away from the promenade and the – somewhat limited – holiday attractions that the town had to offer; and Ginny, never afraid of hard work, had taken a job as a barmaid in a local pub a few nights a week, to make ends meet. It was sometimes a struggle with three children, although they managed a week's holiday each year to Scarborough, Whitby or Filey.

It was heaven, though, to have these two days on their own, and Ginny felt an air of excitement as soon as they set off. The area from the River Tees to the Tyne estuary was an almost continual built-up stretch of houses and factories which had expanded from the time of the Industrial Revolution. At the heart of the region was the city of Durham. As they bypassed it they had a superb view of the castle and the majestic cathedral on a hill overlooking the steep banks of the River Wear. Very soon they were heading through the northern Yorkshire dales where the limestone hills were criss-crossed with drystone walls. Sheep grazed on the upper slopes, and in the villages and hamlets, greystone houses clustered around a village green or beside a rippling stream.

Ginny gazed from the window, pondering for a while about how blissful it would be to live in such a place, but she did not voice her thoughts to her husband. She knew that at heart she was a town girl, and she and Arthur had a good marriage that many might envy. She had not looked back since the time he had rescued her from Burnside House, insisting that he loved her and that he was not going to let their baby be given away to strangers. The thought of what had so nearly happened had been on her mind since Ryan's recent revelation earlier that week. She had shared the confidence with Arthur – they never kept secrets from one another – and he had agreed that they must leave well alone.

'Ryan was bewildered, too,' she had told him, 'when he realized what might have happened to him. I was quite touched when he said what a dreadful thought it was, that he might have been brought up with someone else.'

'Perish the thought!' Arthur had said. 'He's a good lad; they're all good kids. We've been real lucky, pet, haven't we? So far, at least; you never can tell how they're going to turn out.'

'I've a feeling they'll all do alright,' Ginny assured him. 'I've been lucky, too, Arthur. I'm so glad you decided to marry me! And managed to change my parents' minds.'

'I'm the one that's lucky,' Arthur said, as they shared an intimate moment.

'Adoptions can work out well, though,' he said, in a later conversation. 'If – God forbid! – it had happened to Ryan, he might have been OK. This girl Debbie, she's got a good home, hasn't she?'

'Oh, I should imagine so,' said Ginny. 'I don't know, of course, not for sure, but I have a feeling that Claire might have had a hand in the adoption. I hope the girl's happy... but we've decided, haven't we, that it's none of our business? We don't breathe a word to Fiona.'

Arthur broke into her reverie then as they drove along. 'We'll stop at Richmond, shall we, pet, and stretch our legs for a while. Then it won't take us long afterwards to get to Aberthwaite.'

'It'll be busy in Richmond; it's market day,' Ginny remarked, 'but I'd love to stop for half an hour or so if we've got time.'

They parked in a side street near to the market square. 'Come on, Ginny; no time to go shopping!' he told her, nudging her away from the market stalls where she was wanting to linger.

'All right, then,' she said, a trifle reluctantly. 'Actually, I think there's a market in Aberthwaite as well, so maybe I could have a browse there with Fiona. I love markets.'

Arthur smiled indulgently at her as they climbed the hill to the castle high above the River Swale. There was a magnificent view from the road that surrounded the castle keep. Just below them were the colourful awnings of the market stalls and the cobbled streets of the town, and in the distance the green and brown stretch of the dales, sweeping across to the Vale of York.

They sat on a seat thoughtfully provided by the council and enjoyed the coffee that Ginny had brought in a Thermos flask, with her home-made shortbread biscuits. 'Fiona's expecting us for lunch,' she told her husband, 'so don't scoff all those biscuits!'

'Is she a good cook?' asked Arthur. 'As good as you?'

'I don't know,' she replied. 'But I should think she is. She looked after her gran in Leeds for quite a while, and she's probably learnt all sorts of skills as the rector's wife. I'm dying to see her again, Arthur.'

'Come on then,' he said, depositing their rubbish in a nearby litter bin. 'Let's be on our way. Another half hour or so, and we'll be there.'

—

They received a joyful welcome at the rectory. 'It's been far too long,' exclaimed Ginny as she threw her arms around her friend in a tight hug. 'I can't believe it's been so long since we saw you.'

'Yes, nearly three years!' said Fiona, a trifle reproach-fully, but she was smiling and Ginny knew that she understood. 'It's almost three years since Simon and I got married, isn't it, darling?' Ginny noticed that the two of them exchanged a loving glance.

'Yes, time flies, doesn't it?' replied Ginny. 'I'm sorry, Fiona; we kept meaning to come, but you know how it is. One thing after another, and it's not always easy to leave the children. Anyway, we're here now... Let me look at you...' She stood back smiling at her friend. 'You don't look any different, younger if anything! I can see that marriage suits you.'

'It certainly does,' agreed Fiona, laughing. She did, indeed, look radiant. 'And you haven't changed either, Ginny.' If either of them thought that the other looked a little plumper – although Ginny had never been what you might call slim – they did not say so.

'Just a few grey hairs,' said Ginny, patting her glossy auburn hair, cut short, as was Fiona's, in an up-to-the-minute style, 'but I do my best to disguise them…' She turned to look at the little girl at Fiona's side. 'So this must be Stella. Oh, isn't she a little love?' She crouched down to talk to the little blonde-haired girl who was holding her mummy's hand. 'Hello, pet. I'm Ginny, your mummy's friend. I've been looking forward so much to seeing you.'

The child nodded, smiling a little shyly. 'Hello,' she said, then she looked up at her mother for reassurance. She could be a bit wary of strangers at first, although she was continually meeting new people, one of the pleasant – or occasionally less pleasant – necessities of her daddy's occupation.

Simon and Arthur's greeting to one another was less effusive, although they shook hands with a smile, Simon's warm and welcoming, Arthur's rather more diffident. Ginny knew that her husband had felt a little apprehensive at meeting and, what was more, staying as a guest of the Reverend Simon Norwood. They had met only once, at the wedding, when there had been little time for any meaningful conversation. Ginny, too, had only met Simon the once, but she could tell from Fiona's letters that he was a pretty normal sort of bloke who would not preach at Arthur or behave in a pious or overzealous manner.

Ginny and Arthur, like many folk, went to church only on special occasions. They had been married in church, and had had their three children christened, because it was the right thing to do, and had made sure they all went to Sunday school. Fortunately the children had kept up their links with the church through the Scout, Cub and Brownie packs, but their parents were well aware that their own attendance was spasmodic.

'Anyway, come on in,' said Fiona, leading the way into the rectory. 'I expect you're ready for a rest after your journey, although it isn't really all that far, is it? Simon'll take your cases up and show you where you're sleeping; and the bathroom's at the end of the landing. Come down when you're ready. I've made just a cold lunch, salad and cold meat and stuff, and we'll dine in style tonight! Not too much style, mind; I don't mean dressing for dinner! We're just ordinary folk. Oh, it is good to see you again!' Fiona impulsively kissed her friend's cheek.

'She's just the same as she always was,' Ginny remarked to Arthur, when their hosts had gone back downstairs. 'Being the rector's wife hasn't made any difference. There were never any airs and graces with Fiona, although she went to a grammar school.'

'He seems OK, too,' said Arthur. 'Nice friendly chap, isn't he? He's not wearing his dog collar, either.'

'Oh, I expect it's his day off,' said Ginny. 'That is if clergymen ever get a day off. He probably thought it would make us feel more at ease if he wasn't dressed as a vicar. I think they will be expecting us to go to church in the morning. Is that OK with you? I'm sure they wouldn't insist on it, but I think it would only be polite to go along with Fiona and listen to Simon preaching. I'm looking forward to that actually.'

'Yes, that's OK with me,' said Arthur. 'Will Fiona be able to go, though? What about little Stella?'

'Fiona said something about a crèche in one of her letters. The young mothers take it in turns to look after the toddlers so that the parents can attend the service if they want to.'

Arthur nodded. 'I see... Well, let's enjoy today, shall we, and let tomorrow take care of itself? It's grand, isn't it, pet, to have some time on our own?' He went over to where Ginny was standing and put his arm round her. She was gazing out of the window.

'Just look at that view, Arthur! Quite something, isn't it?'

'It is that,' he agreed. 'It's a bit different from our view of folks' backyards and washing lines, to say nothing of cranes and factory chimneys.'

'Oh, come on, Arthur!' said Ginny. 'It's not that bad, where we live. At least we've got a garden, of sorts, and nice friendly neighbours. And the factory chimneys are only in the distance. Five minutes' walk and we're by the sea... well, the estuary at least.'

'Eeh, I'm not complaining,' he said, giving her a hug. 'We're real lucky, you and me, and we've got three grand kids. I know how to count my blessings. I'll have a chance to do that when we go to church tomorrow, eh, pet? And happen it'd be a bit quiet for us here, don't you think?'

'Maybe so,' said Ginny pensively. 'Yes... I'm sure you're right.'

The room they had been given was at the back of the rectory overlooking the garden where late daffodils and tulips were flowering around the stretch of grass. It couldn't really be termed a lawn because it was rather uneven with clumps of daisies and clover amongst the longish grass. At the bottom of the garden there was a swing and a sand pit, beneath a cherry tree which was shedding its pinkish white petals like snow on the ground. The rectory was adjacent to the church, and over the hedge there was a view of the greystone building with its square tower, and the centuries-old graveyard. The old lichen-covered graves were dotted here and there in a haphazard way, some leaning at a crazy angle. Tall elm trees where rooks nested stood sentinel at the rear of the church. In the distance were the limestone hills, shading from deep brown in the shadows to emerald and pale green where a ray of sunlight streamed from behind a cloud. In the near distance were the ruins of an ancient castle, and there was just a glimpse between the trees of a rippling stream wending its way through the valley.

'It's a canny view all right,' remarked Ginny. 'An' I'm real glad that Fiona's had the good fortune to end up here. She deserves it if anybody does. Eeh! I used to feel real sorry for her when we were in that place, and she had to go home to those miserable parents of hers.'

'Well, she's got a lovely little lass now, hasn't she?' said Arthur. 'I'm sure Stella must have made up for the little girl she had to give up.'

'I'm sure she has,' replied Ginny. 'I feel better about it all now that I can see how happy she is… I'll just nip along to the bathroom, then we'd better go downstairs. I won't be a minute, Arthur, then you can have your turn…'

The rectory was a mid-Victorian house, but not as large or as rambling as some of those places tended to be. It was centrally heated too, which was a bonus; Ginny could imagine how chilly it must have been in those high-ceilinged rooms in the days of open fires, which many people still had. Only recently had Ginny and Arthur had central heating installed themselves, and she was still revelling in the luxury of it.

The rectory dining room was furnished in a modern style with a contemporary table, chairs and sideboard in light oak that Ginny guessed – correctly – had come from the newish store, 'Habitat'. They enjoyed the simple meal of home-cooked ham served cold with salad and small potatoes, followed by apple crumble and custard. Stella, in her high chair, coped very well with her own meal, only needing a little assistance now and again with her spoon and fork.

'She's good, isn't she?' remarked Ginny. 'Our Sharon was unbelievably messy when she was that age. She's still untidy though; I'm forever on at her about the state of her bedroom. But that's girls for you, I suppose. You'd think it might be the other way round, wouldn't you, but our Ryan and Carl are real neat and tidy compared with her, aren't they, Arthur?'

But Arthur was listening to Simon who was talking about taking a walk on the moors that afternoon. 'Whoops, sorry!' said Ginny. 'I'm interrupting, aren't I? She's a little treasure, though, isn't she, your Stella?'

'Yes, she's very good,' agreed Fiona. 'We've been very lucky. Of course we may not be so lucky the next time.'

Ginny's eyes opened wide. 'Why? D'you mean that you're…?'

Fiona put a finger to her lips. 'Shush… That just slipped out. I'll tell you later…'

Ginny, of course, was dying to hear more, but she had to wait until later that afternoon to hear what she guessed Fiona had been hinting at. Over lunch the two men had been discussing a proposed walk in the foothills of the dales that afternoon.

'I've no climbing gear, or walking gear for that matter,' said Arthur. 'I did a spot of walking years ago, with my mates, in the Cheviot Hills and the Hadrian's Wall area; but I've not been since Ginny and me were married. Never time, is there, pet?'

'Now you know you could go if you really wanted to, Arthur,' she chided him. 'You know I'd never stop you. Anyway, off you go this afternoon with Simon. You'll enjoy it.'

Her husband looked a little dubious, whether it was at the idea of unaccustomed exercise, or the prospect of spending so much time alone with a vicar she wasn't sure. But she nodded her head and winked at him, and he grinned back at her.

'That's great then,' said Simon. 'I'll lend you a pair of hiking boots. I reckon we're about the same size, eh, Arthur? I take nines.'

Arthur nodded. 'Aye, that's my size too.'

'I promise there'll be no climbing,' said Simon. 'I've never been into rock climbing. We'll just have a walk on the gentler slopes, maybe along to Aysgarth Falls; they're well worth a visit.'

'Be careful you don't get your feet wet,' laughed Fiona. 'You've done that more than once.'

Simon smiled. 'Perhaps you two girls would like to come along with us?'

'No fear!' said Ginny. 'I fancy a visit to the market meself… that is if Fiona agrees,' she added, thinking she might have been a little presumptuous. Maybe Fiona had other plans for them.

'Yes, that's fine by me,' said Fiona. 'There's one on a Wednesday as well that I usually go to, but I'm always ready to visit the market. And Stella enjoys it too; we'll take her in her push chair.'

The market was one of the best that Ginny had ever seen. 'Eeh, it's a real old-fashioned country market, isn't it?' she remarked as they walked between the stalls of fruit and vegetables and home-made produce. She breathed in the mixed aroma of ripe apples and oranges, cabbage and spring onions, and the faint odour of cheese on the air, from a stall a little way distant.

Fiona did a little shopping; a cauliflower and carrots fresh from the earth, apples and pears, then a chunk of cheese and a pat of butter from a stall of farm produce. There were several such stalls, manned by farmers' wives from the nearby area. They sold cheese, mainly of the local Wensleydale variety; pats of butter; newly laid eggs – deep brown, or white if preferred; and jars of home-made jams, marmalade and lemon curd, along with pickled onions and cauliflower and chutneys.

Fiona clearly knew the farmer's wife quite well; in fact she seemed to know most people, and they all stopped to have a word with little Stella who smiled happily at them. They greeted Ginny in a friendly way, too.

'They're OK once you get to know them,' Fiona told her. 'These Yorkshire country folk tend to be rather insular. Anybody who wasn't born here or has lived here for ages is regarded as a foreigner. Incomers, they call us. But they seem to accept me now; Stella has helped, of course. It's amazing what a difference a child makes.'

'Especially one as cute as Stella,' added Ginny.

'Yes, she's a winsome little lady, isn't she?' smiled Fiona. 'Quite a heart stealer. Like I said, I found it a bit hard going with some of the folk, mainly the older women of the parish, but they seem to have come to terms with me – and everything – now.'

'And you're happy, aren't you?' said Ginny. It was more of a statement than a question. 'I can see that you are. I'm so glad about that, Fiona. Now, what was it you were going to tell me earlier, eh?' she asked with a twinkle on her eye.

'Let's go and have a look round the other half of the market,' said Fiona, 'then we'll go and have a cup of tea in my favourite cafe, and I'll tell you!'

On the opposite side of the market cross were stalls selling crockery, kitchenware, clothing for women and children, and what were known as fent stalls, selling materials and dress making requisites, and at the end, the chocolate and sweet stalls.

Ginny bought a box of assorted fudge for her children and a jar of Yorkshire mixture − a selection of humbugs, aniseed, pear drops, fruit rocks of strawberry, lemon and orange, and boiled sweets shaped like little fishes. She was captivated by the array of materials on the fent stalls: floral, spotted, striped and self-coloured in every imaginable shade. She bought enough for two dresses for her daughter, Sharon; a candy-striped pink and a design of daisies and poppies on a blue background. She was tempted by the knitting wools on the next stall, but Fiona nudged her away.

'I have a friend who has a shop on the High Street,' she told her. 'Joan Tweedale; she was at our wedding, but you might not remember her. She has a wonderful handicraft shop. I'll take you there when we've had our cup of tea. I expect you're ready for one by now, aren't you. I know I am.'

The little cafe, 'The Merry Kettle' was situated in the market square. There was a swinging sign outside depicting a large copper kettle, and inside there were a dozen or so round tables covered with lace cloths, with wheel-back chairs round them. The delft rack held an array of small kettles, and teapots in varying styles and designs; shaped like cottages, story book characters, engines and cars, and pretty ones with flowers, country scenes and crinoline ladies. On the wall were framed advertisements from times past: for Typhoo tea, Camp coffee, Huntley and Palmer's biscuits and Cadbury's chocolates.

'Eeh! Isn't that lovely?' exclaimed Ginny. 'It's like something out of another time.'

'Yes, I always come here when I've been to the market,' said Fiona. 'Let's see if we can find a table... Yes, there's one, right at the back, and there's room for Stella's push-chair in the corner. They know us here; Mabel will find some cushions so that she can sit on a proper chair.'

'Hello there.' The said waitress, Mabel, was soon with them, dressed in the blue uniform dress with a frilled apron and mob cap in a paler shade. 'Now, what would you like today, Mrs Norwood? The usual, is it, tea and fruit scones?'

'Er, no. I think we'll push the boat out today and have cream cakes as it's a special occasion. This is my friend from Tyneside; I haven't seen her for ages.'

'How d'you do?' said Mabel, smiling cheerfully. 'What do you think of our little town then?'

'It's real quaint,' Ginny replied. 'A far cry from South Shields! Still, home's home, isn't it?' she added loyally. 'It's nice to visit other places though, now and again. But we've come to see Fiona, not the town... Only a small cream cake, Fiona.' She patted her stomach.

'I don't think any of them are all that small,' laughed Fiona, 'but we'll restrict ourselves to one each.'

Ginny chose a chocolate eclair and Fiona a cream horn from the selection that Mabel brought. The tea was in a silver pot, with rose-patterned china cups and saucers, and Stella had a drink of orange juice and a chocolate biscuit.

'Now, spill the beans,' said Ginny when the waitress had gone. 'I'm dying to know. Did you mean what I think you mean?'

Fiona smiled. 'Actually I'm not quite sure yet. I'm… well, I'm late, you see,' she whispered. 'Only a few days, and I never am, not normally. I knew straight away with Stella, and with… the other one, of course. And I feel a bit different, somehow.' She nodded. 'I'm pretty certain I'm expecting again, but you're the very first to know. Apart from Simon; I tell him everything.'

'That's wonderful news,' said Ginny. 'I do hope you're right. It'll be a nice age gap, won't it, about two years between Stella and her little brother… or sister.'

'Yes, I can't really afford to wait any longer, can I? I'm nearly thirty-four now, and Simon's in his late forties, not that it matters to either of us.'

'I think my child-rearing days are over,' said Ginny. 'At least I jolly well hope so! They're not all as easy as your little Stella.'

'Oh, she has her moments,' replied Fiona. 'But on the whole, yes, she's a remarkably good little girl. You never know what's in the future, though, do you? How they will turn out?'

'She's not likely to go far wrong with you and Simon as parents,' said Ginny.

'Oh, don't be too sure,' replied Fiona. 'I've heard of clergymen's children who've rebelled and kicked over the traces. She may seem to be a little angel now, but only time will tell.'

Ginny knew that she had to bring up what was on her mind, but she also had to be careful to keep mum. 'Do you ever think…' she began carefully, 'you know, about your first little girl? Does it bring it all back, seeing me again?'

'No, not very much; not now,' answered Fiona. 'When Stella was born Simon actually asked me then if I would like to trace her. It was after Greg had turned up. But I said no, and I meant it. And that's how I still feel about it. I just hope she's happy, wherever she is. She may not even have been told about me. She's almost the same age as your Ryan…' She smiled reminiscently. 'It all turned out right for you as well, didn't it, Ginny? I can see how happy you and Arthur are.'

'Yes, and our Ryan's a good lad,' said Ginny. 'I'm real thankful we were able to keep him. I admit I don't go to church all that often, Fiona, but I do thank God for that, and for our other two children.'

'Do you ever see any of the girls who were in the home with us?' asked Fiona.

'No, I've never set eyes on any of 'em,' said Ginny. 'It's strange, that, because they were mostly from the Tyneside area.' She was just about to say that she had seen Claire Wagstaff, but changed her mind. It might lead to more awkward questions.

'Do you remember Hazel Doherty?' asked Fiona.

'Could we ever forget her? Nasty piece of work, she was. I don't think anybody liked her. Why?'

'Because I saw her, just once,' said Fiona. 'At the clinic when I was expecting Stella. I just caught a glimpse of her – you know, how you do sometimes, and you're not quite sure who it is? Anyway, it was after that, that the folk in the parish found out about my first baby, and I guessed it must have been Hazel who told somebody who knew me. And then the gossip started.'

'It sounds just like Hazel,' said Ginny. 'She always was a vindictive bitch. Sorry, Fiona! Must watch my language!'

Fiona smiled. 'No, you're right. She was... not very nice. Anyway, it was a nine days' wonder in the parish. Simon soon put a stop to the gossip, and so did Joan; that's the friend we're going to see now. And I've never seen her again; Hazel, I mean. Odd, isn't it?'

'Maybe she's moved on elsewhere,' said Ginny. 'She didn't seem the type to stay in one place for long. Good riddance to her... That cream cake was delicious. I hope I'll have room for my tea!'

Fiona laughed. 'I think we'd better be posh and call it dinner tonight. I'm cooking something special in your honour, at least I'm trying! I don't think I do too badly in the kitchen. Simon never complains anyway, bless him! Now, if you're ready we'll go and see Joan.'

Nine

Joan Tweedale's handicraft shop on the High Street had always been a source of delight to Fiona. Joan was the wife of Henry, the organist and choirmaster. She was in her early fifties and her husband a few years older. Fiona had felt drawn to both of them on their first acquaintance. Henry had invited Fiona to join the choir, which she had been pleased to do. She had a pleasant mezzo-soprano voice; not a solo sort of voice but she blended in well with a choir.

And Joan had proved to be a real friend in need. It was Joan who had taken Fiona, the rector's new wife, under her wing and had told her not to be intimidated by the diehards of the congregation, mainly the older women of the Mothers' Union, under the leadership of a certain Mrs Ethel Bayliss, who did not take kindly to change. But Fiona, with Joan's advice, had proved her worth in the parish, and now the rector's wife was well known, and becoming very popular in the town of Aberthwaite.

There was no one else in the little shop when they entered. Joan appeared from the back room at the sound of the bell's old-fashioned tinkle. She was an attractive woman with auburn hair, now greying at the temples. Her brown eyes lit up with pleasure when she saw Fiona and her friend and her little granddaughter, Stella.

'Hello there,' she said. 'You must be Ginny. Fiona's told me a lot about you. Have you girls had a good old chinwag together?'

'I'll say we have!' said Ginny. 'We've hardly stopped for breath. Pleased to meet you, Joan. I've heard a lot about you, too; about what a good friend you've been to Fiona.'

'I've tried to be,' replied Joan. 'But it's mutual; we help one another. We stand firm against the opposition, don't we, Fiona?' She smiled. 'Are you all set for tomorrow, you and Simon? It should prove interesting.'

'What's that?' asked Ginny.

'Oh, we're trying something different at the service,' said Fiona. 'I'll tell you later. Actually we've come to buy some wool – at least Ginny has – as well as to see you, Joan.'

Ginny was staring round at the array of goods for sale that filled every corner of the little shop. Knitting wool in every imaginable shade, in ready-to-use balls. It wasn't so long ago, as the women remembered, when wool was bought in hanks, and you had to persuade a willing husband or mother, or somebody, to hold the hank in outstretched hands whilst you laboriously wound the wool into a more manageable ball. There were tapestry sets, of flowers, animals and country scenes with the embroidery silks required; examples of crocheted and knitted garments displayed on hangers; buttons of every shape and size; ribbons, lace, braids and tassels for adornment and, on the counter, large books of knitting patterns.

'Eeh!' exclaimed Ginny – the Geordie remark that had used to amuse Fiona but which she now had come to expect – 'It's a real Aladdin's cave, isn't it?' She looked at it all in wonderment.

'Isn't it just?' said Fiona. 'I was amazed the first time I saw it all. I was never all that good at handiwork, and I still don't sew very much, but Joan got me started on rather more complicated knitting. I could only do plain and purl before she took me in hand. Now, can you see anything that takes your fancy, Ginny?'

'Far too much,' said Ginny, 'but I'll just concentrate on the knitting wool.' She showed Joan the materials she had bought at the market. 'I thought I'd knit a nice lacy cardigan for my daughter.'

Between them they chose a pretty shade of blue that would go well with both the floral and the pink candy-striped fabrics, and an intricate lacy pattern that Ginny was eager to tackle.

'Mind you, I only knit for our Sharon,' she said, 'or for myself, now and again. She's ten, so I don't know how much longer she'll want to wear her mum's home-made things. I don't knit for the lads any more; our Ryan and Carl, they wouldn't be seen dead in a hand-knitted jumper.'

'You're getting me going now,' said Fiona. 'Stella could wear bright colours now, couldn't she? I really like that deep coral shade, or that bright yellow. What do you think, Joan?'

Joan advised her that the coral pink would be better with Stella's blonde hair. They chose a pattern for a lacy cardigan, though not as intricate as the one that Ginny had chosen. Stella was by now fast asleep, oblivious to their plans for her future clothing.

'Well, we'd better be off then,' Fiona said, when they had chatted for a while. 'This little lady's ready for a proper nap, and time's getting on. See you in the morning, Joan.'

They said their goodbyes and set off back along the High Street, then along the side road that led to the church and rectory, only a few minutes' walk from the centre of the little town.

'She's very pleasant, isn't she?' observed Ginny. 'I'm glad you've got a good friend here, although she's probably one of many, is she?'

'Yes...' Fiona answered a little carefully. 'I have quite a few friends. There are some folk, though, who tend to be rather wary of making friends with the clergy, or their wives, as though there's something a little bit odd about us. But they usually decide that we're quite normal! I found it strange at first, being married to the rector, but Simon has never expected me to behave any differently because of my... er... status. Although I do try to exercise decorum when it's expected of me! I have several friends in our Young Wives group. Most of my friends are connected with the church. I must admit it can make you rather insular in outlook if you're not careful. Simon tries hard with what he calls 'outreach', encouraging the folk who wouldn't normally think of coming to church. That's what Joan was referring to. We're trying a new venture tomorrow: a family service with the Sunday school children, and their parents... we hope! Anyway, we'll see what happens. You and Arthur will come along tomorrow, won't you?'

'Yes, we'll be there,' said Ginny.

–

Simon and Fiona explained to their guests a little about the service to be held the following day, whilst they ate their evening meal. Fiona had done them proud with succulent roast pork – with crisp crackling – cauliflower cheese, carrots and peas, roast potatoes and both sage and onion stuffing and apple sauce, followed by Eve's pudding and fresh cream, all home-made. Then they chatted in the lounge over coffee and After Eight mints, the feast completed later with a glass of fine sherry – for the ladies. Simon guessed that Arthur might prefer a beer so he joined him in a pint of Yorkshire bitter.

They tried not to make the conversation too 'churchy'. They talked about the walk that the men had enjoyed that afternoon, about the football teams they supported – Sunderland and Leeds United – and, more seriously, about the recent assassination of Martin Luther King, and Enoch Powell's rantings in Parliament, concerning the Kenyan Asians being forced out of their country, and the possibility of them taking up residence in Britain.

Arthur had come to the conclusion that Simon was a grand sort of chap who took an interest in most things; home and world politics as well as the concerns of his own church and parish, which had to be his primary consideration.

'We're about to make a radical change from tomorrow,' he told them. 'At least, radical for St Peter's. Our Sunday school, from now on, is going to be held in the morning instead of the afternoon. We think it's the way ahead, don't we, darling?'

'Yes, we've noticed that children are staying away because their parents want to go out as a family on a Sunday afternoon,' said Fiona. 'Especially those who have cars, and who can blame them?'

'Of course there are sure to be those who don't agree,' said Simon. 'There are some at St Peter's who take the words of the prayer book literally. "As it was in the beginning is now and ever shalt be, world without end, Amen!'" He gave a wry smile. 'You know, we've always done it this way, so why should we change? We've done it all democratically, though. We took a vote about the proposals at a church council meeting, which is the correct procedure; and it was passed by a majority vote. There were a couple of dissenters and some abstainers, but we got the result needed to go ahead.'

'Why the objections?' asked Ginny. 'I should think it makes sense.'

'Well, apart from what I've mentioned – resistance to change of any kind – there is the view that parents like Sunday afternoons to themselves. You know, pack the kids off to Sunday school, then Mum and Dad have some free time – possibly Dad's only afternoon off – to do whatever they like. Need I say more?' He grinned. 'And some may not like the idea of the family service that we plan to do once a month; the children in church with their parents – we hope – and a much more free and easy form of worship. Anyway, we'll see what sort of a response we get tomorrow...'

–

Parts of St Peter's church dated from the fourteenth century. There was a faint musty, though not unpleasant aroma on entering; of old hymn books and bibles, together with the scent of furniture polish and the spring flowers – hyacinths and daffodils – on top of the closed stone font and on the altar. It did not feel cold and clammy as did some ancient buildings, but comfortably warm with the heat circulating from the iron grilles set in the floor along the central aisle.

Ginny looked round at the massive stone pillars and the vaulted ceiling. The high-backed pews did not look as though they were built for comfort, although there were flat cushions along the length to make it a little easier on the posterior, and kneelers – she thought that the correct name was hassocks – with colourful tapestry covers adding a touch of brightness to the dark oak pews. Fiona told her later that they had been made by a band of willing parishioners to celebrate the coronation of Queen Elizabeth in 1953; designs of flowers of the realm, birds and animals, heraldic beasts, and some in simple geometric patterns.

One's eyes grew accustomed to the dimness as diffused light shone in through the stained glass windows. Ginny's eyes were drawn to the one of Christ in glory over the altar, with scenes of the Nativity and the Crucifixion on either side. The altar cloth of rich red and blue was embroidered with golden lilies, and another focal point was the brass lectern in the shape of an eagle with outstretched wings.

Ginny and Arthur sat in a pew about halfway down the church. Fiona had explained that she could not be with them as she sang in the choir, but Joan Tweedale, a few rows in front, turned round giving them a little wave and a smile. Ginny, taking her cue from those around her, knelt down on entering the pew and nudged Arthur to do the same. At the mid-Victorian church that they occasionally attended in South Shields – Ginny slightly more often than Arthur – the worshippers simply bowed their heads whilst remaining seated. She knew, though, with her limited experience, that there was a good deal of diversity in the Church of England, ranging from what they called Low Church to Anglo-Catholic. She guessed that this church was what you might call 'middle of the road'; there were no candles or incense, neither did they bow their heads to the altar.

The organist who Ginny knew to be Henry Tweedale, Joan's husband, played before the service started – not solemn music but what she recognized as songs from popular shows: 'O, What a Beautiful Morning' – which it was; cool, but bright and sunny – and then 'Who Shall Buy This Wonderful Morning?' from *Oliver*. Then the choir processed round the church, with Simon at the head, to the singing of 'O, Jesus I Have Promised' – to a catchy new tune – then the service began.

Ginny thought there was a goodly number in the congregation, but then she didn't know how many usually attended. At a glance she guessed there could be forty or more children, some with their parents, others obviously with their Sunday school teachers. The very young children, including Stella, were being cared for in the usual crèche. There were two young children, though, whose parents had decided to keep them in church; but they were clearly in need of firmer handling than they were receiving. They shouted out in loud voices, and ran up and down the aisle a couple of times, resulting in annoyed glances and cries of 'Shush!' from a few older members of the congregation.

Simon looked handsome in his regulation white surplice and royal blue stole. Ginny could quite understand how her friend had fallen for him. She guessed that there might have been other young women who had felt the same, but who had been doomed to disappointment. He did not stick rigidly to the set service for morning worship, only using the more necessary prayers and responses. The readings for the day – the collect, epistle and gospel – were read, very ably, by three of the older Sunday school children, which was clearly a break from tradition.

The anthem sung by the choir was far from traditional as well: 'When Morning Gilds the Skies', sung to a very jazzy tune. Ginny watched Fiona singing away joyously and pondered again how contented she was in her new life.

The newly formed guitar group played and sang two rousing numbers: 'When the Saints Go Marching In' and, 'Go Tell It on the Mountain'. And the singing of the hymns, chosen for a younger congregation, almost raised the roof, especially 'Give Me Oil in My Lamp' with the chorus of 'Sing Hosanna', to which the congregation was asked to clap in time to the rhythm. There were many, though, who kept their hands still, and quite a few far from joyful faces. Ginny was comparing it all with the somewhat feeble singing that she remembered from their own parish church. She guessed that it was not always the norm here, but was being done in order to cater for today's more youthful congregation.

Neither was there a sermon as such. Simon's address was geared to the children, with visual aids – cards and objects held up by eager participants – telling of God's care for all his people, not only here but in all parts of the world.

Simon stood at the door after the service, shaking hands with everyone as they left. Ginny and Arthur waited at the back of the church for Fiona to disrobe from her choir regalia in the vestry. No one, except Joan, knew who they were, and they could not help hearing the comments of the people as they passed by.

'Well, it was different; I'll say that...'

'The children enjoyed it anyway…'

'That was lively, wasn't it? Of course, Simon's services are never really dull, are they…?'

'Well then, what did you make of that? More like a pop concert than a service if you ask me!' This comment came from a corpulent, self-important-looking woman wearing a large brimmed hat. She and her companion were standing by the table where pamphlets and church magazines were displayed, not seeming to care if their remarks were heard by others. 'And it won't be only us who disapprove, you mark my words!'

'Yes, it was very noisy, wasn't it?' said the other woman, though rather more diffidently. She was a thin, grey-haired woman, of indeterminate age, with wire-rimmed spectacles and a hat like a pudding basin. 'And those children running wild! Children should be taught how to behave in church.'

'I quite agree; it was disgraceful!' said the larger woman.

Fiona appeared at that moment, and the women stopped their backbiting to murmur, 'Good morning, Mrs Norwood.'

'Good morning, Mrs Bayliss… Miss Thorpe.' Fiona smiled brightly, inclining her head at them. 'Did you enjoy the service?'

'I'd rather not comment,' answered the larger lady, and her friend nodded subserviently.

'Oh well, I suppose we can't please all the people all the time.' Fiona smiled again, turning her attention to Ginny and Arthur. 'Hello there. Let's go and collect Stella, then we'll see about some lunch.' The two women had the grace to look a little subdued.

They had a brief word with Simon, who was still busy with several of the parishioners, collected Stella from the crèche in the church hall, then set off back to the rectory, just a couple of minutes' walk away.

'Who are those two women?' asked Ginny. 'They had quite a lot to say!'

'The larger one is Mrs Ethel Bayliss, a long-time adversary of mine,' replied Fiona, 'although she has seemed a lot better recently, I must admit. And the little one is Miss Mabel Thorpe, one of her minions; too much of a "yes woman" for my liking. At least you know where you are with Mrs Bayliss. What were they saying? Maybe I shouldn't ask, but I think I can guess, anyway.'

'Well, they didn't approve of the service,' said Ginny. 'That's it, really, in a nutshell. But we enjoyed it, didn't we, Arthur?'

'Yes, I must admit I enjoyed it very much,' said Arthur, obviously meaning what he said. He laughed. 'I've changed my mind about vicars since getting to know your Simon. But don't tell him I said so!'

Fiona smiled. 'Not all clergyman are like Simon. He's quite unique, though I would say that, wouldn't I? I'm very lucky, and the people at St Peter's are lucky, too. I think most of them realize it.'

The rest of their time in Aberthwaite passed by all too quickly for Ginny and Arthur. After lunch – a simple casserole dish that cooked itself in the oven whilst they were at church – they walked by the riverside along to the ruined castle. Then, after a sandwich tea they set off back to Tyneside, leaving Simon to prepare for the evening service, and Fiona to get her little girl to bed. As they said goodbye, Fiona and Ginny rather tearfully, they promised it would not be so long this time before they met up again.

'It's been a grand couple of days, hasn't it?' said Arthur, as they drove away. 'And Simon's a smashing fellow. D'you know pet, I almost feel like giving church a go again?'

'We've nothing to lose,' agreed Ginny. 'It might not be anything like St Peter's, but we won't know till we try.'

'I like Fiona too,' said Arthur. 'They're just right together, those two, and that cute little girl. I don't suppose you're too bothered now, are you, about what happened before?'

'No… She's very happy,' said Ginny. 'She probably never thinks about that first baby now… Well, maybe now and again. But I'm convinced, now, that it would be wrong to rake it all up again. She's secure in her own little world, and she doesn't need any complications.'

She said as much to Ryan the next day.

'Well, how was your friend, Fiona?' he asked. 'And the vicar?'

'Very well and very happy,' she answered. 'Now, I want you to promise me, Ryan, that you won't breathe a word about what you know to your friend – well, Shirley's friend – Debbie. It's best to let sleeping dogs lie, as they say.'

'I promise, Mum,' he replied. 'Honestly; cross my heart and hope to die!' He put his hand to his chest in a dramatic gesture.

'No need to go so far, just so long as you understand.'

'Yes, I do,' Ryan assured her. 'I won't breathe a word.'

Ten

The O level results were published in mid-August. Debbie was there at the school at ten thirty in the morning of the big day with her friend, Shirley. There was no school bus provided so Shirley's father had run them there in his car and agreed to wait for them outside.

There was a good deal of pushing and jostling – mainly good-tempered – around the board where the results were listed in alphabetical order. And shouts of, 'Oh my God!! I've got all nine! I don't believe it...' 'Two As, three Bs, three Cs; not bad, I suppose...' 'Oh crikey! Four Cs, four Ds; God knows what my mam'll say...'

Debbie and Shirley grinned at one another as they waited to get near the notice board. Debbie was trying to put on a show of nonchalance. Secretly she wanted to do well. Who didn't? But she liked to give the impression that she didn't care all that much. She was determined not to go along with the plans that her parents had in mind for her. Sixth form, college or university, then a good steady job... According to her mother the pinnacle of achievement was for her to become a teacher. Debbie couldn't think of anything she wanted less.

'We'd be so proud of you, Debbie love...' How many times had she heard the same old tale? 'It's something I would have loved to do but we didn't get the chances, your daddy and me, like you've got. We had to leave

school when we were fourteen...' And so on and so on...
'Besides, you're a clever girl, Debbie. It's such a shame to
throw it all away... to water plants in a garden centre, of
all things!'

Debbie had retorted that if gardening was good enough
for her dad then it was good enough for her. Her father
had smiled, sort of sadly and understandingly, when she
said that. He wasn't as adamant as was her mother about
what she ought to do. He didn't seem to be so fixed on the
idea of teaching. Her dad's thoughts were running more
along the lines of an agricultural college or something of
the sort, after she had spent two years in the sixth form.
Debbie admitted to herself that that might not be too bad
an idea eventually; but she certainly didn't intend to say so
– not yet. She had had enough of school despite Shirley's
odd notion that it would be fun in the sixth form.

Debbie had been working each and every day at
Sunnyhill since the term had ended in July; and she
wanted to go on doing so on a permanent basis. OK, she
would agree to go to night school. It might not be a bad
idea to learn more about horticulture. The more she knew
the better she would be able to do her job. Even she could
see that she wasn't likely to stay at Sunnyhill forever. She
might want to branch out, even have a place of her own
in time. Of course, it all depended on Kevin.

Things were going very well with him at the moment.
Since finishing school she had been seeing him more
regularly, almost every night, in fact. He had even been
invited to the house for tea – Sunday tea at that – and he
had made a good impression on her parents. Of course
her mother remarked, the following day, that Kevin was a
very nice lad. 'But you'll meet lots of other boys, Debbie.
Don't start getting all serious about him and thinking he's

the one for you. You're far too young to know your own mind yet.'

But Debbie was sure that she did know her own mind; and she hoped that Kevin was of the same mind as she was. He seemed to be happy going out with her; and he hadn't said any more recently about her being cleverer than him and how she could do something much better than working in a garden centre. He knew that it annoyed her when he talked like that; and so he had kept off the subject of her career, and he had said no more either about what she had told him of her adoption.

When they managed to squeeze their way in to look at the results Debbie discovered that she had passed in all nine subjects; not that she had expected to fail in any – that would be unheard of – but she had done extremely well; seven As and two Bs, those in her least favourite subjects, French and History.

'Well done you!' said Shirley. She had got two As, in English Literature and English Language, and the rest were Bs and Cs. 'I knew you'd do well, Debs. I suppose I've not done too badly; it's as good as I expected anyway. At least I'll be able to go into the sixth... I do wish you'd decide to stay on as well.'

'What's the point?' replied Debbie. 'And what's the point of you going when you don't know what job you want to do? You don't, do you?'

'No, not really. I might decide to go in for teaching. Or I might be a librarian... I'm keeping my options open.' It was the sort of thing Shirley's mother might have said.

You mean you've no idea what you want to do, thought Debbie, but she didn't say that. 'You could go and work in a library now,' she said. 'You don't need A levels to do that.'

'No, but education's never wasted,' answered Shirley, another old-fashioned phrase that sounded as though she was quoting her mother. Her next words proved it. 'Anyway, that's what Mum and Dad want me to do… Your parents will be pleased, won't they, Debbie?'

'Oh yes; they'll be over the moon!' Debbie rolled her eyes heavenwards. 'I'll never hear the last of it. About how they never had the chances I've had, and I mustn't throw it all away. I must settle down and be a good obedient little girl…'

'You're barmy, you are!' said Shirley, giving her a playful push. 'Suppose you'd done badly. Suppose you'd got all Ds, or even lower grades, like some of 'em have?' There were, indeed, some miserable faces and a few tears being shed. 'You are pleased, aren't you?'

'Of course I am, you idiot!' said Debbie laughing. She pushed her back. 'I'm just sorry that I didn't get all As. I thought I might… but I suppose you don't get everything you want. Look, there's your Ryan just coming in. I'll go and have a chat with Jean and Marjorie. See you later…'

Shirley came to find her about ten minutes later. Ryan was with her, of course. 'Come on, Debbie,' she said. 'We'd better not keep my dad waiting any longer.'

'No… sorry,' said Debbie. 'I'm ready now.' She was feeling a little disgruntled because Jean and Marjorie had not gone overboard with their congratulations on her good results. Sour grapes! she thought to herself. Their results, as expected, had been only mediocre. In spite of that they were two more sixth form aspirants. Was there no one, apart from herself, who wanted a life outside of school?

'How have you done, Ryan?' she asked, trying to be nice to him for Shirley's sake.

'Oh, so-so, you know,' he replied.

'He's done very well,' Shirley butted in. 'You know you're pleased, Ryan. He's got three As!'

'Jolly good,' said Debbie.

Ryan shrugged. 'Not bad, I suppose. Not as good as you, though, clever clogs!' He grinned affably at Debbie, and she decided that he was perhaps not too bad after all.

'See you tomorrow, Ryan,' said Shirley, leaving him to talk with his friends. He gave her a quick peck on the cheek. 'Yeh... See you Shirl... Bye, Debbie; see you around.'

Mr Crompton seemed pleased at his daughter's results. 'You've done well, love,' he said. 'You too, Debbie. Your parents will be pleased.' But he didn't enthuse, nor did she expect him to.

'Thank you for taking me, Mr Crompton,' said Debbie as she got out of the car. She was always polite, as she had been brought up to be. 'See you, Shirley...' she added, the usual farewell words between friends.

'Yes... see you, Debbie...'

She steeled herself then to face the rapturous reception from her mother who was, predictably, ecstatic at her results. She flung her arms round her daughter. 'Oh, you clever girl! Your daddy will be so pleased. I can't wait to tell him tonight. But it's only what we expected, Debbie love. We know how hard you've worked.' Actually, Debbie knew that she hadn't exactly flogged herself to death with her revision. She had a retentive memory, and recalling facts came easily to her. 'Now, sit down and tell me all about it,' said her mother.

'Actually, there isn't anything else to tell you, Mum,' said Debbie, a little edgily. 'I've told you the results, and that's all there is; end of story. I haven't much time now, anyway, because I've promised Mr Hill I'll go in this afternoon.'

'Oh dear!' Her mother's face fell. 'I didn't realize you'd be going in to work today. I thought he might have let you have the whole day off.'

'I offered, Mum. It's no big deal!'

'All right then, love. I'll make you a sandwich, shall I? Will that do?'

'Yes, anything, so long as it's quick. I said I'd be back by two.'

'I'll have a sandwich with you,' said her mother. 'It's all we'll need really, because...' Her eyes lit up excitedly as she went on. 'We've got a surprise for you, your daddy and me. We're going out for a meal tonight! What do you think about that, eh? And then we've booked seats at the Palace theatre – second house – to see the variety show. To celebrate!'

Debbie's heart sank to the soles of her shoes. Oh no! She'd been hoping to see Kevin tonight, although he hadn't actually said so. And a variety show of all things! Yuck! She knew, though, that she must try to look pleased, if she could manage it. She gave a little laugh. 'But how did you know that we'd have something to celebrate?'

'Because we know you, pet,' said her mother. 'We knew you'd do well. Anyway, your dad's finishing work early, and we've booked a table at that new restaurant on the prom. We've heard it's very good.'

A myriad of thoughts were going through Debbie's mind as she listened to her mother's animated chatter. It was certainly a special occasion if her parents – especially her father – were willing to spend an evening away from their home. 'Eating out' was fashionable now, but Stanley Hargreaves was of the opinion that there was no point in going out for a meal when you could eat just as well – probably better – at home, and at a fraction of the cost. And very rarely could the two of them be tempted to leave their fireside and the 'telly' to watch entertainment elsewhere. So long as they could watch *Coronation Street* and *Dad's Army*, and the weekend quiz shows and variety shows they wished for nothing more. So for them to be dining out and going to a theatre both in the same evening was really a red-letter occasion.

There was a nicer side to Debbie. The bolshie attitude she adopted, and of which she knew she had been guilty of recently, was partly an act of bravado. She did know, deep down, that her parents loved her and only wanted what was best for her – in their view. She knew, too, that she loved them, and she realized now how proud they must be of her achievements. And so she decided not to be difficult but to go along with their plans for the evening with the best grace that she could muster. There would be other times she could spend with Kevin. And on Saturday evening there was Carol's party at the seafront hotel owned by her parents, to which several of the girl's form mates had been invited. Debbie had managed to persuade Kevin to go with her, so there was a lot to look forward to. If she went along with them now, then maybe her mum and dad would try to see things more from her point of view. It so happened that she was beginning to waver with regard to school and college and all that, but for the sake of her pride she was determined not to give in too easily.

So she smiled now and said, 'Yes, great! That sounds nice, Mum. I was a bit surprised, that's all. You and dad, you don't often want to go out, do you?'

'No, but like I said, love, this is a time for celebration. Do you think Mr Hill will let you finish a little earlier?'

'Yes, I'm sure he will,' said Debbie. 'I'll come and help you to make the sandwiches, shall I?'

'Thank you, Debbie!' Her amazement showed in her face as she beamed at her daughter. 'A job shared is a job halved, as they say...'

—

Kevin was in a greenhouse at the far end of the garden centre when Debbie arrived at Sunnyhill promptly at two o'clock. 'Oh, hello there,' he said, nodding at her then looking away to carry on with the job he was doing. 'Hang on a minute while I finish watering these toms.' He walked away, further down the row of plants.

She followed him. 'Aren't you going to ask me how I've gone on?'

'What?' He put down the watering can. 'Oh yes, of course; your exams. How did you go on?'

'Seven As, two Bs,' she answered, feeling more than a little miffed.

'Oh, that's good is it?' he asked, grinning at her.

'Of course it is!' she snapped.

'Well, congratulations then,' he said. He saw that she looked somewhat put out, so he put his arm round her. 'Well done!' he added, with a little more enthusiasm. 'But it's what you expected, isn't it?'

She shrugged. 'I suppose so. I'm sorry, though, Kevin; we won't be able to go out tonight because my parents have planned a surprise for me.' She grimaced. 'A meal out, then seats at the variety show. Honestly!'

'What's the matter? That sounds very nice,' he replied. 'Actually, I'd planned to go out with my mates tonight. Perhaps we could go somewhere on Saturday, eh?'

'It's Carol's party on Saturday night,' she answered, sounding more than a little peeved. 'Don't say you'd forgotten?'

'Oh yes, so there is. No, I hadn't forgotten; it just slipped my mind for the moment, that's all.'

'I'd better get on with my work then.' She turned her back and walked away.

'Cheerio then,' he called after her. 'Enjoy yourself tonight.'

Debbie didn't answer. She felt utterly deflated, her euphoria of the morning – she had been pleased at her results despite her show of indifference – fast disappearing.

At least her parents were pleased with her, she consoled herself. She made up her mind she would humour them tonight and show them how nice she could be when she tried. Mr Hill agreed that she could finish early – in fact she could take the afternoon off if she wished. She decided she would do a few little jobs and then depart. Kevin's father, unlike his son, congratulated her warmly on her success, although she didn't much care for his remark that she would soon be leaving them all far behind.

–

Vera was pleased when Debbie arrived home early; in fact she was back again only an hour after she had gone out.

'Mr Hill said I could have the afternoon off,' she said, adding, 'he was pleased to hear about my exam results.'

'I should think he was,' said Vera. 'We're all very proud of you. Was Kevin pleased?'

'Uh-huh, I think so... Er, yes, he was,' she answered evasively. 'He was busy working, so I didn't stay to hinder him.'

Vera thought she sounded a little put out; maybe they'd had a tiff. She, Vera, would not be sorry if this friendship with Kevin came to an end. He was a very nice lad, pleasant and well-brought-up, but Debbie could do much better for herself. It was too soon, anyway, for her to be having a serious courtship – if they called it that any more. He was her first boyfriend, and it sounded now as though she was not quite so keen about him as she had been. Maybe her splendid exam results had made her realize that she should take notice of what everyone was telling her, and continue with her studies instead of working at a job which Vera was sure she would soon tire of.

A fleeting thought came into Vera's mind; she had been not much older than Debbie when she had started going out with Stanley; they had called it courting then. It had been different, though. There had been no question of what they called 'higher education' for either of them. They had been two ordinary teenagers – although the term hadn't been used then – with ordinary jobs, and they had known, almost from the start, that all in good time they would get engaged and then married.

Vera was pleased now that her daughter, for once, seemed to be in a good mood. When Stanley came home, early as promised, Debbie actually seemed delighted to tell him how well she had done; earlier in the day she had appeared very offhand about it all.

'This calls for a little celebration,' said Stanley. 'There's some sherry left from Christmas, isn't there, Mummy?' He often referred to his wife as 'Mummy' when Debbie was there, just as he was 'Daddy'. She was growing up though now, thought Vera, as she listened to him. Maybe they should start treating her more as an adult.

'Yes, I think so, Stanley,' she answered, giving a little laugh. 'I don't know why you keep calling me "Mummy". I'm not your mummy, am I?' She opened the sideboard cupboard and brought out a bottle, still half full, of the dark Emva Cream sherry that she always bought as a treat at Christmas, to sip whilst they were listening to the Queen's speech.

'Yes, I think we could allow ourselves a little tipple,' she said. 'Not too much, though, because I dare say we'll be having some wine tonight, won't we, Daddy... er, Stanley?' She poured the sherry into three gold-rimmed glasses, handing them to her husband and daughter. 'We'd better have a biscuit with it,' she said, 'It goes straight to my head on an empty stomach.'

The tin containing 'Nice' and 'Rich Tea' biscuits was opened and they all took one.

'Cheers, then,' said Stanley, 'and congratulations to you, Debbie. We're proud of you, love.' Debbie smiled graciously as they clinked their glasses and sipped at the unaccustomed treat.

When they were ready to embark on the evening out Vera was relieved to see that Debbie had dressed more suitably than she had dared to hope for. Like all girls of her age, she had a few miniskirts and dresses, some so short that little was left to the imagination. On the other hand, she sometimes wore long trailing skirts in drab shades of black grey or brown, bought from jumble sales or second-hand clothing shops, with a black polo-necked sweater – these were still in fashion from the time of Beatlemania – or a 'skinny rib' that clung tightly to her developing figure.

Tonight, though, she was wearing a conventional summery dress with white polka dots on a red background, which was not too short, with a fashionable chain belt round her waist. Her shoes were strappy sandals, not the clumpy things that she sometimes favoured. Her hair, too, was not so excessively backcombed as usual, and her make-up was more discreet.

'You look very nice, dear,' her mother told her.

She replied, with just a hint of sarcasm, 'Yes, very suitable for the occasion, isn't it, Mum?'

'We're doing things in style tonight,' Stanley remarked with a beaming smile, as a taxi rolled up at the door. It would not have been all that far to walk to the Bayview restaurant on the promenade but, as Stanley said, no expense was to be spared.

The restaurant had been opened about six months previously, and was proving popular with visitors to the resort and with the residents. It was what could be termed homely rather than posh, with red-checked cloths on the tables, contemporary crockery rather than fine china, and paintings by local artists on the walls, which could be purchased at a reasonable price.

Vera was relieved that the menu was not in French, as she knew it was in some places, and there were several dishes that she felt would be to her liking. She and Stanley were very conventional in their eating, which was why they had opted to come here instead of to one of the Indian or Chinese restaurants that were opening up in the town.

'What are you going to have, Debbie?' Vera asked, a little hesitantly, looking to her daughter for advice. 'Can you find something you like?'

'Of course,' said Debbie, with a confident air. 'Quite a lot of things actually. It's quite a comprehensive menu. I shall have prawn cocktail for a starter. It's what everybody's having now. Go on, you try it, Mum. I'm sure you'll like it.'

Vera had never eaten prawns, but she decided to be guided by her daughter. She found the tiny pink morsels, coated in a rich pink sauce on a bed of lettuce and cucumber, to be very nice indeed. Stanley stuck to the more conventional tomato soup.

She could not, however, be persuaded to try duck with an orange sauce, which Debbie had chosen as her main course, but opted for steak, served with chips, peas and mushrooms. 'I'm not sure about the mushrooms,' she wavered. 'They're a sort of fungus, aren't they? I might not like them.'

'Go on, Mum; be a devil!' Debbie urged her. 'They're nice; you'll like them.'

'When have you had them then?' asked Vera. 'Not at home, that's for sure.'

'No; I had them at Shirley's once, when I went for tea. Mushrooms on toast. It was yummy!'

'Oh, I see.' Vera nodded, thinking that Shirley's mum was a good deal more adventurous than she was. 'Go on then, I'll try them… And we must order some wine, Stanley.'

The waiter, noting Stanley's puzzled perusal of the large wine list, suggested that they should try Liebfraumilch. 'A very pleasant wine, from Germany, sir,' he said, a trifle condescendingly Vera thought. 'Quite reasonably priced. I think it should suit all your requirements.'

Stanley was puzzled, too, that he was expected to taste it first; the waiter had poured a small amount into a glass and offered it to him. 'Yes… er, very nice,' he mumbled, and the waiter poured it into their three glasses.

Vera enjoyed the mushrooms, which she ate cautiously at first. There was a large mushroom, too, on the mixed grill that Stanley had ordered. He gingerly tasted a corner of it, pulled a face, then pushed it to the side of his plate. But he ate all the rest – a very substantial meal – with the accompaniment of his favourite HP sauce, and pronounced it very good. 'But your cooking's just as good, any day of the week,' he whispered to his wife, 'The wine's not bad either,' he added. 'A nice treat, once in a while.'

Guided by Debbie, they all decided to have Black Forest gateau for the sweet – or pudding, as Debbie called it – another popular dish of the time.

'And very nice too,' Stanley remarked, patting at his stomach. 'I'm full up now. I don't know about you two. We'll not bother with coffee, eh? Anyway, we'd best get a move on. We don't want to miss the start of the show.'

Vera was a little embarrassed when Stanley studied the bill, trying to find the exact money to give to the waitress. A very pleasant young girl had served them, unlike the wine waiter who had been rather snooty. Stanley fumbled with the half crowns and shillings from his pocket, together with the pound notes, more than he was used to dealing with at one go.

'A tip, Stanley,' Vera whispered, giving him a nudge.

'Oh yes, of course. Er… how much do you think?' he whispered back.

'Oh, give her five shillings,' said Vera, very red-faced by this time.

Stanley parted with two more half crowns, and the girl seemed very pleased. 'Thank you, sir,' she said. 'We hope you'll dine with us again soon.'

'Er, yes… I'm sure we will. Thank you, miss,' said Stanley.

'Whew!' he exclaimed, when they were out on the pavement. 'I was a bit out of me depth there, Vera pet.'

'Never mind, Stanley; you coped very well,' she assured him. 'And it was a lovely meal, wasn't it, Debbie?'

'Yes, smashing!' said Debbie, dissolving into a fit of giggles. She was really in a very jovial mood tonight, thought Vera. She usually made it seem like such a drag when she had to go somewhere with her parents. But maybe it was partly due to the glass and a half of wine she had drunk. Her cheeks were pink and her eyes sparkled. Vera herself felt light-headed; she hoped she wouldn't nod off during the show.

The Palace theatre was just across the road from the restaurant, on the sea side of the promenade; a mid-Victorian building that had been popular through the years with the entertaining variety shows they put on in the summer, interspersed with the occasional play and the annual Christmas pantomime. They did not attract the top flight of performers; comedians such as Ken Dodd, Jewel and Warris, or Jimmy Edwards, who topped the bill at resorts like Blackpool, Torquay and Brighton; or singers like Cilla Black, Shirley Bassey, Dickie Valentine or Harry Secombe. There were so many of these stars now, household names whom most people had only heard on the radio or watched on the television screen. All the same, it was reckoned to be an entertaining show, and Vera settled down into her rather worn red plush seat, ready to enjoy it.

It was, on the whole, quite a good show for a small and somewhat insignificant seaside resort. A group of dancers, reminiscent of the Tiller Girls, opened the show, first and second half, their movements perfectly synchronized and their bright smiles never slipping. There were a tenor and a soprano who sang a duet, and performed singly; a comedian with an accompanying stooge; a ventriloquist; a juggling act; a magician – 'The Magic Malvolio'; and a comedy sketch involving several of the company in different guises. The very small orchestra performed bravely and the audience was very appreciative.

Vera was pleased to see that Debbie was enjoying it; she was keeping a surreptitious eye on her; you could never tell with Debbie. At least she laughed and applauded in the right places, and enjoyed a tub of ice cream with a tiny wooden spoon, at the interval, just as she used to do when she was a little girl.

After they had stood to sing 'God Save the Queen' there was a dash for the exit. Fortunately Stanley managed to hail a taxi almost straight away, and they were home in no time.

'Thank you; that was a nice evening,' said Debbie, so meekly and politely that Vera could scarcely believe it. 'I'm off to bed now if you don't mind.' She actually went so far as to kiss them both on the cheek before dashing upstairs.

Vera made a cup of Ovaltine for herself and Stanley, and they sat and chatted for a little while although it was long past their usual bedtime.

'Well, that was a great success, wasn't it?' said Stanley. 'She seems like a different girl.'

Vera pondered that 'seems' was the operative word, but she agreed with her husband. 'Yes, she's certainly in a better frame of mind.'

'Happen she's realizing that what we say about school an' all that makes sense, eh pet?'

'Let's hope so,' said Vera. 'Best not to mention it again, though, too soon. We'll give it a day or two, then we really must try to make her understand that we want her to make the most of her opportunities.'

'Aye…' Stanley nodded, smiling contentedly. 'I reckon she'll make us proud of her in the end, our little lass.'

Yes, maybe she would, eventually, thought Vera to herself. But she suspected that there might be all kinds of problems ahead before that day arrived.

Eleven

When Debbie returned to work the next day she was relieved that Kevin was more like his old self. She had thought for an awful moment the previous day that he was tiring of her. He met her at the gate as she alighted from her bicycle and walked up the path with her.

'Well, did you enjoy yourself last night?' he asked. 'Your evening out with Mummy and Daddy?' His eyes twinkled mischievously.

'Yes, I did, actually,' she answered. 'We had a fabulous meal that made up for the show; that was a bit of a bore, to be honest. You'd have laughed, though, Kevin. My dad got in a right pickle about giving the waitress a tip, and my mum was as red as a beetroot. They're really not used to dining out an' all that. I couldn't stop giggling.'

He looked at her sharply. 'I expect they did their best, Debbie. Don't be such a snob.'

'I'm not! How can you say that?' she retorted. 'I told you... it was very nice. I said thank you to them. But if they think I'm going to fall in with all their ideas just because they've taken me out for a meal, they can think again!'

'All right, all right! Don't get your knickers in a twist!' He pushed at her playfully. 'I'm looking forward to Carol's party on Saturday. I remember her sister, Sandra, from when I was at Kelder Bank. We were in the same year, not in the same form, though. She was in an A form, not with the thickies, like me.'

'Yes, Sandra'll be there too,' said Debbie. 'The party's for her and Carol. Don't run yourself down though, Kevin. Thickies, indeed! You're as good as anybody else... See, I'm not a snob. How can I be?'

'If you knock about with such as me, you mean?' he smiled.

'No, I didn't mean that at all! Stop picking me up on everything I say, Kevin.'

He burst out laughing. 'You're a funny kid, Debbie, you are really! Oh, by the way, my dad wants to see you when you have your break.'

'What about?'

'I've no idea. He just asked me to tell you.'

'OK; see you later then, Kevin.'

'Yeh... See you, Debs...'

She parked her bicycle in one of the stands and made her way to the garden shop. She was to take a turn there this morning, serving customers from a large range of goods, from cut flowers, seeds and plants, to all sorts of garden requisites. She put on her apple green overall which was the uniform and said hello to Mrs Hill who, seemingly, was also on duty at the shop that day. She helped out where and when she could in the business, as well as seeing to the needs of her home and family.

'I thought I'd make a few floral decorations this morning,' she said. 'You can give me a hand, Debbie. I've noticed you're getting quite a flair for it. How about trying one on your own? Choose the container you want, and here's the oasis...' Debbie set to work with a boat-shaped container into which she placed a block of green oasis. There was a wide variety of seasonal flowers to choose from at the moment. She decided to go for reddish hues, ranging from pale pink to deep crimson and purple; roses, sweet peas, dahlias, small button chrysanthemums, and sweet-scented stock. She was pleased that Mrs Hill had asked her to do one on her own. Kevin's mother usually took charge of the arrangements with just a little assistance. They made artificial ones as well, especially in the autumn and at Christmas time when fresh flowers were not so abundant.

Her thoughts wandered as her hands worked deftly, snipping at the blooms and the greenery. She felt a little vexed with Kevin. He had seemed all right at first, then he had laughed at her and made her feel like a stupid child, goodness knows why! And what did his father want with her?

She went to find Mr Hill at eleven o'clock when Mrs Hill sent her for her morning break. 'That's a superb arrangement, Debbie,' she told her. 'Well done! I wouldn't be surprised if that's snapped up in no time.' They didn't make all that many arrangements as most people preferred to buy bunches of flowers and make their own displays.

Mr Hill had a cup of coffee waiting for her when she joined him in the office, which was really just an annexe to the living room in the family home, adjacent to the garden centre.

'Hello there, Debbie,' he greeted her. 'Sit down, pet. Here; have a biscuit.' She took one from the plate of chocolate digestives.

'Now, I've a little favour to ask of you,' he began. 'We've got a new girl starting on Monday, and I wondered if you would take her under your wing and help her to settle in. She's a bit shy, you see; but she's really keen and she's got such an affinity with plants, like you have.

She's the daughter of a friend of ours; she's just left school and this will be an ideal job for her. Especially as you'll be leaving us soon, won't you, when you go back to school? It's been great having you here for the whole of the summer holidays, but we need someone to take your place... Is something the matter, Debbie?'

She realized that her dismay must show on her face. She had been so happy this morning, working with the flowers. Mrs Hill had complimented her, and she felt she was where she wanted to be, surrounded by plants and flowers, things of the earth; helping to nurture them and make them grow. The idea of another girl coming along and taking her place was... well, it was something she couldn't imagine at all. She knew she had been wavering about returning to school since she had got those good results, but this had brought her streak of determination – it might be called stubbornness – to the fore.

'Er... I hadn't actually decided about going back to school,' she said.

'Hadn't you?' Mr Hill looked at her in surprise. 'Why not, Debbie? You're such a clever girl, and you've got a great future ahead of you. I met your father not long ago, and he was telling me how proud they are of you, and how they were looking forward to you going to college one day...'

'Oh yes, my parents!' She shook her head crossly and almost stamped her feet. 'But that's just their idea...' She looked at him pleadingly. Surely he would understand. 'I like working here, Mr Hill,' she went on, 'and I was thinking that I might be able to go on working here all the time. I mean... you did say once, didn't you, that you'd give me a full-time job?'

'Did I?' He looked surprised. 'Well, yes… I suppose I might have said something of the sort, but I only meant that I would if I could. But a job like this is not for the likes of you, Debbie. We'd still want you during the holidays, of course; that is, if you'd like to carry on with us?'

'Yes, I might…' replied Debbie. 'I must have misunderstood you. It's just that I'm doing exactly the job I want to do; working with plants, an' all that. I can't imagine wanting to do anything else.'

'There's nothing to stop you making a proper career of it,' said Mr Hill. 'There are all sorts of openings for a clever girl like you. You can take courses and degrees in horticulture and agriculture. Or have you thought about landscape gardening? My wife tells me you've an eye for design and colour. Would something like that appeal to you?' He smiled understandingly at her; she could see he was trying to help.

She smiled back, nodding her head. 'Yes, maybe it would…' She knew she must hide her disappointment and her annoyance that other people thought they knew best about what she should or shouldn't do. Besides, it wouldn't do to make Mr Hill aware of the other − not so nice − side to her nature, what her mother called 'nowtiness'.

'Anyway,' Mr Hill went on, 'your love of gardening will always be there, won't it? Whatever job − or career, I should say − you take up, it would still be there as a hobby. There's nothing quite so pleasurable as watching things grow.'

'Yes, thank you, Mr Hill,' she answered politely. 'And I'll look after the new girl for you; what is she called?'

'Julie,' he said. 'Julie Harper. Like I said, she's just left school. Not your school; she went to the secondary modern, but she's a bright little girl. She'll just need a bit of encouragement, that's all. Now, I'll leave you to finish your coffee in peace… Thanks for everything, Debbie. You're a great help to us here, you know.'

But you can manage quite well without me, she thought. She was still feeling miffed, and now she was to act as nursemaid to this new girl. She put on a cheerful face, though, when she returned to the shop; and she was gratified when her floral arrangement was sold, not long afterwards, to a posh lady who said it would make a lovely table centre for a dinner party she was having.

Kevin appeared at the shop when it was time for his midday break, and they found a sunny spot to eat their sandwiches together. At least he had come to find her, she reflected. Maybe he was regretting being so peculiar with her earlier.

'What did my dad want?' he asked.

'Nothing much,' she shrugged.

'He must have wanted something,' he persisted.

'Oh, all right, then. He asked me if I'd look after some new girl that's starting here on Monday. Julie… something or other.'

'Oh yes; Julie Harper. She's a nice kid; a bit on the quiet side, though. But you'll bring her out of her shell, won't you?'

'I might,' she answered. 'It all depends on whether we like one another, doesn't it?' Then, aware that her ill humour was getting the better of her, she decided to change the subject. 'I'm really looking forward to the party on Saturday,' she said. 'Will you call for me Kevin, or shall we meet outside the hotel?'

'No, I'll call for you,' said Kevin. 'I was thinking I might borrow my dad's car and go in style… but perhaps better not, eh? There'll be drinks laid on, won't there? Best not to drink and drive. Anyway, it's doubtful if he'd lend it me.'

Nobody could accuse Kevin of being reckless, Debbie pondered. 'Perhaps we could have a taxi,' she suggested. 'I know it's not all that far to walk, but I'll be wearing my new dress, and might be raining, you never know.'

'OK then. Anything Your Ladyship wants.' He made a mock bow at her. 'I'll come round for you in a taxi. About half past seven?'

'Yes; thanks, Kevin.' She smiled at him; he really was trying to please her. 'I don't know all that much about the party except that's it at the hotel that Carol's parents own. Carol says they're having a band. I expect there'll be drinks, although a lot of us aren't eighteen yet, are we?'

'You speak for yourself; I am!' said Kevin. 'I'll look after you. I dare say Mr Robson'll get round the licensing laws as it's a family party, and no doubt he'll keep an eye on what's going on.'

'It's a fabulous hotel,' said Debbie. 'Carol's parents must be loaded.'

–

Sandylands was, in fact, one of the largest hotels on the promenade of Whitesands Bay. It was privately owned by Mr and Mrs Robson, the parents of Carol, who was in the same form as Debbie, and Sandra, two years older, who had just finished her two years in the sixth form and planned to go to Durham University in September. Her recent A level results had made this a certainty.

To celebrate their daughters' successes their parents had agreed to throw a party for their friends at school and elsewhere, although most of them did attend Kelder Bank. Debbie had been delighted to be sent an invitation, especially as it said she could take someone else along with her, who would, of course, be Kevin. Shirley and Ryan were also invited. There would be around fifty in all, mainly from the fifth and sixth forms of Kelder Bank.

Mr and Mrs Robson had agreed to keep just a cursory eye on the proceedings from time to time, to make sure that things were not getting out of hand. But they trusted that their girls would invite only those who would behave themselves, and Carol and Sandra had agreed with this. The hotel had a good reputation; the functions held there were always first-class affairs, and the same guests came back year after year for holidays to enjoy the hospitality of a family run hotel.

They had hired a group; four local lads who called themselves the Groovy Guys. They sang and played guitars and drums, in a mixture of the style of the Beatles, and of the rather more outlandish Rolling Stones. Beatlemania as such was now a thing of the past, but their songs were still widely played. A female vocalist called Sally Diamond – an aspiring Cilla Black – would be performing as well.

–

Debbie and Shirley had been shopping in Newcastle to buy new clothes for the party. Debbie had saved up quite a lot from her earnings at the garden centre; she had to admit she was lucky because her mother let her keep most of it for herself. Shirley had a Saturday job at a newsagents' shop near her home, and she did a spot of babysitting now and again for neighbours.

First of all they went to C and A. They didn't know whether to go for minis or maxis, but as Carol had told them it would be quite an informal occasion they decided on minidresses. Debbie chose one in bright orange, almost what they were calling psychedelic, with a swirling pattern in black and white. Shirley, always more conservative in dress, went for a plain shift-style in kingfisher blue with lace at the sleeve edges and neckline.

They went to Stead and Simpson's next for new shoes. Heels were becoming thicker and not so high now; possibly less flattering to the legs, but fashionable and certainly easier to dance in. They both chose black patent leather. Shirley's had ankle-straps, and Debbie's had squarish toes with a large petersham bow decoration. They both already had shoulder bags with chain straps, and large white clip-on earrings from Woolworth's added the finishing touch.

'You look very nice, pet,' Debbie's mother told her when she came downstairs, ready for the evening out, after more than an hour spent in the bathroom and bedroom. Perhaps she glanced a mite critically at her daughter's make-up and hairstyle, but she did not pass any comment. It had taken Debbie ages, backcombing and lacquering and teasing her fringe into shape to get the desired effect, and she was wearing more eye make-up than usual. She had used the mascara and green eyeshadow liberally, and had experimented with eyeliner, which she hadn't tried before.

Her mother nodded, whether in approval or disapproval Debbie was not sure, but at least she smiled at her in a cosy, motherly sort of way. 'Won't you be cold, though, in that sleeveless dress?' she enquired. 'Hadn't you better take a cardigan in case it turns chilly?'

'A cardigan! Nobody wears cardigans, Mum.' Debbie laughed. 'They're dead old-fashioned. No; I shall wear this.' She held up a shawl that she had bought from a second-hand clothing shop. It was a lacy design, crocheted in black wool, and where there were one or two larger holes that shouldn't be there she had mended them with black cotton. 'It's a stole,' she said, draping it round her shoulders. 'It looks great, doesn't it?'

'Well, it's what I would call a shawl,' smiled her mother. 'But… yes, it does look rather nice.'

There was a ring at the doorbell. 'That'll be Kevin with the taxi,' said Debbie. 'Bye, Mum.' She kissed her briefly on the cheek. 'Bye, Dad.' Stanley was hidden behind the evening paper.

'Bye, pet. Have a nice time,' he called.

'Don't wait up for me,' said Debbie to her mother, who had insisted on going to the door with her. 'It'll probably be late… ish.'

'You know I always wait up,' said Vera. 'I wouldn't sleep anyway, until you were safely back home.' She opened the door to Kevin. 'Hello, Kevin. I hope you both have a lovely time.'

'Thank you, Mrs Hargreaves; I'm sure we will,' he said politely, adding, 'Don't worry, I'll look after Debbie.'

Debbie scowled a little. It wasn't the first time he had said that recently. Did he think she was a child in the infant school? 'I can look after myself, you know!' she hissed at him as they got into the taxi.

'I know you can,' he replied, putting his arm round her in the back of the cab. There was no hint of reproach in his voice, and she realized she was taking it out on him whereas it was her mother she was annoyed with. Waiting up for her indeed! 'I was just trying to show your mother that I'm not such a bad sort, that's all.' He grinned at her. 'And I must say you look lovely tonight, Debbie.'

'Thank you,' she said, snuggling closer to him. 'You don't look so bad yourself. New jacket, eh?'

'Yes, d'you like it? My mum said it was a bit too mod, but that's mothers for you, isn't it?' He was wearing a suede jacket in a russet brown colour, with a fringe at the bottom edge, teamed with black trousers with a slight flare, a pale blue shirt with a high collar, and a wide 'kipper' tie with a floral design in black and blue. She had never seen him look so trendy.

'I think it's fab,' she told him, her ill humour fading away.

She had never been inside Sandylands before, and she was impressed by the grandeur of the place. As they entered through the swing doors into the spacious foyer both Carol and Sandra were there to greet them. She noticed they were both wearing long skirts rather than minis, and wondered if she might have made the wrong decision, but then she noticed some more girls, in short dresses such as hers, standing nearby.

'Hello! So glad you could come!' Carol flung her arms round Debbie in an effusive manner. 'And you too, Kevin.' She smiled at him.

'Hello, Carol,' he said. 'And... Sandra. D'you remember me?' he asked the older girl. 'Kelder Bank, but I left two years ago.'

Sandra looked at him before exclaiming, 'Kevin Hill! Yes, of course I remember you. You went to work for your father, didn't you, at that garden place?'

'Yes, Sunnyhill, that's right.'

Sandra looked from him to Debbie. 'So, you and Debbie... you're going out together, are you?'

'Yes, we are,' said Debbie, with a confident nod.

'Er... yes, sort of,' added Kevin. He heard Debbie's indrawn breath. 'Well, yes, I suppose we are. Debbie works at our place in the holidays. That's how I met her and we... got friendly.'

Debbie got hold of his arm to pull him away.

'Catch up with you later then, Kevin,' called Sandra.

'Yeh... see you,' he answered.

Carol showed them into a large room at the rear of the hotel. There were small tables round the sides, a large table with drinks at one end, and at the other end the band members were setting up their equipment.

'Come on, let's bag some seats while we can,' said Kevin. 'They'll soon fill up.' Debbie was already heading towards the table where Shirley and Ryan were sitting.

'May we join you?' she asked.

'Yes, please do,' said Shirley, throwing an angry side-ways glance at Ryan, who was standing up to greet Kevin. 'Me and Ryan have had words,' she whispered to her friend.

'Then that'll make two of us,' Debbie whispered back. 'Honestly! I could kill Kevin!'

'Why, what's he done?'

'Tell you later... What's up with Ryan?'

'Can't say just now...'

The two lads were standing there chatting in a friendly way. They had met before a couple of times and had seemed to get on well together. They smiled at the girls now as though there was nothing wrong.

'What do you two girls want to drink?' asked Ryan. 'Carol says her dad's laid on plenty of booze for us... Well, Babycham and lager, shandies and fruit juice; all that sort of stuff. No spirits though. He says there's enough to last us the night, but when it's done then that's your lot! He's making sure things don't get out of hand.'

'Quite decent of him all the same,' said Kevin. 'Come on, Debs,' he said in an aside to her. 'Snap out of it! What do you want? A Babycham?'

'No; just an orange juice, please,' she answered primly.

'OK; suit yerself!'

'I'll have a Babycham, please, Kevin,' said Shirley.

The two lads went off to the drinks table leaving the girls to have a hurried conversation.

'Would you believe it!' Debbie began. 'He actually hinted to Sandra Robson that we're not really going out together. After all this time! I think he fancies his chances with her, actually.'

'No, he couldn't! And what about Ryan, eh? He's only going hiking with some friends next weekend, and he'd said he'd go to my cousin's wedding with me, in Whitby. I thought it was all arranged, but he said he never promised. Anyway, they're not going to spoil our evening, are they? We'll show them we can still enjoy ourselves.' Shirley put a conspiratorial arm around her friend.

'Yes, I suppose so,' said Debbie. But she was still very vexed with Kevin.

It was a lively party with Jeff, one of the Groovy Guys, acting as compere. Dancing was very much a case of doing your own thing. Quicksteps and foxtrots – dances they had heard their parents talk about – were things of the past. There were communal dances, like 'March of the Mods', and the still popular hokey-cokey when everyone stamped and shouted, getting into the party mood. But the dancing mainly consisted of twisting and shaking, gyrating and arm waving and rolling of hips. You could dance opposite a partner, or in a group, or on your own.

They danced to 'Love Me Do', 'Twist and Shout', 'Can't buy me love', 'I Can't Get No Satisfaction'... to the accompaniment of guitars and drums and the shrill voices of the Groovy Guys, who were quite a fair alternative to the more famous bands. And Sally Diamond with the beehive hairstyle, kohl black eyes and white lips sang that the times were a changing, and invited them to 'Step Inside Love'.

Debbie tried to talk to Kevin – what did he mean by hinting to Sandra that they were not really 'going out'? – but he brushed her off.

'For heaven's sake, let it drop, Debbie!' he told her. 'I'm here with you, aren't I? What more d'you want? It isn't as if we're going to get engaged or anything. I can talk to other girls if I want to.'

And so he did, at supper time, when the guests were invited to help themselves from the buffet table. It was a sumptuous spread. Daintily cut sandwiches and vol-au-vents; chicken legs, sausages on sticks; quiches and salads. And for afters, raspberry pavlova, Black Forest gateau, or sherry trifle. Kevin gravitated towards Sandra, and the two of them sat together in a corner chatting and laughing, no doubt reminiscing about old times. Not all that long ago, though; it was only two years since Kevin had left school, and from what he had told Debbie he couldn't wait to get away. Things seemed better looking back on them, she supposed.

By this time she had given up on the orange juice and had had a Babycham and a cider, which had made her feel that she wasn't all that bothered what Kevin was doing. She had danced as though she hadn't a care in the world, and Shirley had done the same. Debbie noticed Ryan dancing with Wendy Perkins, a girl from their form who had a reputation for being rather 'fast'; she had 'been with' most of the lads in their form and several of the sixth formers as well, or so she said. But some of the girls, Debbie included, were not quite sure what she was implying. Shirley didn't seem to have noticed, or maybe she was pretending not to do so.

At supper time she joined Shirley and two more girls from their form, and very soon two of the Groovy Guys – Jeff, the compere, and Max, the lead guitarist – joined them and asked how they were enjoying the entertainment. 'Fabulous!' they all agreed, putting in several requests for later.

'Have you made it up with Ryan?' Debbie asked her friend.

'Sort of…' Shirley gave a shrug. 'I don't much care at the moment. I'm enjoying myself.'

'Where is Ryan now?' asked Debbie. 'I know where Kevin is. Look – he's chatting up Sandra Robson; not that I'm bothered.'

'I expect Ryan's gone out for a fag,' said Shirley. 'Come on, let's go to the washroom, if you've finished eating.'

The ladies' room was a very stylish place with pale pink loos and wash basins, pink fluffy towels and full length mirrors. Debbie could feel a headache threatening, so she decided to go outside and get a breath of fresh air. French windows opened out from the room where the party was being held, on to the garden at the rear of the hotel. She stood for a moment on the veranda, enjoying the coolness of the night air. There were one or two couples in the garden below.

She caught sight of a ginger head near a clump of bushes – it could only be Ryan with hair that colour – and a blonde head near to him. She thought for a moment that it was Shirley, but she had only just left Shirley in the toilets. And this girl was wearing a bright pink dress, not a blue one. It was Wendy Perkins... She saw their heads come close together in a long kiss.

She turned quickly and went inside, not wanting to see any more. What should she do? Should she tell Shirley? Supposing it was Kevin snogging with someone else? Would she want to know? Of course she would. On the other hand, Shirley was enjoying herself and it wouldn't be fair to spoil the evening for her. And it might only be a one-off with Wendy and Ryan. Wendy had such a reputation for flirting. Debbie did have a nice side to her. She felt sorry for her friend now and decided she would say nothing.

Still, she knew what she had seen, and who could tell when it might come in handy? She and Ryan pretended to get on together for Shirley's sake, but she knew that Ryan did not really like her, Debbie, very much, though she was not sure why. But she would keep what she knew to herself, for the moment, at least.

'Where have you been?' asked Shirley when she joined her again. 'You just disappeared.'

'I went outside for a while,' she answered. 'I felt I had a headache coming on, but it seems to have gone now. I'm ready to start enjoying myself again. What about another Babycham, eh?'

'Oh, I don't know,' said Shirley. 'I've had two already. I'd better stick to fruit juice. Carol says her dad's trusting us to behave ourselves. Oh... hi there, Ryan. Where've you been?' Ryan had just joined them, and Debbie noticed that Wendy was at the other side of the room with another group.

'I went outside for a fag,' he said cheerfully, 'but I'm here again now.' He grinned at Shirley. 'Budge up and let me sit down.' He sat down next to Shirley, putting his arm round her.

The cheek of it! thought Debbie. She couldn't resist saying. 'I went outside as well, Ryan. I had a headache but it's better now. It's lovely and cool out there, isn't it?' She smiled artlessly at him, feeling a moment of smug glee at the hint or warning in his eyes, as he tried to smile back at her.

'Yes, it's a lovely evening,' he replied. 'Er… what are you drinking, Debbie? And you, Shirley?'

'Another Babycham for me,' said Debbie, rather too loudly. 'Go on; you have one as well, Shirl.' But Shirley decided to stick to pineapple juice.

'I'll go and get them,' said Ryan. 'Coming, Kevin?' he added, as Kevin, to Debbie's surprise, came to join them.

'Well, they've come back again, haven't they?' Shirley remarked. 'We'd better pretend everything's all right, hadn't we?'

'Whatever you say,' answered Debbie, then she burst out laughing.

'Hey, steady on,' said her friend. But Debbie was feeling reckless all of a sudden, tired of conforming to what everyone expected her to do.

–

As the evening drew on a few more of the party, acquaintances rather than friends, joined the group. Kevin had returned to Debbie after his decision to show her that she couldn't take him for granted. He wasn't sure why he had said what he did to Sandra. He liked Debbie well enough, and they had had some good times together, but he had felt recently that he might be getting in too deep. She was only sixteen, and sometimes he felt that he was years and years older than she was. Debbie was really quite immature, despite the act she put on. He knew he had to stay there now and keep an eye on her. Her laughter was getting louder and shriller, almost hysterical.

He needed to pay a visit to the gents, though, and when he came back Debbie was sitting next to an older lad, one of the sixth formers. Kevin vaguely remembered him from his own time at the school. Sean… something or other; rather a loud-mouthed character with long black hair and an incipient moustache. He was smoking, and as Kevin watched he saw the lad pass the cigarette to Debbie. She took hold of it, put it to her lips and took a deep breath.

Kevin suddenly realized what it was. It wasn't an ordinary cigarette. How many drags had Debbie taken already whilst he was away for a few minutes? He leapt from his seat. 'What the hell d'you think you're doing?' he shouted. 'That's a joint, isn't it?' He snatched it away from Debbie, who pouted at him, then started giggling.

'Get lost, Kevin!' she yelled. 'What's it got to do with you? I'm having a good time.'

'Yeh… cool it, man,' said Sean. 'It's only hash; it's not harmful.'

Shirley suddenly woke up to what was happening. She had been preoccupied making up with Ryan again. 'Debbie, you stupid girl! What d'you think you're playing at?' She turned her attention to Sean. 'And you, Sean Pollock! Carol and Sandra'll go berserk if they see what you're doing, to say nothing of their dad. You'd best get rid of it, quick, before we're all turned out.'

'Alright, alright; we'll be good boys, won't we, Chas?' said Sean to the lad next to him. He had the grace to look a mite ashamed. 'Give it here,' he said to Kevin, who passed over the offending article. Sean stubbed it out and secreted it in his pocket. 'All gone,' he said, spreading out his hands.

'And you'd better go an' all,' said Kevin. 'Buzz off, the pair of you.'

Sean and Chas shrugged and walked away with a jaunty air.

'Debbie, you silly chump!' said Kevin, sitting down next to her and putting an arm round her. But it was too late.

'I feel sick,' she said, putting a hand to her mouth.

'Come on then; up you get.' He helped her to her feet, grabbing her stole from the back of her chair. She clung to him as he steered her out of the room, across the foyer and through the swing doors. No one seemed to be taking much notice; they were all too busy enjoying themselves.

The cool air engulfed them as they stepped out on to the pavement. 'I'm going to be sick,' said Debbie. And so she was, in the gutter in front of the hotel. He held on to her, then wiped her mouth and her damp forehead with his clean handkerchief.

'Better now?' he asked. 'You've got it all up?'

She nodded. 'I think so.' She was not so cocky now, and she tried to smile at him as she said, 'I'm sorry, Kevin.'

'I'd better get you home,' he said, 'then you can go straight to bed. Let's hope your parents are not still up.'

'You must be joking!' she replied. 'My mum'll be waiting up, that's for sure.'

Luckily there was a taxi waiting nearby, and they were at Debbie's front gate in no time. 'Come with me,' she begged. 'They might not be so mad, if you're with me.' She really did sound contrite, and he felt sorry for her; but he was still very annoyed and disappointed with her.

He rang the bell, and Debbie's mother opened the door straightaway, as though she had been waiting there. 'Hello, Mrs Hargreaves,' he said. 'I'm afraid Debbie isn't feeling too well. Er... it was probably the rich food at the party...' He stopped as Debbie was sick again, all over the doorstep.

Her mother sighed. 'Not just the food, I reckon. Get inside, Debbie; straight up to bed.' She sounded cross, as well she might, but she smiled at Kevin. 'Thank you for bringing her home, Kevin. We know you're a good lad, and our Debbie can be quite a handful.'

'Thank you, Mrs Hargreaves,' he said. 'Er... don't be too cross with her, will you?'

She shook her head, looking sad as well as annoyed as he left her. He knew that Debbie would have to face the music in the morning.

Twelve

Debbie undressed quickly and was in bed by the time her mother came upstairs. She knew Mum would be angry with her – she had every right to be, she supposed – but she didn't feel like listening to a long diatribe about her behaviour at that moment. Or at any time, but she knew she would have to face it eventually.

'Feeling better?' asked her mother, putting her hand on Debbie's forehead, as she tried to retreat further under the bedclothes.

'Yes… I'm all right, Mum… I'm sorry!' she almost shouted; not sounding at all contrite. 'Now, just leave me alone, please. I want to go to sleep.' She hadn't really meant to lash out at her mother like that, but it was the look on Mum's face, a look more of hurt and disappointment than anger, that had riled her. As though she was a little girl who had been naughty. It was about time her parents realized that she was not a child any more and that she had a life of her own. OK, she had stepped out of line. She had had too much to drink – she hoped to goodness that the other incident would not come to light! – but so what? It was a party for heaven's sake, and it was the first time she had ever done anything like this.

'Very well, then. I'll leave you to calm down and sleep it off,' said her mother coolly. 'Goodnight, Deborah.'

She certainly was in the doghouse for her mother to call her Deborah. But her head was still spinning and she didn't want to think about it now. She fell asleep in no time.

She still had a slight trace of a headache the next morning. She felt like staying in bed, but she knew she had to face the day, whatever it might bring, primarily the wrath of her parents. Her mother, though, greeted her much as usual.

'Hello, love; I hope you're feeling more yourself this morning.'

Her father looked at her from over the top of his Sunday newspaper. 'Yes; you were a bit worse for wear, weren't you, last night? All right again now, eh?'

'Yes… thank you,' murmured Debbie.

'Your daddy and me, we have decided not to say too much about your behaviour last night,' said her mother, in a patient, yet reproving, sort of voice. 'You were a very silly girl, but we're prepared to overlook it this once provided you promise not to get into that state again, and you must settle down to your studies. We want to have a serious talk to you, later today, about what you're going to do… Now, some breakfast, Debbie? Bacon and egg, seeing that it's Sunday?'

'Ugh, no!' she grimaced. 'Not for me… thanks.' The thought of it made her stomach churn. 'I'll just have some cereal and a piece of toast.'

'I'm not surprised,' said her mother. 'It's a case of the morning after the night before, isn't it? That's what happens when you have too much to drink.' She couldn't resist a dig, could she? thought Debbie, her hackles rising once again. Mum had said they'd say no more about it, but there was a smug half-smile on her mother's face as she pushed the cornflakes packet towards her.

'You're not going to the garden centre today, are you?' she asked, as Debbie ate her breakfast in a moody silence.

'No. Well, not this morning,' she answered curtly. 'I've said I'll do an hour or two this afternoon.'

'Then perhaps we could have a little talk tonight,' said her mother. 'We only want what is best for you, you know, your daddy and me.' It was the way she always said 'Your daddy and me' that made Debbie see red, as though she was a little girl of six instead of sixteen.

She spent the morning reading in her bedroom, well aware that she was being rather 'nowty' as her mother would say, but towards dinner time she was in a slightly better frame of mind. So much so that she told her mother how much she had enjoyed the dinner of roast lamb and mint sauce, accompanied with Mum's usual choice of vegetables, garden peas and carrots, followed by apple pie and custard.

'Glad you liked it, pet!' Her mother beamed with pleasure at the unusual compliment. 'It's very nice of you to say so... Don't forget, will you; we must have our little chat tonight?'

–

Kevin came to find her as she was working in one of the greenhouses that afternoon.

'Glad to see you've recovered,' he said. 'No ill effects?'

'None to speak of,' said Debbie nonchalantly. 'A bit of a headache, that's all, but it's gone now.'

'Well, perhaps you've learnt your lesson,' he said, not very concernedly.

'Oh, don't you start!' she retorted. 'I got enough of a lecture from my parents; well, from Mum at any rate. About the drinking. They didn't know about... the other thing. You won't mention it, will you, Kevin?'

'Of course not,' he replied. 'Why should I? Just don't do it again, that's all.'

'I shan't!' she said, peevishly. Then, thinking better of it, she added, 'Thanks, anyway, Kevin, for looking after me. I'm sorry, really I am.'

'OK, let's forget it then,' he said, with a casual air. 'Actually, Debbie, I've been thinking... Perhaps we'd better not carry on seeing one another, not for a while, anyway.'

'Why not?' She stared at him in surprise. 'D'you mean... you don't want to see me again?'

'Not exactly,' he answered evasively. 'I mean... we can still be friends, and I'll see you here, of course; and perhaps we could go out... occasionally. But you're only young, Debbie...'

'I'm sixteen,' she answered. 'Old enough to leave school; old enough for... all sorts of things.'

'But I'm not so sure that I am,' he replied. 'You'll have a lot of studying to do when you go back to school; and I want to be free to go out and enjoy myself. I don't want to feel that I'm... well... tied down. Not to you, or to anyone. I'm sorry, Debbie, but that's the way it is.'

'You've met somebody else!' she countered. 'That's it; I knew it! It's Sandra Robson, isn't it?'

'Of course not,' he said, and laughed. 'I enjoyed talking to her, that's all. But she's going to uni anyway... Look, we've had a good time together, Debbie, and I'm fond of you, but I really think we should call it a day.'

She was determined she would not cry, although she could feel a sort of hotness behind her eyes. 'All right then,' she retorted. 'If that's the way you want it. See if I care!' She picked up her watering can and turned her back on him.

He actually put an arm around her. 'Sorry, Debbie. But it's for the best; really it is...' He squeezed her shoulder, then he walked away.

–

Debbie was hurt and angry rather than heartbroken at Kevin's words. She knew that she had been dumped; at least that was what everyone would say when they knew about it. And so she must tell everyone that it was a mutual agreement, that they had realized they were not getting on as well as they used to and they had decided to call it a day. She had known, of course, if she were honest with herself, that Kevin had been cooling off. There had been that remark to Sandra last night, and other occasions when he had shown quite clearly that he didn't agree with her.

And how did she feel about Kevin? Although she was loath to admit that her mother was right, Kevin was the first boy she had been out with; and there might well be others, perhaps, in the near future. She had been obsessed with Kevin for a while. He had seemed so different from the lads at school whom she had known since she was eleven. He had a job and more money to spend, and the use of his father's car, and it had all seemed glamorous. But now, as she thought about it, she recognized that what her mother had kept telling her might be true. He was her first boyfriend; that was all. And although Mum hadn't actually said so, she had hinted that Debbie could do much better for herself.

Who better than Kevin? she had thought. He was the owner's son, and she loved working at Sunnyhill, and who could tell where it might lead? She knew now that it had been just a ridiculous fantasy on her part. Kevin had never had any such thoughts about her. He had told her himself that he had left school because he did not have the ability to cope with more academic studies, and that she was far brainier than he was. But she had refuted that at the time.

She was realizing now, rather to her surprise, that she didn't want to go on working at Sunnyhill. It would be difficult, anyway, working with Kevin despite what he said about them still being friends; he had just been trying to let her down gently. She knew now that she did want to go on to the sixth form. And then what? University, or some sort of agricultural college? She wasn't sure. Mr Hill had mentioned landscape gardening. She hadn't thought much about it at the time; she had been annoyed with him for assuming, as everyone else did, that she would return to school. Now, though, the idea was beginning to appeal to her.

Debbie, however, had a stubborn streak to her nature. She didn't like admitting that she was wrong. What should she tell her parents about her change of heart? She didn't want to admit that they had been right all along, or that she was giving in to them because it was what they wanted.

She finished her allotted jobs for the day, said a quick goodbye to Mr and Mrs Hill – Kevin was nowhere to be seen – then cycled home. She was a good deal calmer now, her first feeling of hatred – well, almost – towards Kevin had receded, to be replaced by a determination to show him what she was made of. 'See if I care!' she had yelled at him, and she intended to show him that she was moving on, and quickly too. She didn't intend to tell her parents, though, not yet, that she was no longer going out with Kevin. She would bide her time, and then act as though it had been her decision to end the friendship.

Her mother had prepared a nice tea. Boiled ham and salad, which was the usual fare for a Sunday teatime; followed by sliced banana in a fruit jelly – Debbie had loved this when she was a little girl, and Mum still thought that it was a special treat for her – with fresh cream. This was certainly a treat because they usually had Carnation milk. And the inevitable home-made buns and flapjack.

Debbie was in something of a quandary. She had nothing to gain by being stroppy, which was what often happened when her parents wanted a serious talk with her. No; she would be the opposite, she decided; she would be all sweetness and light, to start with anyway.

–

Vera was quite prepared for a battle, or at least a heated argument. Debbie still seemed to be set on the idea of carrying on working at the garden centre, despite her excellent O level results. She hadn't exactly said so recently as she had been so excited about the party last night; the party that had ended so badly for Debbie. Vera could almost have felt sorry for her if she hadn't felt so angry. Well, perhaps the silly girl would have learnt her lesson. Vera had been surprised to hear that there had been any alcoholic drinks at the party. Most of the youngsters were only sixteen, but with it being a private party they must have got round the restrictions somehow. She hoped – although it was perhaps not very nice of her – that Debbie had not been the only one to get into that state! On the other hand, she had been pleased to see that Kevin had appeared to be sober, and he had certainly taken good care of Debbie.

She had decided not to mention the episode again. Debbie had been moody and quiet at first that morning, possibly embarrassed at her bad behaviour; but as the day went on she had come round and now seemed to be in quite an approachable frame of mind, ready, Vera hoped, to listen to advice.

'I'll help you to wash up, Mum,' she said after they had finished their tea, which was, indeed, a surprise. Then the three of them settled down together in what Vera called the front room, the 'best' room, used on special occasions such as Christmas and when they had visitors for tea. The discussion of Debbie's future seemed to warrant the use of it today.

Vera decided the grasp the nettle, so to speak, straight away, no shilly-shallying around. 'School starts again fairly soon, doesn't it?' she began. 'How long is it, Debbie? About a fortnight?'

Debbie nodded and opened her mouth to speak, which was what her mother expected, but Vera forestalled her. 'We were wondering, your daddy and me,' she went on, 'if you'll be needing anything new in the way of clothes? They're not so strict about uniform, are they, when you go into the sixth form? And what about a nice new briefcase to carry your books in? You've had your satchel for ages, and I'm sure you'd like something more grown-up. It will be our little treat for you, because you've done so well.'

Vera had hardly paused for breath, not giving her daughter a chance to speak. She had been quite expecting her to interrupt with a comment such as, 'Who says I'm going back to school?' But to Vera's amazement Debbie just smiled as though she was finding it all very amusing.

'It's all right, Mum,' she said. 'There's no need to go on about it. I don't need to be bribed with presents and all that. You don't need to worry; I'm going back to school.'

'Well, that's wonderful, love,' said Vera. 'We knew you'd see sense eventually. It would be such a waste of it all if you didn't take the chance to go on with your studying. We never got the chance, did we, Daddy... er, Stanley?'

'No, that's true,' he replied. 'We think it's the best thing you could do. Like your mum says, we're proud of you, and we want to buy you a little something because you've worked so hard. It's not a bribe, Deborah, as you seem to think, so try to sound as though you're pleased, if you can. A bit of appreciation would not go amiss for all that we try to do for you, your mother and me.'

Vera was surprised to hear Stanley speak so forcefully. He usually took the line of least resistance with Debbie. Now, for once, he seemed to be in agreement with his wife. Debbie looked a little taken aback.

'Of course I'm pleased, Dad,' she said. 'It's very kind of you and Mum. Er... thank you very much. What I wanted to say, though, was that I'd already made up my mind to go back to school. I didn't need persuading. I was pleased that I'd done so well in the exams; and I've got an idea now about what I'd like to do in the future. And I've decided that I'm not going to carry on working at Sunnyhill any longer. Well, I shall do the next couple of weeks until school starts again. Actually, Mr Hill has asked me to look after a new girl who's starting there – to show her how we do things and all that – so I've promised him that I will. He was really sorry when I told him I wasn't going to carry on working there. Like I told you before, he said he'd like to employ me full time, but I told him I'd decided to go back to school. He begged me to go back during the holidays, but I said that I didn't think I would.'

'You've changed your tune,' said Vera. She didn't entirely believe what Debbie was saying. 'What's gone wrong? Have you fallen out with Kevin?'

'No, of course I haven't!' said Debbie, sounding very indignant. 'I shall go on seeing him, but we won't be working together any more, not after the next week or two, that's all.'

Vera nodded. 'Yes... I see. Well, we're certainly pleased that you're going back to school, whatever the reason is for you changing your mind, aren't we, Dad... I mean, Stanley?'

Stanley just nodded in agreement, looking somewhat bemused.

'It seems to be a sudden change of heart, though,' Vera went on. 'You were so determined about leaving school and carrying on working at Sunnyhill.'

'I can change my mind if I want to, can't I?' snapped Debbie. 'And it hasn't been all that sudden anyway. I've been thinking about it for... quite a while. I didn't like being pestered, that's all. I do have a mind of my own, you know.'

Stanley gave a wry chuckle. 'I think we know that only too well, don't we, Vera? And happen you don't want to admit that your parents know best; that's the truth, isn't it, Debbie?'

Vera was still amazed at the way Stanley was speaking to their daughter. She had felt that he had been too lenient with her sometimes, too ambivalent about her changes of mood, and that she, Vera, was not getting the support she wanted. She could see a stubborn look on Debbie's face now, so she decided to play her husband's remark down a little.

'Oh, we all like to think we know best when we're young,' she said. 'I expect we were just the same with our parents, weren't we, Stanley? We thought they were old fuddy-duddies.'

'I don't know so much about that,' he replied. 'We were taught to respect 'em, and not to answer back, I know that.'

'Well, like Debbie says, young people have minds of their own these days. It's all this schooling. They're encouraged to give their point of view. That's right, isn't it, Debbie?'

The girl nodded, rather sullenly. 'Yes, I suppose so.'

'Anyway,' Vera continued, 'you were just saying that you'd got an idea about what you'd like to do in the future. So… are you going to tell us about it?'

Debbie shrugged. 'I suppose I could,' she said, in an offhand manner. 'It's only an idea. It was something Mr Hill said, about there being a good future in landscape gardening these days. You know; designing gardens – rockeries and water features and ornamental flower beds and all that sort of thing. Some people – posh people – are paying the earth now to have their gardens restyled. And just ordinary people are going in for it as well, on a smaller scale. And I've got a good eye for colour and design. Mr Hill says so, and Mrs Hill as well, when I did those floral arrangements.'

Debbie was looking more animated now. She had seemed loath to tell them her ideas at first, but as she warmed to her subject a note of elation had come back into her voice.

'So… what are you saying?' asked Vera. 'That you'd like to be some sort of a gardener?'

'Yes… I've just said — a landscape gardener. You've heard of them, haven't you? Capability Brown — he was the most famous one. He designed the gardens at Blenheim Palace.'

'By heck! You're aiming a bit high, aren't you, lass?' said Stanley.

'I'm not saying I'd be as good as him! I'm not thinking of anything on that scale, but I'd like to design gardens for people. That's what I'm saying. And I think I'd be good at it!' There was a touch of defiance in her tone, as though she had added, 'So there!'

Vera had no idea who this Capability Brown was — that couldn't be his real name, surely? — but it sounded as though Stanley had heard of him, probably with him being a gardener himself. But it all sounded very improbable to her. 'Isn't it more of a job for a man, Debbie, love?' she asked, 'I mean — all that digging and carting stones and stuff about. And water features? Do you mean ponds for goldfish, and fountains an' all that? It all sounds very ambitious to me. Not that there's anything wrong with ambition. But when you said you didn't want to go on working at the garden centre, I thought you meant you were giving up the idea of gardening altogether. That you'd train to be a teacher… or something of the sort.' That had long been the apex of Vera's ambitions for her daughter, as Debbie now reminded her.

'That's all you ever think of, isn't it, Mum? How many times do I have to tell you that a teacher is the last thing I want to be? I can't think of anything worse.'

'No, you don't want to end up coping with girls like you, do you Debbie?' chuckled her father.

'I thought you said you were proud of me,' retorted Debbie. 'You said how hard I'd worked. And I'm very well behaved at school, not like some of them.'

'You mean you save your nowtiness for us when you get home, eh?' laughed Stanley.

'That's enough, Stanley,' said Vera. She turned to Debbie. 'He's only teasing; he doesn't mean it. Anyway, pet, we're glad to hear that you're going back to school. And all this gardening business; we'll have to see about it, won't we? Perhaps it seems like a good idea now, but you might change your mind. We'd love to see you go to university, your daddy and me. We'd be so proud of you! There's one in Durham, isn't there? That would be near enough for you to get home at weekends. There's a teacher training college there, too... Yes, I know what you said, love,' she added, as Debbie tutted and cast an exasperated glance in her direction. 'But I'm just saying, that's all...' No one spoke for a few moments, and Vera decided that maybe enough had been said for the moment.

'Well, I think we've had a nice little chat, haven't we?' she said in conclusion. 'We've sorted out a few things. And you and me, Debbie, we'll go into Newcastle next week and choose a nice briefcase for you from that posh leather shop. And how about a new skirt and coat from C and A?'

Debbie nodded. 'Yes... thanks, Mum. That'll be lovely...'

Thirteen

Debbie set off early on Monday morning, not because she was eager to get to the garden centre early; it was because she didn't want to spend any more time than she needed to at home. Her father started his gardening work early, but her mother worked only three afternoons a week at the fancy goods shop, and she had ample time in a morning to chat over the breakfast table.

Debbie was in a state of confusion. Her parents thought that the all-important discussion last night had gone well; at least her mum seemed to think so. Debbie was still bewildered, though, at her father's sudden change of attitude towards her. She had always thought she could rely on him to support her, or at least to try to see her point of view, if her mother was too intransigent. Mum still seemed to think that she and Dad had got their own way; that it was only because of her parents' persuasion that Debbie was returning to school. They thought they could wear her down. She was under their roof, and so would be under their control whilst she attended school, like a good little girl, for the next two years. And if she didn't stick up for herself they would do their utmost to make sure that she went to a university of their choice, near to Whitesands Bay. The main idea of going to college or uni as far as Debbie – and thousands like her – were concerned, was to break free from the apron strings.

Apart from feeling smothered by her possessive parents, she was still smarting from Kevin's rejection. She would never admit to anyone that he had ended their friendship – in other words that he had dumped her – but that was, in truth, what had happened, and Debbie's self-esteem was damaged. She could pretend to herself that she didn't care, but deep down she knew that she did.

She was determined, however, to put on a happy face at work. She greeted Mr Hill with a smile, and she had a cheerful grin, too, for the new girl, Julie, to whom she was introduced.

'Hello, Debbie,' said Julie, sounding very nervous and unsure of herself. 'Mr Hill says you're going to help me. I'm really glad, because I find it hard to talk to strangers, like the customers, I mean, and I'm scared of getting it wrong.' She was a small, thin-featured girl with fairish hair tied back in two bunches. She was a year younger than Debbie having left school at fifteen, but she seemed even younger than that. Debbie found herself feeling sorry for the kid – for that was how she thought of her – although she herself had never suffered from such lack of confidence.

'Now stop worrying,' she told her. 'You'll be fine; really, you will. You won't be dealing with the customers all the time, and they're usually very nice. They wouldn't come if they weren't interested in gardening. Most of them know exactly what they want, but sometimes they need a bit of advice; they like to have a chat about what sort of plants would be best.' She could see a look of apprehension – fright, almost – on Julie's face so she went on hurriedly. 'Mr Hill won't want you to deal with the customers just yet. Anyway, there's far more to the job than that. We spend a lot of the time in the gardens and the greenhouses. There's a lot to learn but I'm sure you'll soon pick it up. It's the job you wanted to do isn't it?'

'Oh yes, I do!' The girl sounded quite eager now. 'I love helping my dad in the garden. But neither of us really know much about gardening, about the different plants and soil and all that.'

'Well, you'll soon learn,' said Debbie cheerfully, 'then you'll be able to show off to your dad, won't you? That's how I got interested, with helping my dad, but he knows a lot about it because he works as a gardener as well… Come on, now, and we'll make a start in the far greenhouse. The tomato plants need pruning, and there'll be some more ripe ones ready to take off.'

Far from feeling resentment at having to look after the new girl, Debbie thought that she might enjoy it. Julie was looking at her with eyes that shone with admiration and she felt that she had already helped to make the girl feel less anxious. They worked closely together all day. Debbie made sure that she kept herself and Julie busy. She saw Kevin briefly, once or twice. She managed to speak civilly to him, without showing any hint of bitterness or regret.

–

There was something else, though, on Debbie's mind; something that she had been thinking about, on and off, for a while, and now it was looming large again. Ever since she had found out that Claire Wagstaff had known the person who had given birth to her, and had probably had a hand in the adoption as well, she had wanted to know more. The mother must have been quite a young girl at the time – an unmarried mother – and Debbie found herself wanting to know, quite badly, what she was like. Not all the time; there were times when she almost managed to put it out of her mind, but at other times it became very important to her that she should know. It was one of those times now.

Debbie knew that her adoptive parents – her real parents now, by law – loved her very much. She knew, also, that she loved them. But as well as loving them she was often annoyed and angered by them. It was at those times that she wondered about her real mother, what she would have been like with her, Debbie, if things had worked out differently. Mum had always told her that the girl had loved her but had been unable to keep her. And there was that little pink teddy bear which proved – didn't it? – that she had wanted there to be some sort of contact with the child she had been forced to give up.

Debbie knew there was no way she could get any more information from her mother; besides, Mum would be very hurt. Debbie knew that only too well, but it didn't stop her from wanting to find out more. And so she had worked out a plan. Tomorrow, Tuesday, was her half-day off from the garden centre. She intended, after lunch, to cycle to Burnside House in order to see Claire Wagstaff. She would need to find out, though, if Claire would be there that afternoon; if, in fact, she was still working there. If she wasn't, then Debbie knew that her search would come to an end; she didn't know of any other way of finding out. A phone call from Sunnyhill on Tuesday morning, however, told her that Claire would be on duty that afternoon.

It was only a couple of miles through the winding country lanes from Debbie's place of work. She had butterflies doing a wild dance in her tummy as she stood at the door of Burnside House, ready to ring the bell. This, then, was the place where she had been born. It was a large greystone house set in its own grounds, with a lawn in front surrounded by colourful flower beds. She had imagined something more like a prison, but this seemed to be quite a pleasant place. She pressed the bell and waited.

To her surprise – what a stroke of luck! – it was Claire who opened the door. They hadn't seen one another for quite a while, and they looked at one another a trifle unsurely. Claire didn't really look much different, possibly a shade plumper and her hair was greying a little; but she still had the same friendly smile as she recognized Debbie.

'It's Debbie, isn't it?' she said. 'You've grown up quite a lot since I last saw you, and your hair's shorter. It took me a minute to place you. Anyway, come along in, and you can tell me why you're here.' She looked at her rather more closely. 'I take it there is a reason? Your mum and dad are both all right, I hope?'

'Er... yes; it's nothing like that,' said Debbie. 'They're both very well.' She followed Claire into a smallish room at the back of the house, furnished with easy chairs, a bookcase and a television set. 'It's... well, it's something I wanted to ask you,' she went on. 'Something that I want to know.'

'Well, sit down then,' said Claire. 'This is the staff sitting room. We won't be disturbed, and I can spare you a few minutes. I expect I can guess why you want to see me, Debbie. I can't think of any other reason; but I can't help hoping I'm wrong.' Her smile was replaced by a look of concern, although she didn't seem annoyed.

Debbie gave a sigh and shook her head. 'No, I don't suppose you're wrong... unless...' A sudden thought struck her. 'You don't think I'm pregnant, do you? Because it isn't that!'

'No...' Claire gave a wry smile. 'I didn't think it was that; and I suppose that's something to be thankful for!'

'I've come to ask you about my mother; I mean... the person who gave birth to me,' said Debbie.

Claire nodded. 'Yes; that's what I guessed.'

'I've always known I was adopted,' Debbie went on, 'and from what Mum told me once I guessed that you might have had something to do with it. So... I just wanted to know about her. I feel I have a right to know,' she added, a little more assertively, now that she was gaining in confidence. 'Mum told me that she – the girl, I mean – didn't really want to part with me.'

'I'm afraid, Debbie, that you don't really have a right to know, as you put it,' said Claire, rather sternly. 'It was Vera's choice to tell you about your adoption, but as for your birth mother, I don't know of her whereabouts, and even if I did I wouldn't tell you. The adoption was confidential. Your parents – Vera and Stanley – never knew whose child you were, just as your birth mother never knew who was adopting you. She had to let you go because it was the right thing – the only thing – for her to do. I dare say she has made a new life for herself now. I'm sure she won't have forgotten you, but I also believe that it wouldn't do any good for you to try to find her now... I presume that is what you want to do?'

'I don't know,' said Debbie. 'I'm not really sure. But I so desperately want to know what she was like...'

'What has brought this about?' asked Claire. She gave a half-smile. 'Have you had a row at home and decided the grass might have been greener elsewhere? It isn't always, you know. And I'm sure you've had a good home and loving parents; well, I know you have.'

'We haven't had a row,' said Debbie. 'Well, more of a difference of opinion about me going back to school. I don't always see eye to eye with them; they're older than most of my friends' parents, aren't they? Anyway, I'm going back to school, so that's all sorted out… But I've still got this longing to find out. There was that little teddy bear, you see. Mum told me where it had come from, and I knew that she – the girl – really must have loved me.'

'Ah, yes, the little pink bear. I remember that Fi… your mother gave it to Sister Travers at the last minute. I wasn't there, but Sister told me about it. She tucked it into your shawl; she said she was very touched by it, although Travers was usually a 'no nonsense' sort of woman. It's a moving little incident, but that doesn't mean… Look, Debbie, I really can't tell you any more.'

'You must have known her quite well though,' Debbie persisted. 'Was she a nice sort of girl? I'm sure she must have been.'

'Yes, she was a lovely girl,' Claire answered. 'Not very understanding parents, though, from what I gathered. They were adamant about having the baby – you – adopted. Yes, I admit I had a soft spot for… her, and for her friend, Ginny. We're not supposed to get too friendly with any of the girls, but you can't help taking to some more than others.'

'Ginny?' said Debbie. 'She had a friend called Ginny?' The name had rung a bell with her, and it didn't take her long to remember where she had heard it. Ryan Gregson; his mother was called Ginny. She knew because Shirley was always going on about how nice Ryan's mum was, and how she had asked her to call her Ginny instead of Mrs Gregson. But it couldn't be the same one, could it? Why would Ryan's mother have been in Burnside House? She decided to enquire a little further, but sort of... casually.

'Yes, Ginny... I can't remember her other name,' said Claire evasively, but looking rather ill at ease.

'And did they all live near here,' Debbie asked, 'the girls who were having babies?'

'Most of them did; they still do,' replied Claire. 'But the babies are not usually placed anywhere near to the birth mother. All I will tell you is that with you it was the other way round. Your... birth mother was from much further away, and your parents, Vera and Stanley, were from this area, as you know. As you've gathered, I had a hand in the adoption because I knew how much they wanted a little girl and I knew what splendid parents they would be. And my advice to you, Debbie, is to try to put it all to the back of your mind. I'm sorry, pet, but you'll not get any more information from me. I can promise you, though, that what you've asked me will go no further. I do see your mother from time to time, but I won't say anything. I just hope that you'll try to put it all behind you. Now, if you'll excuse me, I must carry on with my work. I can't say give my love to your mum, but it's what I would say, if I could. Your mother and father think the world of you, you know...'

–

Claire had a few anxious moments when she had said goodbye to Debbie. She realized she had almost given away Fiona's name by a slip of the tongue, Debbie might not have noticed, and even if she had it wasn't likely to be of much help. And maybe she shouldn't have mentioned Ginny – the name had slipped out unintentionally – but it was unlikely that Debbie would know her. She recalled then that Ginny had told her that her son, Ryan, was at Kelder Bank School. And so was Debbie; in the same year, maybe in the same form. She hoped against hope that Debbie would not make the connection. She felt sure, though, that she might well be a determined little madam once she got an idea into her head. The only real lie that she, Claire, had told was in saying that she did not know the whereabouts of Debbie's birth mother. Ginny had told her about Fiona's new life and about how happy she was. Claire trusted that nothing would happen to mar her happiness.

–

Debbie was not entirely disillusioned as she cycled home. She had known, if she were honest with herself, that she was not likely to find out very much from Claire Wagstaff. There was so much secrecy attached to adoption. They were honour bound, she supposed, not to divulge private information; and Claire, also, would not want to do anything that might hurt her friends, Vera and Stanley. And Debbie knew, at the heart of her, that her parents would be deeply distressed if they knew what she was doing. At the same time, she so badly wanted to know; it was becoming an obsession with her.

Claire, however, had let a few little things slip out. The name of the girl; she had started to say something that began with the letter F... or Ph... then she had pulled herself up sharply. Phyllis, Phoebe, Fiona, maybe? It didn't mean much on its own, but coupled with the name Ginny – there was no doubt about that name – she might have something to go on. The person to see was Ryan Gregson, but before that she would have to see Shirley.

There was no one in when she arrived home as it was one of the afternoons when her mother was working. She didn't know what they would be having for tea, but to show willing she set the table for the three of them. Then, when Vera came home she helped her to prepare the meal; cold chicken with salad and new potatoes as it was a warm day, followed by strawberries and ice cream.

'I think I'll go and see Shirley tonight,' she said casually.

'You're not seeing Kevin then?' asked her mother, in quite a normal manner.

'No, not tonight. Later in the week, maybe.'

'We must arrange a time for us to go to Newcastle,' said Vera. 'Thursday would be best for me; I'm working the other days. D'you think you can get the time off?'

'I don't see why not,' said Debbie. 'Today was my half-day, but Mr Hill should be easy about it. He knows I'm leaving soon, anyway.'

'Thursday then,' said her mother, sounding very cheerful and excited. 'I might even treat myself to a new bag from that leather shop we're going to, and a new coat from C and A.'

'Yes, why not, Mum?' said Debbie. 'You deserve it.' Which was the truth and she meant it, although she felt a pang of guilt as she thought of the half-formed plan in her mind.

—

Shirley was in her bedroom listening to The Beach Boys on her record player when Debbie arrived. They listened to the last track, 'Barbara Ann', then Shirley turned it off.

'Have you recovered from Saturday?' she asked, laughing. 'Did you get into a load of bother?'

'Don't mention it!' groaned Debbie. 'I know I was an idiot, though. I won't do it again, I'll tell you! Mum and Dad were OK though, after the first outburst, but they just thought I'd had too much to drink. They didn't know about... the other thing. You haven't said anything, have you?'

'No, of course I haven't!'

'And they're real chuffed now that I've said I'm going back to school.'

'Are you, really?' said Shirley. 'That's terrific! And have you made it up with Kevin?'

'Yes,' said Debbie, briefly. 'But I want to talk about something else. You said that Ryan's mum is called Ginny, didn't you?'

'Yes, she is,' said Shirley, looking at her friend curiously. 'Why?'

'Well, I know this sounds silly, but do you think she could have been in Burnside House – you know, that place for unmarried mothers – at the same time as... well, when I was born there?'

Shirley looked alarmed, so much so that Debbie felt she might well be on to something. 'Why?' Shirley asked again. 'I don't know; I mean, how could she have been?' She was going red though, and flustered. 'Don't ask me, Debbie,' she said. 'I can't tell you.'

'You do know though, don't you?' coaxed Debbie. 'I know you do. Come on, Shirl, tell me. We're supposed to be friends.'

Shirley looked more worried than ever. 'What are you up to?' she said. 'You're not trying to find out about...

what you told me once before, are you? About you being adopted?'

'Yes, I am, actually,' said Debbie. 'I went to see that woman, Claire, who knows all about it. She wouldn't tell me, of course; I never really thought she would. But she mentioned that she — my real mother, I mean — had a friend called Ginny. It was Ryan's mum, wasn't it?'

'Yes... yes it was,' said Shirley, in a small voice. 'She — Ginny — wasn't married when she had Ryan; they got married later. But like Ryan says, it's no big deal.'

'No, I don't suppose it is,' said Debbie, 'about them getting married later. But why was his mother there, in Burnside House?'

'Because her parents were annoyed with her,' said Shirley, sounding cross and agitated. 'They wanted her to have the baby adopted, but Arthur stepped in — that's Ryan's dad — and talked them round. So she was able to keep the baby; Ryan, I mean. But I do wish you hadn't asked me, Debbie. I can't tell you any more. Ryan wasn't supposed to tell me anything about it.'

'But you do know, don't you? You know more than you're letting on. You've known all along, haven't you? You went all peculiar once before when I mentioned it. Come on, Shirl; you've got to tell me.'

Shirley sighed. 'OK, I'll tell you a bit of it. Ginny told Ryan that she and his dad were going away for the weekend to see a friend — it was earlier this year — somebody who had been expecting a baby at the same time as she was. So it all came out about Burnside House. Then Ryan said he knew a girl who had been adopted, and that she — you — had been born there as well. And so Ginny realized they were talking about the same person...'

'My… mother,' said Debbie. 'You knew all the time, and you never let on.'

'I couldn't! Ryan said I mustn't. He'd promised his mum. I'm not going to tell you any more.'

'I shall ask Ryan then…'

'He won't tell you!'

'Oh, I think he might,' said Debbie with a little smile. 'Anyway, you can't stop me asking him.'

After a little persuasion Shirley admitted that she was seeing Ryan the next night at the coffee bar, Katy's Kitchen, in the town centre, a popular meeting place for the teenagers when they didn't want to go to the pub. Debbie knew that her friend wasn't happy about it, and she promised she wouldn't hound him too much if he didn't want to tell her. She rather thought, though, that he might.

—

They met at eight o'clock as arranged at the cosy little cafe with the brightly coloured Formica topped tables and the psychedelic posters on the walls. It was obvious that Shirley had already warned Ryan about Debbie's desire to find out all she could.

'I'm having nothing more to do with it,' she said. 'I think you should leave well alone, Debs. You'll only go and upset your mum and dad, and you might upset… the other lady as well. And Ryan'll get into trouble if his mum finds out. Anyway, I'll order us some drinks, and then I'll go and have a word with Jean over there…' There was a trio of girls from their form in the opposite corner. 'What d'you want to drink?'

They all decided on strawberry milkshakes, and Ryan pulled a pound note out of his pocket and handed it to Shirley.

'Ta,' she said briefly. 'I'll leave you to it.'

'Shirley's right, you know,' said Ryan, quite reasonably, as she left them. 'You could cause an awful lot of bother. And my mum's going to be real mad with me if I tell you anything.'

Debbie grinned. 'Not half as mad as Shirley's going to be if I tell her about you snogging with Wendy Perkins at the party.'

Ryan looked horrified. 'You wouldn't?!' he gasped.

'Try me!' laughed Debbie.

'It was nothing, honest.' He shook his head. 'Shirley and me had a row, and you know what Wendy's like. It didn't mean anything, and we're OK again now, me and Shirl.'

'Well, if you want it to stay that way, you'd better tell me what you know, hadn't you?'

Ryan closed his eyes for moment, shaking his head. Then, 'OK, OK,' he said. 'My mum had a friend in the home. She was – is – called Fiona. My mum and dad were going to see her… oh, about four months ago, I think it was. I realized who it might be, and I showed Mum that form photo of us all… and she said that you were the image of her friend. Different colour hair, but she didn't seem to be in any doubt about it, that you were the baby who was adopted.'

'Your mum didn't tell her friend, though, did she? About what she'd found out?'

'No, of course not. Fiona's married now; she's very happy, and they've got a little girl. So I think you should leave it alone, Debbie. I've told you all I know.'

'You haven't, though, have you? Where do they live? And what's her name? Fiona... what?'

'For goodness' sake, Debbie! I don't know! I can't remember.'

'Then think about it,' retorted Debbie. 'Shirley told me that you were very nearly adopted yourself. If you had been, then you'd have wanted to know all about it, same as I do.'

'Well, I wasn't, was I?' He screwed up his face, frowning in concentration. 'I'm trying to think... I know she's married to a vicar.'

'A vicar!' Debbie cried out in astonishment. A thought flashed through her mind. What might she be getting into? Mum and Dad were a bit odd and old-fashioned. What would the woman married to a vicar be like, and the vicar himself? It might be a case of out of the frying pan and into the fire... if she went through with it.

'He's called a rector, though,' Ryan went on, 'because it's a country parish. They live in Aberthwaite in North Yorkshire. He's the rector of St Peter's church... Wait a minute... The Reverend Simon Norwood, that's his name. So that's it, Debbie. End of story.' He almost smiled at her. 'I suppose I can understand how you feel. I got a shock, I can tell you, when Mum said how close I'd come to being adopted. But your parents are OK, aren't they? I know you've got a good home and... everything.'

'Yes, I have,' she admitted. 'I get annoyed with my parents sometimes, but I suppose everybody does. It's just nagging at me, though, this... wanting to know.'

'My mum says that the vicar – rector or whatever – Simon, he's a jolly nice chap, good fun, not like you'd imagine a clergyman might be. And Fiona's real pretty with blonde hair. They've only been married about three years, and the little girl's called Stella. So now you know as much as I do.'

Shirley had come back now and had heard the last few remarks. She gave Ryan an odd look. 'You've told her, then?'

'I had no choice, had I?' he replied ambiguously, with a meaningful look at Debbie. 'It's not fair that we should know all about it, when Debbie doesn't.'

'Fair enough, I suppose,' said Shirley, uncertainly. 'We're going to get into awful trouble, though, Ryan, when your mum finds out that we've told her.'

'If she finds out,' said Ryan. 'It depends on what Debbie's going to do about it. I've told her to leave well alone, haven't I, Debbie?' He smiled at her in a more friendly way than he had ever done before; and she found herself quite liking him. She wouldn't have told Shirley about Wendy, despite what she had threatened.

'On the other hand, I know how Debbie feels,' he went on, 'because I was nearly in the same position myself.'

'But you're not are you? It didn't happen to you. Anyway, I'm having nothing more to do with it.' Shirley turned away crossly and took a long drink of her milk-shake. Debbie could tell she was disgruntled, maybe because she and Ryan, for the very first time, had formed a bond.

'But I think you'd be making a big mistake, Debbie…' Shirley was still harping on about it. 'I'd forget about it if I were you.'

'But you're not me, are you?' snapped Debbie. 'You've no idea how you'd feel. Anyway, you've just said you don't want any more to do with it.'

'I don't… but I'm just saying what I think. I shan't say any more. But I think you should start counting your blessings.'

Debbie burst out laughing. 'You sound like my mother! She's always saying things like that.' And so was Shirley, she pondered; she was a great one for trite little remarks.

'Then maybe you should listen to her,' countered Shirley, 'instead of chasing after something you can't have.'

'Girls, please!' said Ryan. 'Calm down. We're not going to fall out about it, are we? We've told Debbie what we know, whether we should have done or not. Now it's down to her.'

'Sorry, Debbie,' muttered Shirley. 'I don't want you to get hurt, that's all. Or anybody else…' she added.

'I know,' said Debbie. 'I do, really. Anyway, thank you, both of you. I'm sorry if I've made you break a promise.'

Shirley and Ryan exchanged glances. She really did look sorry, and a contrite Debbie was something they had never expected to see.

Fourteen

Debbie had a good deal of information now, enough for her to continue her quest, if she decided to do so. She hadn't imagined it would be so easy to find out as much as she had. Her birth mother was a lady called Fiona Norwood, married to the rector of St Peter's church in the market town of Aberthwaite, in the North Yorkshire dales.

She looked up Aberthwaite in the map book her parents owned. It was not far from Richmond, which seemed to be the largest town in that area. She didn't know if there was a railway station there. Most probably there wouldn't be. She remembered that a few years ago, in 1963, there had been something called the Beeching Report – she had heard her parents talking about it – and a lot of the smaller branch lines had been axed, and the railway stations closed, to make way for improved road travel, or so they had said.

Whitesands Bay still had their railway station. She and her mother sometimes caught the train there to Newcastle, some twelve miles away. There might be a train from there to Richmond, or maybe it would involve another change at Durham. These were places she had heard of but never visited. She remembered seeing Durham castle and the cathedral perched on a hilltop when they had been travelling on the train to Whitby, or was it Scarborough? Her knowledge of Yorkshire was limited to those seaside resorts, and once they had gone to Butlin's holiday camp at Filey. They had even visited Blackpool on a rare occasion when her father had had a pay rise.

On the whole, though, her parents were quiet stay-at-home people, content with what they had and with little desire to travel and see the world or even their own country. Shirley's dad had a car – Shirley had gone to Scotland with them earlier that year – and so had Ryan's dad, and Kevin's, of course. And Kevin was saving up for one of his own. She was determined, though, not to think about Kevin and what he was or wasn't doing. She had other more important things on her mind. If she intended to go ahead with her plan to find her birth mother she would need to do it very soon, before she got cold feet.

She was trying to behave normally at home, to keep out of bother with her parents and not to get into any arguments. Ironically, though, they might well regard that as unusual behaviour, considering how she sometimes carried on.

She went to work each day, helping Julie, the new girl, to find her feet, and treating Kevin in a casual manner whenever she saw him. Which was not often, as he seemed to be avoiding her.

'You're very quiet, pet,' her mother said to her on the Wednesday evening. 'There's nothing wrong, is there? With... Kevin, perhaps?' she asked tentatively.

'No, not at all,' Debbie replied evenly, although it would have been more normal for her to have answered rudely as her mother had already asked her if they had fallen out. 'At least, not how you mean,' she amended. 'Kevin's got a bad cold and he's not at work. That's why

I've not been seeing him.' She crossed her fingers, as she did when she told a lie, hoping she would not be found out.

'Oh dear! I'm sorry about that,' said Vera. 'Never mind, we've got our trip to Newcastle tomorrow. Are you looking forward to it?'

'Yes, Mum, I am,' Debbie answered truthfully. She always enjoyed looking at the big shops, the ones that they didn't have in Whitesands Bay, and it would take her mind off other pressing issues. She enjoyed travelling by train, too. It always gave her the feeling that something exciting was happening, even if they were only going a short distance to the nearest big town.

She stared at the hustle and bustle around her when they got off the train at Newcastle on Thursday morning. She wondered which platform it would be for the trains going further south. There were destination boards giving instructions, and stairs and lifts and walkways leading hither and thither. Most people seemed to know where they were going, although a few were looking puzzled. There were railway officials and porters there, however, who would deal with enquiries. Debbie had a moment of near panic as she remembered what she would be embarking on… if she had the courage to go through with it. A journey into the unknown, in all sorts of ways…

'Come on, love, we'd best get moving,' said her mother. 'What's the matter? What are you looking at?'

'Nothing,' she answered. 'Well… all these people, I suppose, wondering what they're all doing, where they're going.'

Vera laughed. 'You're a funny lass and no mistake! That enquiring mind of yours, always wanting to know the ins and outs of everything. Well, we know where we're going, don't we?' She tucked her arm companionably through her daughter's as they walked out of the station.

Their first stop was the leather shop, not far from the station; the sort of shop where you usually looked in the window but didn't go inside. But today was different. Vera marched in confidently and Debbie followed.

'We'd like to purchase a briefcase,' Vera said to the woman assistant who approached them. 'For my daughter...' She turned to smile at Debbie. 'She's going into the sixth form, and she'll be able to use it later when she goes to university.' Debbie was tempted to say, 'Oh, do shut up, Mum!' But of course she didn't. She just smiled, trying not to look too embarrassed.

They looked at a selection, many of which were too big and clumsy, very ostentatious, for city business men. Eventually they chose one in a light tan leather that was not too heavy or too outrageously expensive. Debbie was feeling guilty about all sorts of things, and had decided she must keep the cost down as much as possible.

Then Vera, after a lot of 'iffing and butting', was persuaded to buy a bag for herself. Debbie coaxed her away from the old-fashioned style of black or dark brown leather with a clasp, and urged her to buy one in soft fawn suede, with a zip and a fancy large button fastening.

Vera parted with a sheaf of pound notes that were tucked away in her capacious purse. 'May we leave these parcels and call back for them later?' she asked. 'On our way back to the train. We've come from Whitesands Bay. We're here for the day, and we've some more shopping to do; new clothes for Debbie for when she goes back to the sixth form.'

Debbie felt herself go pink. *Shut up, Mum!* she thought again. *She doesn't want to know our life story.*

But the assistant just smiled and said, 'Certainly, madam; I hope you enjoy your day,' in a very friendly manner.

They had lunch at Woolworth's cafeteria; salmon sandwiches and large cups of coffee, followed by vanilla slices with lots of custardy filling and sticky icing.

'Lovely!' said Vera, wiping her mouth and fingers with a paper serviette. 'We're having a grand time, aren't we, pet?' Debbie agreed they were. 'And now we'll go to C and A,' she went on, 'and get you a nice new coat, and you need a new skirt for school, don't you, love?'

'I might,' said Debbie. 'But I don't want you spending all this money on me, Mum. I've got plenty of clothes, really I have. I'd rather you bought something for yourself.'

'I probably will,' said Vera. 'Your daddy gave me quite a lot of money. "Go and treat yerself," he said; and I've got some money saved up myself out of my wages. It isn't as if we often go on a spending spree, and we want you to have everything you need for your schooling, your daddy and me.'

Debbie chose a cherry red coat, 'for best', insisting that her other one was more than adequate for school. The red one was 'just above the knee' length rather than a mini, mainly to appease her mother. It was quite trendy though, with a stand-away collar and large black buttons. Vera opted for a 'just below the knee' length, in russet tweed with a mock fur collar. She looked smart in it, and Debbie told her it made her look ten years younger. Vera smiled contentedly, and Debbie couldn't remember when she had seen her mother look so happy.

They went to Marks and Spencer to buy Debbie's school skirt, and she insisted on paying for a jumper herself; a skinny rib sweater in emerald green with a turtle neck. She also treated her mother to a nylon scarf with a pattern of bright green leaves and orange flowers; it would go well at the neckline of the russet brown coat. Vera was so touched that tears came into her eyes.

'Now, stop it, Mum,' said Debbie. 'It's just a little thank you, that's all… for everything you do for me.'

—

'We've had a lovely day. I can't tell you how nice it's been,' Vera said to Stanley as they ate their evening meal. 'We've each got a new coat, haven't we, Debbie? And she's got her briefcase, and I treated myself to a handbag. The assistant was ever so nice and friendly. And we had a lovely lunch in Woolies.'

'Good,' said Stanley, tucking into his steak and kidney pie. 'And what did you buy for me, eh?' He winked at Debbie to show he was only joking.

'Oh dear!' said Vera. 'Poor old Daddy! It was just a girls' day out; we never thought, did we, Debbie? But you know how fussy you are, Stanley. Anything I chose would be wrong. Happen we could go to Newcastle again, just you and me, when Debbie's gone back to school. You're about due for a new suit, aren't you, Stanley?'

He chuckled. 'I never have much cause to dress up, do I? I was only joking, lass. So long as you and our Debbie are pleased, then so am I.'

'She's been grand today,' Vera said to her husband later that night. 'I could hardly believe it was the same girl. Whatever was wrong with her, I think she's got over it. All that business about leaving school, and all that carry-on at the party. I think that taught her a lesson, Stanley. I really do believe she's turned over a new leaf.'

Debbie had, truly, enjoyed the day with her mother. They had been so much more at ease with one another. How then, she asked herself, could she even consider carrying on with the plan she had in mind?

It wasn't as if there was a particular bone of contention between herself and her parents at the moment, although there had been in the past; and they still tended to annoy her with their old-fashioned way of looking at things and their tendency to treat her like a child, their precious little girl. But maybe no more so than other parents did. And she supposed she was precious to them, having waited so long for a child and then given up hope. She remembered her mother telling her how they had chosen her specially, and had been so thrilled that they had got their own little girl at last.

She knew that she was the most important person, the most important part of their lives, she guessed, apart from their love for one another. She knew that her parents got on very well together; it was not romantic or passionate love, she imagined, not now – had it ever been? – but she had never known them to have a serious quarrel or to bicker at one another. Their lives revolved around the family unit, just the three of them, and other issues – work, friends, holidays, leisure activities, churchgoing – were of lesser importance than their happy family. And now, was she bent on destroying it?

There were times when Debbie wished she didn't know quite so much about her background and the circumstances of her birth. Might it have been better if she had never known about her adoption, if her parents had kept the true facts from her? She had accepted the story when she was a little girl; she had thought it was a lovely story. It was only later that she had wanted to know more. Her mother had commented on her enquiring mind only the other day, as she had done many times in the past. Debbie was never content until she had got to the root of the matter, had found out the answer to every question. Having discovered where she had been born had not been enough. She had ferreted away until she knew, now, much more than she had ever expected to discover. So how could she leave it alone, when she had this desire to find out everything niggling away at her.

It wasn't as if she was storming out after a family row, she told herself; she had heard about girls leaving home in such circumstances. She obviously couldn't say where she was going, though. Her parents would be terribly upset – angry, maybe – if she let them know of her intentions. They would no doubt be upset, anyway, when they found out. But if she went about it in the way she intended, in secret, then they would be so relieved at finding her again that they would forgive her. It would be all right... wouldn't it? She wasn't intending to leave home; she just wanted to find the person who had given birth to her. Should she leave a note? she wondered. No; she decided it was best not to. She didn't want them hot on her trail before she had achieved her object...

–

She set off on Monday morning as usual, supposedly for work, on her bicycle. In her saddle bag she had the sandwiches that her mother always made for her – chicken leftover from their Sunday dinner – and a piece of homemade gingerbread. Debbie had also included an apple, a banana and a packet of crisps, a chocolate biscuit, and a screw-top bottle of orange juice.

She didn't know how long it would take her to get to Aberthwaite; it would all depend on the times of trains and the connections. She hadn't had a chance to find out in advance, but she trusted that it would be quite simple. It wasn't all that far – only the next but one county. It wouldn't be like travelling abroad, or even as far as London. All the same, it was a massive step for her to be taking, because she had never before travelled away from her home town on her own.

She couldn't take any luggage, nor would she need very much. She didn't even know if she would be invited to stay for the night, or if they would turn her away, not wanting to know. Surely not... Fiona – which was how she was now thinking of her – was married to a vicar. Surely they would listen to her.

She pushed a few items of underwear into a small bag, then, on the spur of the moment, she put in the little pink teddy bear. That would give credence to her story.

She kissed her mother on the cheek, as she always did, not making any more fuss than usual.

'Have a nice day,' said Vera. 'Your last week, isn't it? I hope Kevin's feeling better. He should be back at work today, shouldn't he?'

'Er... yes; I think so, Mum. See you later then...' She could have said that she was going on somewhere after work, to see Shirley or one of the other girls from school, but she decided not to. Better not to drag Shirley into it.

She turned the opposite way at the end of the street, heading towards the railway station on the outskirts of the town. What about her bicycle? It would be too much of a bother to take it with her, on and off trains and into the luggage vans. She had a lock and key for it, although common sense told her it would still be easy enough to steal if anyone wanted to. She had to take some chances, though. She locked it and left it propped up against a wall in the car park.

The small station was not busy. A lot of people used it between nine and ten o'clock, travelling further afield to work, to Newcastle or South Shields, but they had all gone by now. She stood behind two other people at the ticket office, hoping she wouldn't see anybody she knew. Fortunately she didn't, but she could hear her voice quavering a little as she asked the middle-aged man behind the glass partition if she could have a ticket to Aberthwaite.

He scratched his head. 'Aberthwaite? There's no trains that go there. There isn't a station, pet. The nearest you can get is Richmond; you'll be able to get a bus from there. No, hang on a minute... It'd be best to go to Northallerton. There's not many trains to Richmond now, not since that there Beeching plan. They wanted to close it altogether and it seems as though it's on its last legs. You'll be able to get a bus from there an' all.'

'From where...? From Northallerton?' asked Debbie, starting to feel rather confused.

'Aye, that's what I said. Now, d'you want a single or a return?'

'Oh, a return I think,' she replied. 'Yes, a return, please.'

'Very well then.' After a minute or two he pushed the ticket towards her. 'Change at Newcastle and Darlington.'

'Both of them?' she asked.

'Aye, it'll be quicker in the long run. T'other stops at every little station. Don't look so worried, lass.' He smiled at her. 'Travelling on your own, are you?'

'Yes; I'm going to see some friends. Er… what time will I get there?'

'It should be two thirty into Northallerton, if you catch the connection. There's not much time, though. The next one's an hour later. Then you've to catch your bus. What time are they expecting you?'

'I said I wasn't sure. Sometime in the afternoon…'

The railway clerk looked at the clock. 'The Newcastle train's just gone. I thought you were cutting it fine. The next un'll be in half an hour.'

He was a right Job's comforter, she thought – one of her mother's expressions. But he probably didn't have silly indecisive girls like her to deal with very often. She parted with her pound note for the ticket and put the change away. She had been saving up and had a couple more pounds and some silver for emergencies.

'Over the bridge to platform two,' said the man. 'Hope you have a nice time with your friends. Cheer up, love, you'll be OK. You can always ask one of us chaps if you get lost.' It was almost as though he knew what she was doing.

It was a fine day, not very sunny, but pleasantly warm as she sat on the platform bench waiting for the first train. Newcastle, Darlington, Northallerton, she said to herself. The last town was unknown to her, but as the man said, she could always ask her way. It was only four days since she had taken the Newcastle train with her mother, so this part of the journey was familiar. She alighted at Newcastle and asked a porter to direct her to the platform for the next train to Darlington.

It was quite easy to find a seat. She felt a little self-conscious on her own, but nobody took any notice. She watched the other passengers humping huge suitcases and bags on to the racks, and was glad she was travelling light. The train was one that had little tables between the seats. Her earlier feeling of panic had subsided now, and in a few moments, though a mite self-consciously, she took out her packet of sandwiches and the bottle of orange juice. She was feeling rather hungry as she hadn't eaten much at breakfast time because of the turmoil inside her. Fortunately her mother hadn't noticed, or had made no comment. The lady opposite her smiled at her in a friendly way as she munched away at her chicken barm-cake, but didn't say anything. Debbie was glad because she didn't want to get into conversation with anyone.

She looked out of the window at the scenery that was still familiar. This was the longest leg of the journey from Newcastle to Darlington. A largely built-up area, with factory chimneys and the winding gear of coal mines on the horizon, and hundreds of streets of terraced houses. The train stopped at Durham, where the sight of the majestic cathedral on the hill was a pleasant contrast to the industrial landscape. As they journeyed south the scenery was more rural in parts with isolated farmhouses, green hills and pasture land.

Debbie guessed they could not be all that far from Darlington when the train stopped, between stations, for no apparent reason. The minutes – five, ten, twelve – went by, and she looked anxiously at her watch. The ticket man had said there was not all that much time for the next connection, and it seemed now as though she was likely to miss it.

'Perhaps there's a cow on the line,' said the elderly lady to her husband. They didn't seem overly concerned, and Debbie guessed that this was a joke. The lady smiled at her. 'This often happens, dear,' she said. 'Don't worry, it'll start moving again soon. British Rail! I don't know...' She shook her head in desperation.

There was a sudden jerk, and the train started up again, slowly, only to travel a mile or so before stopping again. 'I reckon we've caught up with that there cow again,' joked the man, and his wife laughed.

But Debbie didn't feel like laughing. She gathered her few belongings together as the train drew near to Darlington. She made a hasty exit when it stopped, then stood on the platform staring helplessly around. It was even busier than Newcastle. She remembered learning at school that it was known as the birthplace of the railway, and George Stephenson's engine, 'Locomotion', was on show somewhere in the station. But there was no time for sightseeing.

She jostled her way through the midday crowd, stopping to ask a porter the whereabouts of the train to Northallerton. 'I think you've missed this one, pet,' he said. He looked at the station clock. 'Yes, you have. Next one's in an hour, platform four, over the bridge.'

'Thank you,' she said although things were not going well at all. Now she had an hour to wait. She went to the ladies' room then browsed at the WH Smith bookstall, buying a puzzler book and a copy of *Girl* magazine. Then she went into the snack bar and bought a cup of coffee. It was hot and she sipped it gratefully, glad of the warmth because the day was turning chilly.

She found that the hour soon passed. She located the platform and the train, then settled down in her seat, relieved that she was coming to the last part of her journey. It took less than an hour to get to Northallerton, but this neck of the woods was completely unfamiliar to her. She asked directions and made her way to the market square from where she would be able to catch a bus. She was aware, on the fringes of her mind, that it was a pleasant market town with old houses grouped around the church, and a market cross in the middle of the square.

At the side of the cobblestoned area there was a bus stop with a seat next to it; there was no one sitting on it. Debbie tried to decipher the times on the timetable that was attached to the bus stop. The printing was very small and complicated to follow. It showed times for all the buses to the nearby towns and villages from early in the morning, then every hour, or forty-five minutes or whatever, up to the evening. She searched for Aberth-waite. It seemed that there were not many buses at all to that place. She was going cross-eyed staring at the small print. From what she could make out there were only two buses a day, one at 11.30, and the other at 15.30. Most people were not wholly conversant yet with the twenty-four hour clock; she calculated that that was three thirty in the afternoon. She glanced at her watch; it was already a quarter to four! She had missed it, the last bus of the day, by fifteen minutes.

She studied the timetable again, trying to make the numbers say something else. Perhaps she was mistaken; but she knew that she wasn't. What on earth was she going to do now? She flopped down on to the seat feeling utterly miserable and dejected. To make matters worse the early promise of the day had not held out and it was starting to rain; a fine drizzle but the sort that could soak you through in no time. Luckily her coat had a hood and she pulled it up. She opened her bag and took out the Kit-Kat biscuit; she couldn't think of what else to do.

She didn't know the phone number of the rectory. There was a phone box nearby, and she thought you could find out numbers if you rang the operator. But what could she say if she got through? How could she explain it all on the phone? There seemed to be nothing for it but to go back home. She couldn't stay here all night, and she hadn't got enough money to go to a bed and breakfast place.

Her head drooped and she felt tears forming in her eyes. Debbie didn't often cry – her mother said she was a plucky little lady – but now it was all too much for her. The tears began to fall and she started to sob; just gentle sobs but enough to be noticed by someone passing by. She felt dreadfully embarrassed when a lady stopped by the seat, then sat down beside her.

'Whatever's the matter, my dear?' she asked. 'Please forgive me for asking... but I saw you studying the timetable when I went into the shop over there. I thought you looked worried, and now it's obvious that you are, very worried. Have you missed a bus?'

Debbie looked up at the kind face of a middle-aged lady – well, sort of young middle-age, perhaps a bit younger than her mother – with gingerish hair and a nice smile. It was the smile that did it, as though the lady really cared. Debbie tried to control her sobs as she told her that she had missed the last bus to Aberthwaite, '...and I don't know what to do because I don't know the phone number, and they're not really expecting me.'

'Well then, there's no need to worry any more,' said the lady. 'I'm going to Aberthwaite; I live there. I've been visiting an old aunt, and now I'm going home. So that's lucky, isn't it? You can come with me. I'm afraid buses to Aberthwaite are very few and far between.'

'Oh... thank you! That's so kind of you.' Debbie stopped crying at once. It went through her mind that her mother had warned her not to talk to strangers, especially about not accepting lifts. But this was different; you couldn't think of this kind person as a stranger.

'Come along then, dear,' she said. 'My car's over there.' Debbie followed her a short distance to where a Morris Minor car was parked. She climbed into the front seat and the lady closed the door.

'Off we go then,' she said. 'It won't take long – less than an hour.'

The thought of what lay ahead had momentarily been set aside in Debbie's mind when she had found herself stranded in the middle of nowhere. Now the forthcoming meeting began to loom large again. She would be there soon. What should she say to... Fiona?

'Are you going to see friends in Aberthwaite?' asked her companion.

'Yes... well, a relation really,' replied Debbie. 'She's my aunt... Aunty Fiona, but, like I said, she doesn't know I'm coming.' Now, what on earth had possessed her to say that?

The woman turned to look at her, quickly, before turning her attention back to the road. 'It isn't Fiona Norwood, is it?' she asked. 'The rector's wife?'

'Yes, it is... actually,' said Debbie, in a subdued voice.

'Well, fancy that! They say it's a small world, don't they? Fiona's a friend of mine.' She turned again to smile at Debbie, rather curiously. 'I'm sure she'll be pleased to see you.'

'I hope so...' replied Debbie.

It was pleasant countryside; leafy lanes with now and again a glimpse of a rippling stream, greystone cottages at the side of the road, a country pub or two, sheep grazing on the hillsides and a ruined castle in the distance. To Debbie's relief, her companion didn't say any more.

Then the sign said Aberthwaite. They drove through a street of shops, around a market square, then along a tree-lined road, heading towards a church. 'That's St Peter's,' said the lady, 'and here is the rectory. But I expect you know that, don't you?' She looked at Debbie quizzically.

'Er... it's a while since I was here,' she answered. 'Thank you very much; you've been really kind. I'll be alright now.' She gathered up her belongings and jumped out of the car.

The lady smiled at her. 'Good luck, my dear,' she said, for some reason.

Debbie opened the gate and walked up the garden path between flower beds gay with late summer blooms, to the big old house. She rang the bell...

Fifteen

'Well, what's your verdict then?' Simon asked his wife, as they walked home after the evening service one Sunday at the end of August.

'I thought he was good, very good indeed, to say it was his first sermon,' said Fiona. 'I was pleasantly surprised. And he was not too... what shall I say?... outlandish! I was trying to see how Ethel Bayliss was reacting, without making it obvious that I was watching her.'

Fiona had a good view of the congregation from her seat in the choir stalls. She didn't always attend the evening service as she needed to stay at home to look after Stella; but Simon's parents were staying for the weekend and they had volunteered to babysit the little girl. They were delighted to do that as they saw her only every couple of months.

Simon and Fiona had been discussing the Reverend Joshua Bellamy, Simon's new curate, who had been preaching his first sermon at St Peter's that evening. He had been in the parish for only a month, and had already proved to be a talking point and had raised a few eyebrows.

Simon had been surprised and very pleased that his request for a curate had, eventually, been granted. The young man, aged twenty-five, was in his probationary year as a curate, and would be officially ordained in September, if he was deemed suitable. He had served several months in a church in the centre of Halifax, and was now being transferred to a country parish. Simon was not told the reason for the move, but he had agreed to interview the young man, about six weeks ago, one morning in mid-July. Their meeting had taken place in the rectory study, and Fiona had kept out of the way until Simon came to find her and asked if she would make coffee.

'What's he like?' she had asked, agog with curiosity.

'Wait and see!' said Simon. 'You'll soon find out.' He was laughing so Fiona had not known what to expect.

She laid a tray with the best china and a plate of chocolate biscuits and carried it into the lounge to where they had adjourned. The young man stood up as she entered, which showed, whatever else, that he knew his manners. He was tall, about six foot, and slim with dark brown hair that hung down to his shoulders. He had bright blue eyes with a friendly glint in them as he took his first glance at Fiona, and he wore an earring, a plain gold hoop, in one ear. He was casually dressed in denim trousers and a green anorak, but she was pleased to see he was wearing his clerical collar.

She put the tray down on the coffee table and held out her hand. 'How do you do?' she said. 'I'm Fiona, Simon's wife.'

He grasped her hand firmly, smiling into her eyes. 'How do you do? Pleased to meet you Mrs Norwood,' he said. 'I'm Josh.'

He had made a good start, in her opinion, by not being too familiar, despite his rather unconventional appearance. The 'Mrs Norwood' had pleased her, although she preferred to be called Fiona. They sat down again and she handed round the coffee and biscuits. Simon started the conversation.

'Josh has been telling me about himself and his ideas,' he said, 'and I have already decided that he will fit in very well at St Peter's. I shall recommend to the church council that we take him on as our curate, and he will be ordained here in September, God willing.'

'That's very good news,' said Fiona. 'It's been hard going for Simon recently. The congregation has increased – not tremendously, but the numbers are encouraging, aren't they, darling?'

Simon nodded. 'Yes, so they are. It's probably due to our decision to move the Sunday school from the after-noon to the morning. I've been telling Josh about our family service once a month, and how quite a few of the parents now come along with their children. Josh has an interest in youth work,' – he smiled encouragingly at the young man – 'so I would like him to be responsible for the family service each month. I am sure he will have a lot of new ideas. And he has also agreed to take over the running of the Youth Club.'

'So you've got your work cut out already, Josh,' said Fiona. 'You're being thrown in at the deep end, aren't you?'

'I don't mind,' he replied, 'I shall look forward to it. And I've been telling Mr Norwood that I play the guitar.'

Now, why doesn't that surprise me? thought Fiona. She guessed that he would be pretty good at it as well.

–

The parochial church council had accepted Simon's recommendation, and Joshua Bellamy had made his first appearance the following Sunday at the morning service. Fiona had watched with interest the reaction of Ethel

Bayliss, the churchwarden's wife, as the new curate took his place in his appointed seat opposite that of the rector. Ethel's mouth dropped open and her eyebrows shot up in alarm; then she nudged her neighbour, Mrs Blanche Fowler, the wife of the other churchwarden and they whispered together during the singing of the first hymn, the cherries on Blanche's hat bobbing about as she nodded in agreement with her friend's remarks. Fiona guessed, though, that Blanche Fowler might not entirely agree with the other woman. She sometimes did so to keep the peace, but she had been known at times to voice her own opinion. On that particular Sunday Joshua's input to the service was limited to a few of the prayers and responses and the reading of one of the lessons, which he did in a deep resonant voice.

It was at the family service two weeks later that he made a more startling impression. He disappeared into the vestry just before the sermon. It was always more of a children's address on these occasions, but designed to be of interest to the adults as well as the children. Josh emerged a few moments later dressed as the devil, in a red suit complete with horns and a forked tail. There were gasps of surprise – mixed horror, amazement and a few of delight – from the adults and laughter from the children. Simon and Fiona both agreed afterwards that his talk was very good and thought-provoking; its message was to beware of the temptations of the devil which could come in many guises, often when you were least expecting it.

The verdict of the congregation, on the whole, seemed to be that the new curate was unusual to say the least, but go-ahead and modern in outlook, and if Simon approved of him who were they to disagree. He was well received at the Youth Club, and Graham Heap, the leader of the guitar group was glad of his assistance there. As had been anticipated, Josh was a very competent musician.

There were mutterings, though, from elsewhere in the church as might only have been expected. The ringleader, as usual, was Mrs Ethel Bayliss, and she soon had a few of her minions in agreement with her, the chief being Miss Mabel Thorpe. Fiona had learnt to be wary of them as they were the ones who had caused trouble for her – or tried to – when the news of her former pregnancy had leaked out. They had been heard to say now – and their mutterings were soon scattered abroad – that they intended to write to the Rural Dean, or even to the Bishop of the Diocese, setting down their views about the curate with long hair and an earring who pranced about dressed like a pantomime character.

Simon doubted that they would carry out their threat. They just liked to cause bother and to make sure that their opinions were made known, but he had other things to worry him. There had been a violent storm one night in June, following a week of sultry weather, and when Simon went into the vestry the next morning he found that there were pools of water in several places. He called for his churchwardens, and they quickly did a mopping-up operation and placed buckets at strategic places in case it happened again. The roofer who was called in said that he could do a temporary patch-up job, but the roof was leaking in several places and the damage had been worsening for some time. What was required was a complete overhauling and rebuilding of a large section of the roof. Simon had no reason to doubt his word. They had used him before for minor repairs on the Sunday school building and the rectory and found him to be reliable.

Simon doubted that there would be much financial help from Diocese funds. He had already applied for a curate so they were unlikely to look favourably at another request. He decided that it was more essential to have some help with the parish work; and they would try to raise the money themselves for the roof repairs.

There were those in the parish who could afford to donate a sum of money; some folk were more financially secure than others, of course. There were some, though, who found it difficult to make ends meet. At an emergency council meeting held soon after the rainstorm it was decided that they should have a 'Gift Day'. Each person in the congregation the following Sunday, at both the morning and the evening services would be given an envelope into which they could place their contribution, anonymously, if they wished. Simon guessed that there would be some who would donate a decent-sized cheque. He stressed, though, that any gifts, large or small, would be appreciated.

Several more ideas were mooted at the meeting. They already, from time to time, held special events such as spring or summer fayres, a Christmas bazaar and sale of work, and concerts with members of the congregation and the choir taking part. One suggestion was that they should invite special guest artistes from elsewhere to give a concert; there was a thriving male voice choir in the area, and brass bands abounded in the Yorkshire towns and villages.

'It'll cost yer though,' one of the men remarked. 'They'll not perform for nowt.' The verdict of a true Yorkshireman, and there were several mutterings of agreement.

'Nor would we expect them to give their services free,' smiled Simon. 'But the idea is that we could ask considerably more for tickets than we do for our own little efforts. Yes, I think that is something that we could look into. Not that I'm decrying the work that you good people do here,' he added, just in case he was treading on anyone's toes. 'But it would make a change, wouldn't it, and might draw in people from further afield.'

It had been decided earlier that year that the usual summer fayre would be held in the church hall and grounds, but the plans had not been finalized. It was suggested now, by a comparative newcomer to the church council, that this could be done on a much larger scale. The lady who spoke up was Mrs Florence Catchpole. She and her husband, who was a retired mill owner from the Bradford area, had come to live in Aberthwaite earlier that year. They had started to attend the services at St Peter's, and Mrs Catchpole had been invited to join the Mothers' Union. She was soon seen to be a very sensible and helpful person, young looking and spritely despite being in her mid-sixties. She had now retired but she had worked in local government, holding a position of authority. There were a few of the women who could see her, hopefully, as a challenge to Ethel Bayliss. But Florence Catchpole kept her own counsel and, as a newcomer, didn't say very much. However, when a vacancy occurred on the church council, Simon lost no time in asking her to become a member.

The suggestion she made now, about the garden party, was greeted with general approval. 'The house where Arnold and I live has quite a large garden,' she told them. It was, in fact, very large, surrounding one of the grandest houses in Aberthwaite; but, as they had already discovered, she was by no means a boastful person despite her wealth and once prominent position.

'I would be very willing – and I know Arnold will agree with me – to hold the garden party there, later in the summer. We could serve afternoon tea – strawberries and cream perhaps – and have stalls and games, whatever you like. That is, if you think it's a good idea…' Her voice petered out as they all looked at her, listening carefully. 'It's just a suggestion…' she added, a little self-effacingly.

'And an excellent one, if I may say so,' said Arthur Bayliss. He looked round at the council members and was answered with nods of approval and murmurings of 'Hear, hear!' 'It's a very generous offer, Mrs Catchpole,' he went on, 'and I would like to suggest that we go along with it. With your approval, of course, Simon?'

Simon nodded. 'I'm in full agreement, and we do thank you very much, Mrs Catchpole. We must get the opinion of the meeting, though, in the usual democratic way. Could we have a show of hands, please, that we take up Mrs Catchpole's offer?'

All the members, without exception, raised their hands, a few rather more slowly, but there was no one who would dare to disagree. The last hand to go up, Simon noticed to his wry amusement, was that of Mrs Bayliss. Most of the company were smiling and nodding at one another. Ethel looked… not exactly angry, more abashed and discomfited. She did not like anyone else to be the centre of attention, more particularly, Simon guessed, when it was a newcomer who was already proving popular with the members of the Mothers' Union.

'That's unanimous,' he said, 'just as I expected. Thank you, everyone. Now we must decide on a date…' It was agreed that the garden party should be held on the last Saturday in August. That would give them almost two months in which to prepare, and the last week in August often turned out to be fine and warm, a last glimpse of summer before autumn set in. There was no guarantee of fine weather, of course. But Mrs Catchpole seemed quite happy to compromise should the weather turn inclement.

'There's plenty of room indoors,' she said cheerfully. 'And the kitchen's large enough to cope with the catering, whether it's fine or not.'

It was agreed that the catering would be one of the chief considerations; they would need a small committee of ladies to take charge. Church people loved their committees, mused Simon, as he watched the womenfolk raise their hands, volunteering to be part of the little – elite – group. He saw Mrs Bayliss smile contentedly – he forbore to think of it as smugly – in her element again when it was suggested that she should be the leader of the group.

'And perhaps us chaps could see to the rest,' said Jonas Fowler, Blanche's husband. 'You know – games and sideshows and that sort of thing. I suppose we've no objection to raffles and tombolas and the like, have we?'

'No... I think we're rather more liberal than our Methodist friends when it comes to raffles,' said Simon. 'Some folk see it as gambling, but we're not playing poker or throwing money away at the casino, are we? We're just trying to raise money and have a bit of fun at the same time.' He smiled. 'I remember when I was a curate, there was a great to-do about it at one church, as to whether they were games of skill or games of chance. You were allowed to knock down skittles, or play hoop-la, because they involved skill. But you weren't allowed to buy a raffle ticket... I never saw the difference myself.'

'What about naming the doll?' asked someone. 'Is that skill... or is it luck?'

'Or guessing the weight of a cake?'

'That's definitely skill…'

'Or how many sweets in the jar?'

'Or finding the right spot on the map?'

Suggestions were coming thick and fast, and there was a general hubbub of conversation until Simon called the meeting to order. 'As far as I can see those are all good ideas, and if anyone wants to organize… a doll, or a cake, or whatever, then please go ahead and do so. Thank you all for your enthusiasm.'

There was one more suggestion that evening that was well worth considering. 'This raising money for the church roof will be an ongoing thing, won't it?' asked Graham Heap, the treasurer, who was as much concerned as anyone.

'Yes, and who knows how long it will take?' answered Simon. 'We may be able to secure a loan to tide us over, but it may take a long time.'

'Then why don't we take this catering business further and start doing it for visitors?' said Graham. Most of the company looked puzzled, so he went on to explain. 'Some churches in pleasant surroundings – as we are in Aberthwaite – have started catering for church outings; coach trips from other towns, maybe not too far away. We've a lot to offer here in Aberthwaite. It's a very attractive little town. There's the river, and the castle, and nice gentle walks round about, and the market on Saturday. It would usually be a Saturday, of course, that people would choose for a day's outing. And what could be nicer than a ham salad tea to round off the day? I've seen adverts in the church newspapers, and the Yorkshire magazines as well. So… why shouldn't we do it?'

Simon was thoughtful, and so were many others. 'Yes, you might have an idea there, Graham,' he replied carefully. 'But it would involve a lot of hard work for... well, just a few people. I would really hesitate to burden our catering ladies with any more work. They have already agreed to do the garden party... I suppose you mean... to put on meals in the church hall?'

Graham nodded. 'That's the idea; yes. To put an advert in the church newspaper, and to see what happens. It would be mainly a spring or summer thing. People don't usually want to travel far afield in the winter time.'

Mrs Florence Catchpole spoke up again. 'I think it's a brilliant idea, and I, for one, would be willing to help. I'm retired now, but I've still bags of energy and I'm always looking for new projects.'

Ethel Bayliss, not to be outdone, immediately said that she would be willing, and so did several others.

'Phew...!' breathed Simon. 'This is getting out of hand. Well, no...' he corrected himself, 'not quite. But it all needs thinking about seriously. We have plenty of food for thought... Please excuse the pun! It wasn't intentional. I suggest we bring the meeting to a close now. Graham and I will discuss that idea further, and maybe – just maybe – we could go ahead. One way and another we're going to be very busy. Now, let's have a word of prayer before we go home.'

—

Fiona had not been at the meeting, so she was interested to hear about what had taken place.

'I've met Mrs Catchpole a few times,' she said. 'It's a pity she's not of the age to join our Young Wives group.

We could argue that she's young at heart, and that's what matters. But it might cause bother. The Mothers' Union women seem to agree that they have their meetings and we have ours.'

'And never the twain shall meet?' joked Simon.

'Not exactly, but we each have a different role to play. Perhaps the Young Wives will be able to help with the catering. We'll do what we can, but it's difficult with most of the women going out to work.'

'Young Wives… and Friends.' Simon reminded her. 'Don't forget the "friends".' It had been decided at the start not to limit the group to married women, mainly so that they could include Ruth Makepeace, a local school-teacher who had been a widow. Since then, however, she had married the headmaster and was now Ruth Saunders.

'I don't think we have any friends now,' said Fiona. She laughed. 'No, that's not right, is it? What I mean is that since Ruth got married we are all wives. But we'll leave it as it is; everyone's welcome. It sounds as though the garden party could turn out to be quite a grand affair. Perhaps we could invite your parents to come for that weekend, Simon. They're due for a visit.'

The fundraising campaign for the church roof fund went on apace. The Gift Day proved to be an excel-lent start with several substantial cheques being presented by members of the congregation, amounting to the first several hundred pounds. Everyone threw themselves wholeheartedly into preparations for the garden party. By that time, Joshua, the new curate, had arrived, keen to prove his worth in all sorts of ways.

The morning of the big day started off cloudy, and everyone held their breath and said a few silent prayers.

By midday the sun had appeared, and it was decided that the stalls and games could be held outside as planned.

Afternoon tea was served in the spacious lounge and dining room – dainty sandwiches, scones and fancy cakes – with strawberries and cream as an extra temptation, which hardly anyone could resist. There were games of skill and of chance, as had been discussed at the meeting. Skittles and hoop-la; a tombola stall; a raffle with better than usual prizes; and various guessing competitions – the name of a doll, the weight of a cake, the number of Smarties in a jar, and pinpointing a place on a map of Aberthwaite and district. And numerous stalls selling fancy goods, bric-a-brac, books, and handmade gifts.

The doll was not the usual baby doll but a large-sized clown doll, denoted by Mrs Catchpole. It was dressed in a harlequin costume of diamond-patterned satin, a lavish creation designed to sit on a bed and enhance the decor of the room. To counterbalance this there was also a teddy bear to be named, which was of more interest to the children. The new curate, who was by now becoming well known – and generally well liked – volunteered to be in charge of this stall. It was soon seen as an excuse for him to dress up again, this time as a clown with baggy trousers, a red nose and a comical hat. He drew a good crowd who joined in the fun, and a few adverse comments from the same little group who had objected to his former appearance as the devil.

However, when the pre-arranged selection of names had all been chosen Josh changed into his normal clothes and went to help in the kitchen with the mountain of washing-up. Mrs Catchpole had a dishwashing machine – to the envy of several of the ladies – but there was still a colossal amount of clearing away to be done.

'A job shared is a job halved, ladies,' he said cheerily, grabbing a pot towel. He won the thanks and the approval of most of the helpers, but just a few remained tight-lipped, ignoring his presence.

When the day's takings were added up and the amount for expenses deducted, the treasurer told the now exhausted, but contented, helpers that more than five hundred pounds had been raised for the church roof fund.

Simon made the announcement at the morning service the next day; he went on to thank everyone who had helped or taken part in any way. There was a round of applause and a few cheers, something that at one time would have been frowned upon in church, but was now becoming acceptable in places where worship was seen to be not just piety and prayers, but a cause for celebration as well. The atmosphere that day at both services was one of unity and friendship.

'You've got a good church going there, lad,' Simon's father remarked when they sat together in the evening, Fiona, Simon and his parents, with Stella fast asleep upstairs. 'I had my doubts at first when you told us you wanted to be a parson.' He turned to his wife. 'Well, we both did, didn't we, love? But we changed our minds long ago. You're doing a grand job, you and Fiona. You should be proud of yourselves.'

'Pride doesn't come into it, Dad,' replied Simon. 'At least it shouldn't do. We have a splendid congregation there who all support us – well, almost all – in what we try to achieve. And now... I believe we have a good curate as well. You didn't hear him tonight, Dad, nor you, Mum, but we thought he was great, didn't we, darling?'

'Yes, I think most people were pleasantly surprised,' smiled Fiona.

'It's been a lovely weekend all told,' said Simon's mother. 'The garden party – that was so enjoyable – and hearing Simon preach this morning. And seeing you all again, of course. Stella's growing up fast, isn't she? And now you have the next one to look forward to; that's wonderful news. Don't do too much and tire yourself out though, will you, dear?'

'I'll try not to,' said Fiona, 'but it's not easy. There's always something to be done.'

–

Simon's parents departed quite early the next morning in a flurry of hugs and kisses and goodbye waves.

'Now, remember what you've been told, and try to take it easy today,' Simon told his wife.

'Yes, I probably will,' said Fiona. 'I must admit I do feel rather tired after that hectic weekend.'

She had a mainly quiet day, finding time to read and do some knitting whilst Stella was having her afternoon nap. The little girl had an early tea at five o'clock, whereas Simon and Fiona dined later after she had gone to bed. Stella had finished her tea and was playing quietly with her dolls, when the doorbell rang.

'Now, I wonder who that can be?' said Fiona. It was her usual – though fatuous – response to an unknown caller.

'Shall I go?' called Simon.

'No, it's OK, you stay there,' she replied. Her husband was enjoying a few minutes' relaxation with the evening paper.

She opened the door. There was a girl standing there. Fiona didn't know her, at least she didn't think she did, though she looked, somehow, familiar. The girl stared at her for a moment, then she said, 'Excuse me, but are you… Fiona?'

'Yes, that's me,' she answered brightly. 'And you are…?'

'My name's Debbie,' answered the girl. Then she burst into tears. 'I think you might be… my mother.'

Sixteen

Fiona gasped, feeling her heart miss a beat. She reached out a hand and touched the girl's arm. 'Come along, dear. Come inside, and tell me about it.' The girl looked at her unsurely, her brown eyes brimming with tears.

'I'm sorry,' she said. 'Perhaps I shouldn't have come...'

'Well, you're here now, aren't you?' said Fiona, putting an arm round her and leading her over the threshold. 'Come along in. Try not to cry, dear... We'll sort it all out.'

She led her into the room they called the living room; the family room at the back of the house, as opposed to the more spacious lounge where they entertained guests and groups from church. The living room was a more intimate place, and Fiona felt that she needed the support of her husband.

'This is Debbie,' she said. Simon looked up from his paper, and Fiona nodded at him in a meaningful way. She could tell from the look on his face – of surprise, bewilderment, then of gradually dawning realization – that he knew what she was trying to convey to him, and that he had guessed who this girl might be. 'She's come to tell us something. Debbie, love – this is my husband, Simon, and our little girl, Stella.'

'Hello,' said Debbie timidly, trying to smile through her tears.

Simon sprung to his feet. 'Take your coat off, dear, it looks rather damp. Now, sit here…' He coaxed her into a small armchair. 'Just relax and calm down, there's a good girl. You don't need to worry about anything at all. Just… take your time.' He patted her shoulder consolingly.

Stella got up from the hearthrug where she was playing with her dolls. She looked curiously at the visitor, then she went across and put her little hand on Debbie's knee. 'Don't cry, lady,' she said. 'Why you crying?'

It made Debbie give a loud sob, although she had been trying to stem her tears. But she smiled as well. 'Aren't you a little darling?' she said, stroking the child's hair. 'Don't worry, pet. I'm just being silly.'

'I'm Stella,' said the little girl, 'and this is Betsy.' She placed a soft-bodied doll, rather grimy with much loving on Debbie's knee. 'And this is Growly Bear.' An equally loved teddy bear, rather bald in places.

'Now leave Debbie alone,' said Fiona. 'I expect she's rather tired. I think we'd better all have a nice cup of tea.'

Debbie looked up and smiled. 'That sounds like my mum; she always says that… Oh dear!' She put a hand to her mouth. 'I'm sorry… but you know what I mean.'

Fiona smiled. 'Of course I do, my dear.' The words had certainly slipped out unintentionally, and it proved to Fiona that the girl had a loving mother, despite the fact that she had landed on their doorstep. 'That's what mums always say, isn't it?' She laughed. 'A nice cup of tea's an answer to everything.'

'I'll make the tea,' said Simon. 'Come on, Stella; you can help me. We'll let Mummy have a talk to Debbie.'

Fiona sat down opposite the girl. 'Now, my dear,' she said. 'Why do you think that I might be… No…' she said, shaking her head. 'I'll rephrase that, because I've no reason to doubt you. What I mean is… how did you find out? How did you know where to find me? To start with, where do you live, Debbie?'

'In Whitesands Bay,' Debbie replied. 'You know, up in Northumberland. I'm called Debbie – well, Deborah Mary really – Debbie Hargreaves.'

It was no surprise to Fiona to hear that she was from up north. She had that sing-song way of speaking, common to the people known as Geordies. She still remembered it from her time in Burnside House, and it was the way that Ginny and Arthur spoke.

'And… I've got this.' Debbie reached for the bag at the side of her chair and rummaged about in it. Then she drew out a little pink teddy bear and held it out to Fiona. 'My mum gave me this when I was a little girl. She said that you… I mean, the lady whose baby I was – she didn't know it was you, did she? – that she had left it with me, and that it showed that she – that you – had loved me…'

Fiona took hold of the little bear. 'Oh… yes!' she breathed. 'I remember…' Her eyes filled with tears, too, as she looked at the pink bear, recalling how she had tucked it into the baby's shawl when she handed the child over to the nurse; recalling, too, how she had first been given the teddy bear. 'I'm so pleased you've kept him. I'm glad your mother gave him to you.'

Debbie smiled. 'Actually, I always thought it was a girl bear, with it being pink. I called it Rosie. I didn't play with it very much, though, because Mum said it was special.'

'It was special to me as well, Debbie,' said Fiona. 'I'll tell you, later, how I came to have it. Now tell me… how did you find out?'

'Well…' Debbie frowned. 'It's complicated. My parents told me – at least Mum did – when I was only a very little girl, that I was adopted. So I always knew, and I didn't mind, because they said I was special, you see, because they'd chosen me.'

'Yes, I see…' Fiona nodded. 'I understand.'

'Do you remember Claire Wagstaff?' asked Debbie.

'Claire? Yes, of course I do,' said Fiona. 'She was one of the helpers at the home. She was very kind to me. Do you mean… Claire told you?'

'No, she didn't,' answered Debbie. 'She wouldn't tell me anything, really, 'cause she knew she wasn't supposed to. But I went to see her because Mum had told me I was born in that place, Burnside House.'

'I see…' Fiona was beginning to realize now what must have happened way back in 1952. 'So Claire… she had something to do with your adoption?' She had thought it strange that the girl lived in Northumberland, so near to the place of her birth. She had imagined that the child would have been taken much further away.

'Yes, it was Claire who told them, the adoption people, whoever they were, that my mum and dad – Vera and Stanley, they're called – that they wanted to adopt a baby girl. And that they'd be good parents. Claire knew them, you see.'

'And they are, aren't they?' asked Fiona. 'They're good parents? You've not come here because you're unhappy at home, have you, Debbie?'

'No,' said Debbie. 'I'm not unhappy. But I had this urge to find out; it was driving me mad. And I couldn't ask Mum anything else.'

'They don't know you're here, I take it?'

'No… I just got on a train and came here, well, I managed to get part of the way. I didn't know where Aberthwaite was, really. There's not a station here, so I was going to get a bus. But the bus had gone, and then a nice lady – she says she knows you – gave me a lift here. She saw me when I was waiting at the bus stop in… where was it? Oh yes, in Northallerton.'

'Oh deary me! It sounds as though you've had quite an eventful journey. Look, here's Simon with the tea.' She poured it into three cups. 'Sugar, Debbie?'

'Yes, one and a bit, please.'

'Now, drink it while it's hot; it'll make you feel better. You must be worn out after that journey. And you'd better have something to eat with us, too. Then we must let your parents know where you are. They'll be frantic, Debbie, when they find out you're missing. Didn't you think about that, dear?'

'Yes… yes, I did, sort of,' said Debbie, looking a bit shamefaced. 'But like I told you, I wanted to know… about you. And I knew that if I didn't do it now, I never would.'

Simon pulled up a chair and sat next to her. 'What is it, Debbie?' he asked kindly. 'Have you had a bit of an upset at home? Is that why you're here?'

'No… not really,' she began.

'No, she says not,' added Fiona. 'She's just been telling me how she found out… about me.' She turned to smile at Debbie. 'So Claire wouldn't tell you what you wanted to know?'

'No; she said she didn't know where you lived, and even if she did she couldn't tell me. But she mentioned somebody called Ginny, a friend of yours. She is, isn't she?'

'Ginny… yes, she was with me in the home. And we saw her – she and her husband came here – not long ago. Do you know Ginny? Did she tell you?'

'No, I don't know her,' said Debbie, 'but I know her son, Ryan. He's in my form at school, and he's the boyfriend of my friend Shirley.'

Fiona shook her head in bewilderment. This was getting very complicated. 'Ryan… yes, I remember Ryan. He was only a little boy when I last saw him. So it was Ryan, was it, who let the cat out of the bag?'

'Yes, but only because I made him. He didn't want to. He said his mum would kill him if she found out. Well, she wouldn't really have done; we always say that, don't we? She'd have been mad at him, though, 'cause she'd told him not to say anything. He showed his mum a photo, you see, of our form, and she said that I looked just like you, except for the colour of my hair.'

'Yes, of course…' Fiona leaned back on her chair, sighing deeply. 'It's just beginning to sink in. You are… my daughter! It's like a miracle, after all this time.'

Simon chuckled. 'The second miracle, eh, darling? Who said that lightning doesn't strike twice!'

'That's another story,' said Fiona, in answer to Debbie's questioning look. 'For another time. I'm so pleased you've come, my dear. It must have taken some courage. I can see that you're quite a determined young lady, aren't you?'

'Yes, and inquisitive, too,' said Debbie. 'I always want to find out. My mum says I'm too nosy for my own good.'

'Yes, and we must let your parents know you're here,' said Simon, a little sternly. 'We'd better ring up and tell them. I hope you won't get into too much trouble?'

'I don't think I will,' said Debbie. 'I know I shouldn't have done it, really, but I just… had to. We're not on the phone, though,' she added.

'Then perhaps there's a neighbour who could take a message?' suggested Simon.

'There's my friend, Shirley Crompton. They live nearby, but I don't know the number.'

'That's easily found out. But first things first.' Simon rubbed his hands together. 'A meal, then you'll be staying the night with us, won't you?'

'Oh… I don't know.' Debbie looked confused. 'I hadn't thought about it.'

'You didn't think we'd turn you out, did you?' laughed Simon. 'We've got a spare room, and Fiona can find you a nightdress.'

'Yes, come along, my dear.' Fiona put an arm round Debbie as she stood up. 'Let's get you sorted out. I dare say you'll want the bathroom as well, won't you?'

'Yes, I do actually,' Debbie said with a grin.

She seems a nice sort of girl, thought Fiona, obviously well-brought-up. Rather wilful, though, and she was probably something of a handful. But not lacking in courage, nor in character. Whatever she was like, though, she was here. It was almost too much to comprehend just now; but Fiona was glad, so very glad, that she had found her baby girl at last.

—

When Debbie came out of the bathroom Fiona showed her into a bedroom at the back of the house, overlooking the garden. 'I'm sure you'll be comfortable in here, Debbie,' she said. 'It's where Ginny and Arthur slept when they came to see us…' She hesitated. 'I wonder if Ginny knew about it then?' she said, almost as if talking to herself. 'I've a feeling she might have done, but maybe she thought things were better left as they were. I'm really pleased about it, though, Debbie, love. It's strange isn't it… but come here and give me a hug.'

Debbie felt herself enveloped in loving arms, and as she returned the embrace, a little diffidently, she breathed in the scent of a flowery perfume; gardenia, perhaps? Her mum liked Coty's L'aimant, but it wasn't that. It was a lighter, younger fragrance. Fiona kissed her cheek, then stood back, looking at her.

'You must call me Fiona,' she said. 'Let's get that settled straight away. Because you've got a mum, haven't you, who loves you very much? And I can tell by the way you talk about her that you think a lot of her, don't you?'

'Yes, I do,' said Debbie. 'And my dad as well. We hadn't had a row – like I said, that's not why I came – but I sometimes get annoyed with them.'

Fiona smiled. 'All girls get annoyed with their parents sometimes; I know I did.'

'They're a bit old-fashioned, you see,' Debbie went on. 'Of course they're older aren't they, older than you? They're turned fifty, both of them. They wanted a baby; they'd been married for ages and nothing happened. So they adopted me.'

'And it's all turned out very well, hasn't it?' said Fiona. 'Look, Debbie; I'm going to leave you to sort yourself out. I'll get you a nightie, and a towel and flannel. You won't have brought a toothbrush, will you?'

Debbie shook her head. 'No, I just shoved in some... underwear, that's all. And something to eat, and the little bear... to show I wasn't making it up. Would you like it back? You said it was special.'

'No, you keep it.' Fiona looked sad for a moment. '...but I'll tell you the story about it... later.'

She left the room and came back a few minutes later with a pretty blue nylon nightdress, a towel and flannel, and a toothbrush and toothpaste. 'There you are, dear.

Come down when you're ready. I must go and see to our meal. We're having a chicken casserole, so there's plenty to go round. See you in a little while…'

Debbie looked out of the window at the garden. Her keen eye told her that Simon and Fiona were probably not expert gardeners, as her father was and as she hoped to be, one day. The lawn needed cutting, and the flowerbeds surrounding it held summer bedding plants – begonias, marigolds, asters – nearing the end of their flowering, and a few rose bushes. There was a stunning view, though, of trees and a stream and distant hills, and nearby was the church where Simon was the rector. She noticed the sand pit and the swing at the end of the garden…

Stella was a lovely little girl. Debbie had taken to her at once, although she had never had much to do with children. She was her… half-sister, wasn't she?

One of the first things that Debbie had noticed about Fiona was that she was pregnant; a few months so, she guessed. Debbie already liked her very much. She was young looking and very pretty, with golden hair in an elfin style. Debbie could see the resemblance to herself, but Fiona's features were more delicate than her own rather stronger ones. She thought that Fiona looked tired. It couldn't be easy, being the wife of a rector… but Simon seemed very nice as well; kind and helpful, but strong, too, she guessed, and determined.

It had all gone very well so far, after the stressful journey. It was then that she remembered her parents. Would they have found out by now that she was missing? She suddenly felt dreadful; there was a sick feeling in her stomach as she thought of Mum worrying about her. It came to her then, like a flash of lightning, that Vera was her mother. She always had been, ever since she had taken charge of her as a tiny baby, and she always would be. Fiona was… well, she was just Fiona. Debbie would no doubt get to know her better and grow fond of her. But Vera was… Mum. And Debbie realized now that she loved her very much.

—

Debbie was usually home by six o'clock. The staff who worked at the garden centre stopped work at five thirty, although Mr Hill sometimes stayed open later to accommodate people who might want to call on their way home.

When she hadn't arrived home at six fifteen Vera started to feel anxious.

'Now don't start worrying,' Stanley told her. 'She's not all that late. Perhaps she's got held up with a last-minute customer, or maybe she's chatting to Kevin.'

'Or she might have had a puncture,' said Vera. 'Oh dear! I do worry, Stanley, when she's out on her bike. I don't think she's any idea how to mend a puncture…' Or she could have had an accident, Vera thought to herself, but didn't say. The country lanes were pretty quiet, but the cars sometimes went too fast round the bends. There had been a report in the paper recently about such an occurrence: a cyclist knocked off her bicycle and badly injured.

'Our meal's ready now,' said Vera, 'but I don't want to start without her.'

'What are we having?' asked Stanley.

'Braised steak with carrots and onions, and there's mashed potato.'

'Put our Debbie's on a plate, then, and leave it in the oven. She won't be long, and I'm starving!'

They started their meal, in fact they finished the first course and started eating their rhubarb crumble, and still she hadn't arrived. Vera pushed her dish to one side. 'I can't eat any more, Stanley; I'm that worried. Wherever can she be?'

'For heaven's sake, Vera, calm down!' said Stanley. 'Don't start thinking the worst. I'll just finish my pud, then I'll nip along to the phone box and ring Mr Hill at the garden centre. She might be working late.'

'Then she should have let us know...'

'How could she?' said Stanley. 'I keep telling you that we ought to get a phone put in. We can well afford it now.'

'But we hardly ever use the phone.' Vera had never seen the need to go to the unnecessary expense.

'Well, we need it now, don't we?'

'I'll go,' said Vera, feeling she couldn't wait any longer. She was all churned up inside, and she had to do something – anything – to stop her thoughts running out of control. 'You finish your pudding.'

'Have you got the number?'

'Yes; it's in my diary. Debbie gave it me, but I've never used it.' She grabbed her bag and ran to the phone box at the end of the road. She put in the money and dialled the number, all fingers and thumbs as she hardly ever used a phone. She could tell by his voice that it was Kevin who answered.

'Hello, Sunnyhill garden centre. How can I help you?'

'Oh, hello, Kevin,' she said. 'It's Mrs Hargreaves here, Debbie's mum. We're rather worried because she hasn't got home yet. Did she leave at the usual time?'

There was a pause before Kevin answered. 'Er... Debbie hasn't been to work today, Mrs Hargreaves. We were wondering why she hadn't let us know.'

'Oh dear! Oh no… where is she then? She didn't say anything to you, did she, Kevin, about any plans or… anything?'

'No, I'm afraid not. Actually, I'm not seeing Debbie any more. I see her at work, but that's all. We decided… well… to call it a day. With her going back to school and… everything.'

'Oh, I see. She didn't tell me. I'm sorry about that.' Despite her early misgivings Vera did feel sorry as she knew now that Kevin was a decent sort of lad. 'Are you feeling better?' she asked. 'Debbie said you had a bad cold and that was why she… wasn't seeing you…'

'I'm fine, thanks. Actually… I haven't been ill at all.'

So Debbie had lied about it. Breaking up with Kevin must have upset her quite a lot. Had that got something to do with her being missing now? she wondered.

'I'm sorry I can't help you, Mrs Hargreaves,' said Kevin, sounding concerned. 'Perhaps you could go and see Shirley Crompton? I know they're very friendly. She might know something… although I'm sure there's nothing to worry about,' he added.

'Yes… yes, I will. Thank you, Kevin. Bye for now.'

She ran all the way home and was breathless when she arrived. She collapsed, panting, in the chair. 'She's not there, Stanley,' she gasped. 'She's not been at work all day. Oh, dear God! Wherever can she be?'

'At least she's not had an accident on the way home. That's what you were thinking, wasn't it? I could tell you were.'

'Kevin said Shirley might know something. They're thick as thieves, you know, and girls don't tell their parents what they get up to, not by a long chalk.'

'Right; we'll nip along to the Cromptons' place then. Buck up, love. We'll find her. I feel sure we will. Happen she's gone off somewhere with Shirley.'

'Then why didn't she tell us? Oh, Stanley, I'm scared, I really am.'

'Come on, then, let's get moving.'

The Cromptons' house was at the far end of the avenue. Madge Crompton, who was a friend of Vera, mainly because of their daughters' friendship, opened the door.

'Hello there, Vera, Stanley. This is a surprise. Do come in.'

'Is our Debbie here?' asked Vera, without preamble. 'She hasn't come home from work.'

'No, she isn't.' Madge looked puzzled. 'I haven't seen her since… sometime last week. She came round to see Shirley. Let's see if she knows anything.'

'Debbie hasn't been to work today, and we don't know where she is,' said Vera. 'Have you any idea, Shirley, pet, where she might be?'

Shirley was reading a magazine. She put it down, looking a little uneasily at Vera and Stanley. 'Er… no. I'm sorry, I don't know where she is.'

Vera thought, though, that she did know something, but it wasn't her place to push her any further. Shirley's father, however, looked at her shrewdly. 'Are you quite sure you don't know anything, Shirley?'

The girl looked down at her feet. 'No, well… not really.'

'Now come along love,' said her mother. 'You won't get into trouble. Has Debbie said anything to you? Look, her mum and dad are worried. Just think how worried we would be if it was you.'

'I might know something…' Shirley looked nervously at Vera, seeming close to tears. 'I don't know whether she really meant to do it but…'

'Go on,' said her mother gently. 'You must tell us, love.'

She started then on a tale of Debbie's adoption and wanting to find out about her birth mother. Vera listened in a stunned silence. Claire Wagstaff was mentioned, although Shirley didn't know her, and a boy called Ryan, who was Shirley's boyfriend. His mother had been in Burnside House with a girl called Fiona, and the crux of the matter was that Debbie had found out. She had pestered Ryan until he had told her that his mother, Ginny, was still friendly with Fiona, and when Ryan showed her a photograph, this Ginny had said that there could be no doubt about it: Debbie bore a striking resemblance to her friend.

Vera could scarcely take it in. Stanley put an arm round her. 'Don't fret, love. If that's where she's gone, then she'll be safe… Where does she live then, this… Fiona?' he asked.

'In Aberthwaite, North Yorkshire,' answered Shirley, a trifle unwillingly. 'Ryan'll get into awful trouble, though. He wasn't supposed to say anything.'

'I don't think he will,' said her mother. 'Anyway, it's too late now to be worrying about that. We'd all better go round to Ryan's house and sort it out. Is that OK with you, Bill?' she asked her husband.

'Yes, we'll go right away,' he answered. 'I'll get the car.'

'Oh, no, we can't put you to all that trouble,' said Vera. 'Where do they live?'

'In South Shields,' said Shirley, in a timid voice.

'But that's miles away!'

'Not all that far,' said Madge. 'We'll soon get there. It seems that these kids have really set the cat among the pigeons. So we'll go and see what we can find out.'

The car was a large Hillman with plenty of room for the Crompton family plus Vera and Stanley. Shirley's parents had not met Ryan's mother and father, so there was a lot of explaining to do when they arrived.

'I'm sorry,' said Ryan. He kept saying it, again and again. 'I'm sorry, Mum… I'm sorry, Mrs Hargreaves…'

Vera felt confused, amazed beyond words at the turn of events. She recalled how curious Debbie had been at one time, about the circumstances of her birth, but she hadn't mentioned it recently.

'She just wanted to know,' said Shirley. 'She wasn't unhappy at home, or anything like that. She said it was just niggling away at her. But I really didn't think she'd do anything about it.'

'That's our Debbie alright,' said Vera. 'She won't let anything rest till she's got to the bottom of it. But we don't know for certain where she is, do we?'

'I'm going to find out right away,' said Ginny. 'I'll ring Fiona…'

She went out into the hall, and they all waited in silence, able to hear only a muffled one side of the conversation.

Ginny returned, smiling brightly. 'Yes… she's there. And… Vera, Debbie wants to speak to you…'

Seventeen

When Fiona left her Debbie had a quick wash and cleaned her teeth. She hadn't brought any make-up as she had packed in such a rush – well, not really packed, just shoved some things into a bag – but it didn't matter about lipstick and powder. She had remembered a comb, though, and she quickly combed her hair and pushed it into place.

Rather diffidently she went downstairs, heading for the back of the house where she guessed the kitchen might be. There was an appetizing smell, and she realized that she felt hungry. She had only had her lunch sandwiches, and a biscuit and a banana.

'Hello,' she said shyly, pushing open the kitchen door. 'Can I come in?'

'Of course,' said Fiona, smiling pleasantly. 'Come on in, dear. I'm just mashing some potatoes for us to have with the chicken casserole. Do you like chicken?'

'I like anything,' replied Debbie. 'Well, nearly everything. Chicken's one of my favourites.'

'I expect your mother's a good cook, isn't she?' asked Fiona.

'Yes, she is. She says she's just a plain cook, nothing fancy, you know. That's because my dad's a bit set in his ways; he doesn't like trying anything new. I've only just got them to try mushrooms.'

Fiona laughed. 'Well, there's some in the casserole, so you should enjoy it.'

'It sounds good… smells good, too,' said Debbie. 'And I'm hungry. Er… can I do anything to help?'

'Yes, why not? You can set the table, please, Debbie. Simon and I find it easier to dine in here when there's just the two of us. We use the dining room on a Sunday – though I don't really know why! – and if we have visitors. But you're family, aren't you, dear?' That made Debbie feel very happy.

'Yes… I hope so,' she replied.

There was a large pine table in the centre of the kitchen. It was a cheerful room with yellow working surfaces and cupboards, and yellow and blue flowered curtains at the window. Fiona opened a drawer and took out a blue-checked tablecloth. 'There you are,' she said. 'Knives and forks in that drawer, and table mats in the cupboard below. So I'll leave you to it. Simon's gone up with Stella, to get her ready for bed. We like to have our meal in peace,' she said, laughing, 'but she's a good little girl, not much trouble at all.'

'When is your baby due,' asked Debbie, 'if you don't mind me asking?'

'No, why should I?' smiled Fiona. 'It's getting rather obvious, isn't it? I seem to be much bigger with this one. It's due at the beginning of December. Stella was born in December, on the eleventh, so I don't know whether it's good planning or not, to have them both with birthdays in the same month.'

'Just one birthday party instead of two?' suggested Debbie. She was finding it very easy to talk to Fiona.

'Maybe, it just depends, doesn't it? Children have their own ideas.' Fiona put the dish of mashed potato in the oven and turned to look at Debbie. 'We must try to contact your parents very soon, dear. I can well imagine how worried they will be... It was really rather naughty of you, wasn't it?'

'Yes, I know it was,' Debbie admitted. 'But I think they might have found out where I am; well, Mum might at any rate. You see, my friend, Shirley, and Ryan – I told you about Ryan – they might guess where I've gone. And I know that the first person Mum would ask would be Shirley, and she'd have to tell them, wouldn't she? Oh dear! Shirley and Ryan'll get into awful trouble, and it's all my fault.'

'It's a bit late to worry about that now,' said Fiona. 'Anyway, I doubt that they'll be in serious trouble. All's well that ends well, as they say... Ah, here's Simon. I was just saying, darling, that we must contact Debbie's parents as soon as possible. Maybe after we've had our meal... I'll just go and tuck Stella in, then I'll serve it out. Debbie's set the table for me...'

'I think we should try straight away,' said Simon. 'I wanted to get Stella to bed first. Your parents will be very worried about you. Didn't you think about that?' He looked rather stern, and Debbie suddenly felt like crying again. Her face crumpled. 'Yes... I'm sorry, really I am,' she said.

'Come on, now, don't get upset... I understand.' He patted her shoulder. 'It'll be OK. And Fiona and I have decided that after you've stayed the night with us, we'll take you home tomorrow. In the car, I mean.'

'Oh, thank you, that's really good of you,' said Debbie. 'I'm sorry to be such a nuisance.'

'You're not, not at all. Now, I'm going to ring the operator and get your friend's number. What did you say her name is?'

Debbie gave him the name and address of the Crompton family. He was just about to go into the hall to use the phone when Fiona came back. 'I'm going to ring now,' he said. 'No time like the present.'

But the phone started ringing before he had the chance to dial. It was Fiona who went to answer it.

'Hello, St Peter's rectory, Mrs Norwood speaking. How can I help you?'

Her face registered shock. 'Ginny...? Well, how amazing!... Yes she is... She's here... Oh, about an hour ago... Yes, of course I will... You go and tell her...'

Fiona returned to the kitchen. 'That was my friend, Ginny,' she said. 'Your parents are there, at her house. Come along, Debbie, love.' She handed her the receiver. 'Come and speak to your mum.'

Simon and Fiona stayed in the kitchen whilst Debbie went to speak to her mother. She felt her hand shaking a little as she took hold of the receiver.

'Mum...' she said, in a small voice. 'Mum, I'm sorry, really I am, but I just had to find out, you see. I didn't mean to worry you...' There was a sob in her voice, and her mother answered quickly.

'Now, don't start upsetting yourself, darling. Of course we were worried, your daddy and me. But now we know where you are, and that you're safe with... Fiona, isn't it?'

'Yes, Fiona and Simon,' said Debbie, 'and their little girl, Stella. She's lovely, Mum, the little girl, I mean, and they're all nice and friendly. But I'm coming home, you know. I wasn't running away or anything like that. I just... had to find out.'

'I understand,' said Vera, quietly. 'At least, I'm trying to. But why didn't you tell me how you were feeling, pet? I would have tried to understand. I suppose I knew that you would want to know more when you got older.' Debbie could hear a sort of laughter in her voice. 'You're such a little nosy parker, aren't you?'

'Yes, I suppose I am,' she replied. 'Shirley and Ryan, they didn't get into awful trouble, did they? It was my fault, Mum. I made Ryan tell me.'

'No, his mother wasn't cross with him, and we were all so relieved to know where you were. Ryan's a nice lad, and his parents as well. Ginny told us about how she met… Fiona. It's strange how it's all worked out. The main thing is… you're all right?'

'Yes, I'm OK, Mum. I'm staying here tonight, then they're going to bring me home tomorrow, Simon and… Fiona.'

'That's kind of them.'

'Yes; it's lovely here, Mum; the countryside, and everything. But I'll be glad to be home… You're not terribly cross with me, are you?'

'No, of course not.'

'And… Dad?'

'He was upset, but I think he understands.'

'Good; tell him I'm sorry.' Then Debbie said something she hadn't said for ages, not since she was a tiny girl. 'I love you, Mum,' she said.

'I love you too,' said Vera, with a catch in her voice.

'Bye then. See you tomorrow…'

Debbie was about to put the phone down when her mother said, 'I'd better have a word with Fiona, hadn't I? Would you go and tell her, pet?'

Debbie went back to the kitchen. 'My mum would like to speak to you… Fiona,' she said. It was the first time she called her by her name.

'Very good,' said Fiona brightly. She went out, closing the door behind her. Debbie gave a sigh.

'It was all right,' she told Simon. 'I tried to explain to Mum why I had to come, and I think she understood… I'm sorry for causing so much trouble,' she said again.

'Now stop that, Debbie; you haven't,' he said, quite positively. 'In a way, I'm glad it's happened like this. I know that Fiona has wondered about you from time to time. Then Stella arrived, and I was glad she'd had another little girl.' He smiled at her. 'And now we've got another family member. We must keep in touch now you've found us, if your parents agree, Debbie?'

'I think they will,' she replied. She knew she would like to visit Aberthwaite again, but quite openly next time.

Fiona didn't divulge all that she and Vera had said to one another. She just said, 'That's settled then. We'll start out early tomorrow, Debbie, and take you home. Your mum has very kindly offered to make us a meal, then we'll have to set off back again. Simon's his own boss, aren't you, darling? But he can't be away for too long… Now, you must be starving, Debbie. Sit yourselves down, and I'll serve the meal.'

The chicken casserole was delicious, and Debbie forgot all the worry and tension of the day as she tucked into it. Simon opened a bottle of wine, a sweet German one that he said was a favourite of theirs. She guessed he was quite a 'go-ahead' sort of vicar. He poured her a small glass.

'A little celebration,' he said. 'It isn't every day that we find another member of the family.' He smiled. 'I'll tell you sometime, Debbie, how I met my long-lost son.'

'A story for later,' said Fiona. 'We've a lot of catching up to do.'

After they had eaten the plum tart that followed, Simon offered to do the washing-up.

'Off you go, you two girls,' he said, 'and when I've finished this lot I'll make us all some coffee.'

Fiona took Debbie into the lounge, a more elegant room than the homely living room, with a three-piece suite in moss green, with toning velvet curtains and bright scatter cushions in a floral design of green, orange and brown.

'Simon's a good husband, isn't he?' said Debbie, to open the conversation. 'Does he help you a lot?' She knew that most husbands did not do so. Her own father, for instance, very rarely helped to wash up, and her mother never seemed to mind waiting on him hand and foot.

'Yes, I'm very fortunate,' answered Fiona. 'Simon's a wonderful husband. He doesn't wash up all the time.' She laughed. 'Tonight's a special occasion... We haven't been married all that long,' she went on. 'Just over three years, that's all. I was single for a long time after... well, you know what happened, don't you?'

'Not exactly,' said Debbie. 'But I can guess.'

Fiona nodded. 'Yes... I wasn't much older than you are now, Debbie, when it happened... Let me tell you about the little pink teddy bear. My boyfriend, Dave, gave it to me. He won it at... a hoop-la stall, I think it was, in Battersea Pleasure Gardens. We'd gone on a church trip to see the Festival of Britain, in 1951.'

'And he, your boyfriend, Dave... he was...?'

'Yes, he was your father, Debbie. But he never knew about you. And I never saw him again after that holiday.

He's married now with a family, and living in America, so he doesn't come into it, I'm afraid.'

'But you must have... loved him?' Debbie was sure that Fiona had not been a flirtatious girl, the sort who would go with anyone.

'I thought I did,' Fiona smiled sadly. 'He was my first boyfriend. We were both in the sixth form at our schools... in Leeds, it was. Anyway, there was this visit to London, run by the church, and my parents allowed me to go. We, Dave and I... got carried away; the first time away from home and all that. And so... it happened. We didn't mean it to, but it does, Debbie, you know.' Fiona looked at her seriously. 'And it only needs to happen once. I was frantic when I found out I was pregnant, absolutely scared to death.'

'And you didn't tell him... Dave?'

'No. You see, I was taken ill while we were away in London, and when we got home the doctor discovered I had glandular fever. So I was in isolation and couldn't see any of my friends. Then... well... I realized I was having a baby. The doctor was marvellous, so very kind to me. He helped me to tell my mother. She was furious, of course, and my father; they were so ashamed of me.'

'So they made you have... the baby... adopted?'

Fiona nodded. 'They told everyone at church – they were great churchgoers, you see – that I'd had a break- down. They sent me to an aunt and uncle up north, as far away as possible. They were kind to me, though, so understanding and forgiving, so much more so than my parents. Then I went to Burnside House, as you know, to wait for the birth. That's where I met Ginny, and we've stayed friends ever since. She was allowed to keep Ryan, of course, at the last minute. Then she married Arthur, and they're still very happy.'

They looked at one another, Fiona and Debbie, mother and daughter, for several moments, both of them lost for words.

Then Fiona said, 'I was only allowed to hold you for a few minutes. But when I looked at you I knew – somehow – that it couldn't have been wrong, what I did, when I had given birth to such a beautiful baby. I wanted to keep you, really I did, but of course I couldn't. Then I remembered the little bear, and I tucked it into your shawl, hoping that... some day... you might understand.'

'Yes, I do understand,' said Debbie. 'Thank you for telling me about it.'

'Simon has a favourite text from scripture,' said Fiona, 'about all things working together for good. And they have done, haven't they, in the end?'

'What about your parents?' asked Debbie. 'Did they forgive you?'

'I don't think they ever did, not entirely,' said Fiona. 'I went back to Leeds, and it was never mentioned again. It was as though it had never happened. Then they were both killed in a coach crash a few years later. I went to live with my gran. I'd always been very close to her, and I lived with her until she died. She lived until she was ninety. I came to Aberthwaite soon afterwards and got a job in the library here. And the rest you know. I married Simon, we had Stella... and now we're expecting another one!'

'That's nice,' said Debbie, 'to have two so close together, so they can be friends. I sometimes used to wish I had a little brother or sister. It can be lonely, being the only one.'

'Well, now you have,' said Fiona. 'I could see that Stella had taken to you, and you took rather a fancy to her, didn't you?'

'Yes, she's lovely,' said Debbie. 'But I didn't mean that. I was thinking about when I was growing up, at home. I thought how nice it would be, but my parents were older and… oh dear! I'm getting myself in a muddle aren't I?'

Fiona laughed. 'Yes, it is all rather strange, isn't it? We hope you'll keep in touch with us, Debbie. We know that you will be living with Vera and Stanley, that's where you belong… but now that we've found one another again, I'd like to see you from time to time. It was probably meant to happen, eventually.'

'You mean… like fate?'

'Well, perhaps. Simon might say it was God's hand in it all; I don't know. But whatever it is, I'm very glad about it.'

Simon appeared with a laden tray. 'I was just saying, darling, that Debbie must keep in touch with us,' said Fiona.

'I've already told her that,' said Simon. 'Now, here we are; coffee and Fiona's home-made gingerbread. Now, are you going to tell us a little about yourself?' he asked, when they were all supplied with a cup of coffee and a biscuit. 'You're still at school, are you? Let's see; it would be your O level year?'

'Yes, that's right. I did quite well, actually,' she said, not wanting to sound boastful. 'Mostly As and Bs. And I'm going into the sixth form. Gosh! It's next week. I'd almost forgotten.'

'And then… what do you plan to do after you leave school?' asked Fiona.

'I'm not sure,' she replied. 'What I'm most interested in is gardening...' She told them about her father's occupation and her part-time job. 'I'd like to do landscape gardening. I'd need to take a course at college, or get a degree in... I'm not sure what. I really wanted to go on working at Sunnyhill, and leave school now. But my parents wanted me to go into the sixth form.'

'Very wise,' said Simon. 'So did mine, but I took no notice. I thought I knew best, of course. I went out to work – office work – when I was sixteen, then when the war started I joined the RAF.'

'Then you became a vicar,' said Debbie.

'A curate first, then a vicar, or rector, in my case... God moves in mysterious ways,' he added with a wry grin. 'But that's another story.'

'So it's the sixth form next week,' said Fiona. 'I think you'll enjoy it, Debbie. It's not the same as ordinary school. I had a year in the sixth, then... well, you know what happened. I would most probably have gone on to teacher training college, but it wasn't to be.'

'That's what my mum really wants me to do,' said Debbie. 'But I don't want to be a teacher. I can't think of anything worse!'

Fiona chuckled. 'That's strange. It seems to be what mothers always want. I think it was my mother's idea, really, that I should be a teacher. It's something to do with having the chances that they never had.'

'Yes, that's what Mum says,' replied Debbie. 'But I think she's satisfied now that I've decided to go back to school. My friend, Shirley, will be there, so I expect we'll enjoy it.'

'And Ryan?' asked Fiona.

'Yes, Ryan as well. We've all been in the same form all through our time at Kelder Bank. I didn't get on very well with Ryan at first, but I quite like him now. You know him, don't you... Fiona?' She used the name a little warily.

'Yes, but I haven't seen him for ages. He's got his mother's ginger hair, hasn't he?'

'Yes, but I've never met his mum, nor his dad. They live in South Shields, but you know that, of course...'

After they had chatted a little about Northumberland, Simon told Debbie how, after more than twenty years, he had discovered that he had a son. 'I'm afraid he was the result of a wartime romance,' he said. 'No... that's not what I mean at all,' he corrected himself hurriedly. 'That sounds as though I'm regretful, and I can assure you I'm not. Greg's a grand young man, and we're pleased to have him as a member of our family. It's becoming quite an extended family, isn't it? I had no idea at the time; Yvonne had disappeared from the scene... and I just carried on with my life – quite an eventful one as it turned out – until Greg came to find me.'

'How old is he now?' asked Debbie.

'Greg's twenty-three. He works as a solicitor in Manchester.' He turned to Fiona. 'I think we're about due for a visit from him, aren't we, darling?'

Debbie pondered that if Greg was anything like his father, then he would be a good-looking young man. Simon was handsome, and very... personable; she thought that was the right word. Quite old, though; he must be not far off fifty. Younger than her parents but quite a bit older than Fiona. They seemed very happy together, she mused, calling one another darling as though they were teenagers... and still having babies.

'Now Debbie, I'm sure you must be tired,' said Fiona, at half past ten. Conversation had flowed easily, interrupted twice by telephone calls for Simon about parish matters. 'We'll have an early start in the morning, so we'd better get our beauty sleep. Would you like a cup of hot chocolate, dear? That's what we usually have.'

Debbie said that would be lovely, and it was even nicer when Fiona brought it up to her bedroom. 'Goodnight, my dear,' she said, kissing her cheek. 'God bless...'

She's nice, thought Debbie. I like her. Even though her mind was full of the events of the day, she soon dropped off to sleep.

Fiona felt a little apprehensive as they set off the following morning. She felt sure that Debbie must be feeling anxious, too, at the thought of seeing her parents again. But Simon was great in difficult situations; he always knew how to act and what to say.

Debbie had been delighted to hear that Stella was coming with them. She and the little girl were sitting together in the back of the car. Fiona could hear them reciting the nursery rhymes that Stella knew. It was lovely the way that they had bonded, and the child would help to distract Debbie from the thought of meeting Vera and Stanley again. Stella wasn't used to long car journeys, and Fiona had insisted that she should wear a nappy today, 'just in case'.

'Big girl now,' Stella had argued. She had been remarkably quick with her toilet training, but it was better to be safe than sorry. They had a 'comfort stop' halfway, when they refreshed themselves with a biscuit and coffee from the flask that Fiona had prepared.

The scenery was gradually changing as they drove north. The first sight of the slag heaps and winding gear, and the factory chimneys, brought back memories to Fiona. She had not travelled this way since the time, sixteen years ago, when her uncle had brought her back from the home – in the other direction, of course – after the birth of her baby. And now... here in the car with her was the same baby, now grown into an attractive and lively young woman.

Fiona had visited Whitesands Bay only once, when the girls had been taken out on a trip, a treat away from the strictures – though never unduly harsh ones – of the home. They drove along the pleasant promenade with its bright flowerbeds. She remembered the sandy beach, and the lighthouse on the rocks. Then they turned off the promenade, and Debbie directed Simon through the streets of the town, until they stopped at a terraced house with a small paved area at the front. There were two large planters filled with geraniums, begonias and blue lobelia; the paintwork on the house was a glossy green, and the brass letterbox and door knocker gleamed as though they had been recently polished. A very welcoming sort of house.

'Here we are,' said Debbie in a small voice. 'I'll go and knock, shall I?'

Simon smiled at her. 'Go on, Debbie. We're here with you; it'll be all right, you'll see.'

The door opened and Fiona saw a smallish woman – Debbie was a few inches taller – with a pleasant smiling face, dark hair that was greying slightly, and warm brown eyes behind tortoiseshell-framed glasses. Her eyes filled up with tears as she saw Debbie, and she enveloped her in a tight hug.

'Oh, Debbie, pet!' she cried. 'It's so good to see you. You've had quite an adventure, haven't you?'

'I'm sorry, Mum,' Debbie began. 'Really I am. I didn't mean…'

Vera cut her off quickly. 'Now, now, we don't want to hear any more sorrys, and don't start getting upset. We're just so glad, your daddy and me, that you're alright… And how nice to see our visitors as well.' Her glance took in all of them.

Fiona stepped forward. 'Hello, Mrs Hargreaves. I'm Fiona, and this is my husband, Simon.'

'Oh, call me Vera,' she said, shaking hands with both of them. 'I'm very pleased to meet you. And who is this little sweetheart?'

'This is Stella,' said Fiona. 'Our little girl; she's nearly two.'

Vera stooped down to her. 'Hello, pet. You're a little poppet, aren't you?'

'Hello… lady,' Stella said, rather shyly. She was staring round, overawed by the strangeness of her surroundings.

'I think we'd better pay a little visit, Vera, if you know what I mean,' said Fiona. 'It's been a long time to sit in the car.'

'Of course,' said Vera. 'Come on in, everyone… The bathroom's at the top of the stairs… Fiona.'

When Fiona came down again they were all sitting in the room at the front of the house, the one, she guessed, that was not used all the time but just for special occasions. The man, whom she knew must be Stanley, stood up as she entered. He was small, like his wife, a wiry man who looked – but probably wasn't – quite a lot older than Vera. His face was lined and ruddy with outdoor work and his grey eyes were serious. He smiled in a friendly way, though, as he shook hands with Fiona.

'And you must be Fiona. How d'you do, pet? Pleased to meet you, though I must say it's all been a bit of a shock. Thanks to Miss Nosy Parker here!' He turned to look sternly at Debbie. Then he chuckled. 'She's always been the same, never happy till she knows the whys and wherefores of everything. So I reckon we shouldn't have been all that surprised.'

'I've said I'm sorry, Dad,' Debbie repeated, a little edgily this time. 'I keep saying it.'

'Aye, and that's the end of it now, pet,' he said. 'We won't mention it again.'

'And we've made some new friends, too,' said Vera. 'We met Ginny and Arthur; such a nice couple. And now... Simon and Fiona.' She beamed with pleasure. 'And little Stella... and another one on the way. Am I right?'

'You are indeed,' smiled Fiona. 'Early December, not all that long now.'

'I'm not going to ask you whether you want a boy or a girl,' said Vera, 'because I know it won't matter, with loving parents like the two of you... Now, I reckon it's time we had our dinner. It's all ready in the oven. I'll just go and see to things. Won't be long.'

'I'll come with you, if I may?' said Fiona, following her into the kitchen. 'This is a strange situation, Vera,' she began. 'It could have been awkward, but you've taken it all so well.'

'I can't pretend I wasn't upset at first, when I found out what she'd done,' replied Vera, 'and worried to death when she didn't come home. But I suppose I should've known what she'd do, some day. We'd made no secret of it, you see, her being adopted. And she was such a pretty little girl, she still is… And now I know why. You're a bonny lass, Fiona.'

She smiled. 'We're the way God made us, I suppose. It's more important to be nice on the inside, though, isn't it? Debbie's turned out to be a grand girl, and it's thanks to the upbringing she's had… A bit of a handful, though, at times, I should imagine?' she added.

'You can say that again!' replied Vera with feeling. 'No, she wasn't always an easy child, but it's been worth it. And we love her as though she was our own, Stanley and me.'

'Yes, I can see that you do,' said Fiona. 'Thank you… for everything.'

'Well, I'd best get this lot served out,' said Vera. 'I've already set the table for five of us, and Stanley found the highchair we had when Debbie was small. He won't throw anything away.'

They sat round the table in the living room, a smallish room, as was the kitchen; but the drop-leaf table would allow more room when the meal was finished. The shepherd's pie with the crusty potato topping was declared delicious, as was the rice pudding, nicely browned with nutmeg on the top.

Fiona noticed that Debbie was quiet and seemed preoccupied during the meal. She guessed the girl was overwhelmed by it all, but no doubt relieved that her reckless behaviour – although it had taken some courage – had turned out all right in the end. More than all right. Fiona was satisfied now that the child she had given up so reluctantly had had the very best of homes. And she, Fiona, need worry and wonder no longer.

Debbie showed an interest, though, when Vera said to her, 'Guess what, Debbie? Your daddy has said that we must have a phone put in. Isn't that splendid?'

Debbie nodded. 'Yes, it's a smashing idea, Mum.'

'Just in case you decide to go walkabout again,' said Stanley, laughing. 'No, I don't mean it, pet. It's about time we moved into the twentieth century. It'll be useful for us. And we'll be able to keep in touch with our new friends.'

There was time to spare afterwards for the inevitable cup of tea, which followed every northern meal. Then Stanley proudly showed them around his garden; the vegetable plot, the herbaceous border, and the greenhouse where he grew tomatoes and cucumbers and, this year, even courgettes and aubergines. 'Not that I'm right keen on them meself,' he said, 'but apparently they're popular now, according to our Debbie; they grow 'em at the garden centre, so I thought I'd give 'em a try.'

'It's a splendid show,' said Simon. 'I'm very impressed. And it looks as though Debbie's going to follow in your footsteps.'

'Aye, she's not doing so badly,' said Stanley, smiling at her fondly. 'We're proud of her, you know. She's worked hard at school, but she was always a clever lass.'

'Give over, Dad!' said Debbie, looking a little embarrassed. Fiona put an arm round her shoulders. 'We're all very pleased with you, Debbie love. And you must come and see us… quite soon, if that's OK with your parents? And I know one little girl who'll be delighted to see you again.' Stella was quiet, and had her thumb in her mouth, indicating that she was ready for a nap.

'We'd better be on our way,' said Fiona. 'Thank you, Vera, for a lovely meal… and both of you for making us so welcome.'

She didn't make too much fuss of Debbie as they all said goodbye, just a quick hug and a kiss on her cheek; and Simon shook her hand and winked at her in a matey sort of way. Fiona kissed Vera's cheek, too, as they shook hands, just saying, 'Goodbye… and thanks for everything.' She felt that they had reached a very good understanding of one another.

Fiona sat in the back of the car this time with Stella on her knee. The little girl was soon asleep. 'That went off very well,' she remarked to Simon. 'They're lovely people. I couldn't have wished for anyone better.'

'I'm glad you're happy, darling,' he replied. 'It must have been a tremendous shock for you.'

'No more than it was for you with Greg,' she answered. 'In fact, that must have been much worse, because you had no idea.'

Simon laughed. 'Another revelation for the folk at church, eh? All in good time, of course. But I don't think anything we do can surprise them any more!'

Eighteen

Fiona had a phone call that evening. She recognized Joan Tweedale's voice straight away.

'Hello there, Fiona,' said Joan. 'I rang before, but...'

'Yes; we've been out all day,' said Fiona.

'Please forgive me for being nosy,' said Joan, 'but I've been wondering... how did you get on with your little visitor?'

Fiona laughed. 'Oh, it was you, was it? I rather thought from Debbie's description that it might have been you. Thank you for coming to her rescue. I dare say you might have guessed who she is?'

'She told me you were her aunty,' said Joan. 'Then I looked at her more closely and I thought it could be...?'

'Yes, she is... my daughter. She's called Debbie, Deborah Hargreaves. And she lives in Whitesands Bay, up in Northumberland.'

'I guessed from the way she spoke that she was from somewhere up there. She said she'd missed the bus. Poor little lass! She looked so sad and sorry for herself, sitting there on the bench. I take it you weren't expecting her?'

'Good heavens, no! I had the shock of my life when I opened the door. I guessed who she was almost at once.'

'And how was it? Did you find that you were able to bond with her? I should imagine she's quite a lively lass normally. She was really down in the dumps, though, when I found her.'

'Thank heavens you did,' said Fiona. 'Yes, we all got on well together after the initial shock. We both agree that she's a grand girl, though she's probably been a bit of a handful to bring up. Her... mother says so. That's where we've been today, taking her back to Whitesands Bay. Her parents are a lovely couple – Vera and Stanley, they're called – very homely and down-to-earth. She couldn't have had better parents... Anyway, I'll pop into the shop and see you, Joan, maybe tomorrow. Then I can tell you more. Thanks so much for looking after her. What were you doing up in Northallerton, anyway?'

'I had a sudden phone call. My aunt Phyllis has had to go into a residential home. She can't look after herself any longer, and I'm her closest relative. So I closed the shop for the day and went to see her.'

'And how did you find her? Is she happy enough there?'

'Yes, she's a sensible person and she realizes it's the best thing to do. She has quite a few friends from the church, so she won't be short of visitors. And Harold and I will go up when we can.'

'Very fortuitous as it happened, that you should be there,' said Fiona. 'And now my mind's at rest knowing that Debbie's got a good home, and that I'll be able to keep in touch with her. She was quite a hit with our little Stella; they took to one another right away.'

'Another shock in store for the congregation,' said Joan, laughing.

'Quite so, but I think we'll leave it a little while. We've enough on our plate at the moment. Cheerio for now, Joan. Thanks again, and see you soon...'

The fundraising for the rebuilding of the church roof was progressing satisfactorily. Notices in the church newspapers advertising 'High teas served in pleasant surroundings' had resulted in three bookings so far from other churches within comfortable travelling distances.

The catering committee consisted of the usual coterie of women, and it was decided that Mrs Bayliss should be the one in overall charge. Florence Catchpole, the newcomer, had agreed graciously with this – in fact it had been her suggestion – so what could have been rivalry between the two women had developed into a wary sort of friendship.

The first visit was from a church in Malton. They were to spend some time in York first of all, where there was much to see and do, and then travel on to Aberthwaite for high tea. This took place in mid-September and turned out to be a great success. Mrs Bayliss had purchased succulent home-baked hand and tongue – at a discount for a large amount – from a local butcher. Served with salad and new potatoes, and home-produced pickles, beetroot and chutney, it was a sumptuous spread. It was followed, inevitably, by the trifles for which Ethel Bayliss and Blanche Fowler were renowned.

Both Simon and the curate were there to welcome the group, and to wish them God speed and a safe journey home.

'Well done, ladies,' said Simon. 'An excellent start to our catering idea. I must admit I had my doubts at first, but you have proved me wrong. When is the next booking?'

'In a fortnight's time,' Ethel told him, with a touch of pride. 'A church from the Bradford area. Then there's another one from up north, somewhere near Durham, a couple of weeks later. And we think that will be the last, for this year at any rate.'

'Probably so,' agreed Simon. 'It's doubtful that folks will want to travel in the late autumn and winter; Aberthwaite's a summer sort of place. But there's always next spring and summer to look forward to. So keep up the good work, ladies.'

'Yes, hear, hear! And may I say that it was a really scrumptious meal,' added Joshua Bellamy, the curate. 'That trifle…' He licked his lips. 'It was quite something!'

'We're glad you enjoyed it,' replied Ethel, a little frostily. She still had not taken to the new curate, as most people seemed to have done. He had appeared again in his clown outfit that he had worn at the garden party for the next children's address.

There had been a good deal of talk about what he might appear as next. The children in particular looked forward to his entertaining talks, and most people had to admit that they were relevant and meaningful, with a message for both the young and the older folk. They were not disappointed at the next family service when he appeared as a spaceman. There was a good deal of speculation as to when – or if ever – a man would land on the moon. A lot of nonsense, according to Ethel Bayliss; and his latest 'Walter Mitty' appearance did nothing to change her opinion of the Reverend Joshua Bellamy.

–

The next church tea, for the party from Bradford, was to take place on the last Saturday in September.

Fiona had an appointment at the antenatal clinic a few days previous to this; a routine check that she had every month. It was no secret now in the parish that the rector's wife was expecting their second child, and everyone, bar none, was delighted about it. It had become obvious, though, even before she broke the news officially; one needed only to look at her normally slim figure to know that it was so.

Fiona herself was becoming quite concerned about her size. 'Two and a half months to go yet,' she exclaimed to Simon. 'At this rate I'll be as big as an elephant by December. I've tried to be careful, as they told me to be. I've cut down on salt, and I don't overeat; "eat for two", as they say. I'm far bigger than I was with Stella.'

'Perhaps it's a boy,' suggested Simon. 'Would that make any difference?'

'I doubt it,' said Fiona. 'Stella weighed seven pounds, and that was quite enough to part with! Anyway, we'll see what the doctor says when I go to the clinic.'

'I'll come with you,' said Simon. He usually drove her to the hospital and picked her up again later, but this time he decided to wait, and Fiona, somehow, felt that she needed him to be there.

She was in the consulting room rather longer than usual, and when she came out she was accompanied by a doctor. Simon could see by the startled look on her face that there was something unusual, but she smiled at him so he didn't think there was anything wrong.

'We have some news for you, Mr Norwood,' said the doctor. 'Your wife is expecting twins!'

'Oh! Oh, my goodness!' exclaimed Simon. He hurried over to Fiona and put an arm round her. 'Are you alright, darling?'

'She's fine,' the doctor answered for her. 'We detected two heartbeats, so there's no doubt about it. It's twins!

Everything seems to be progressing normally and there shouldn't be any complications. Just take extra care Mrs Norwood. Keep an eye on your blood pressure – you can do that with your family GP – and try not to put on too much weight. Congratulations to you both! We'll see you in another month's time.'

When the doctor had gone Fiona had to sit down for a moment. 'I'm amazed!' she said. 'I can't quite take it in. Perhaps I should have realized with me getting so big, but I never thought about twins.'

'Are you pleased, though?' asked Simon.

'Yes… I think I am,' she answered. 'Very pleased.' She smiled. 'What about you?'

'I'm delighted!' he said. 'Come on, let's get back and pick up Stella.' The little girl was being looked after by a member of the Young Wives group who had a daughter the same age.

They hadn't told Stella, yet, as some parents liked to do, that she would soon be having a baby brother or sister. 'Soon' didn't mean much to a child of her age, so they had decided to wait until the birth was a little nearer. Then, what could they tell her to look forward to? Simon and Fiona talked about it, inevitably, and wondered. What would they be? Two boys? Two girls? Or one of each? Identical… or not? It was useless to speculate, and they agreed that it didn't matter at all. The only thing that concerned them was that the babies should arrive safely, and that Fiona would come through it with the least possible trouble.

–

The first person that Fiona told was her friend, Joan. She went to visit the shop the next morning, with Stella in her pushchair. She sat down on the chair provided for customers whilst Joan dealt with a lady buying knitting wool. She was finding that she needed to sit down now when she had walked a fair distance, something that rather annoyed her. She had always been so active, hardly ever feeling tired, even during the last stages of her two previous pregnancies. Of course she knew the reason for her lassitude now – two babies for the price of one! – so she must try not to worry about it but to think that it would be worth it in the end.

'Hello there, Fiona, and hello to you, Stella,' said Joan when the customer had gone.

'Hello, Aunty Joan,' said the little girl.

Fiona didn't stand up immediately, causing Joan to say, 'Feeling a bit jaded today, are you, love? Social visit is it, or do you want to buy something?'

'Just a bit jaded,' smiled Fiona, getting to her feet. 'What do I want? Well, double the amount of knitting wool might not be a bad idea!'

Joan looked puzzled for a moment, then her eyes opened wide. 'What do you mean? You're not having twins, are you?'

'Yes, I am.' Fiona laughed. 'What a fool I was not to realize. Yes, I found out at the clinic yesterday.'

'Well, that's wonderful news,' said Joan. 'At least it is… if you think so?'

'Yes, we do,' replied Fiona. 'We're very pleased. Simon's thrilled to bits, more so than I am, I think. But men don't have to give birth, do they?'

'No, that's true,' agreed Joan. 'You've not had much trouble before, though, have you?'

'No, they were quite normal births… both of them. It might be different this time, though. I'm not unduly worried, except about the amount of weight I've put on. I'm really trying to be careful about what I eat, and everything else.'

'Yes, you must take care, and rest when you can,' said Joan. 'There are plenty of other folk to cope with the parish duties. You're not part of this new catering committee, are you?'

'No… Simon advised me not to get involved this time. Mrs Bayliss is in her element, being in charge, and Mrs Catchpole's a great asset to the group. They did a splendid job with the first tea party, and no doubt the one on Saturday will go off just as well. I shall pop in and see how they're going on.'

'Yes, make an appearance as the rector's wife, and chat to the visitors,' said Joan. 'They'll like that. But keep out of the kitchen! There's enough of them to cope with it all. I wouldn't bother doing any knitting this time, if I were you. When this news breaks all the women will be getting busy. You'll have matinee coats and bootees by the dozen!'

'Everyone was so kind when Stella was born,' said Fiona. 'The garments were mostly blue or yellow, or white, hardly any pink.'

'Yes, people choose what they call safe colours, that'll do for either sex. Doubly difficult this time, isn't it?' She laughed. 'Quite a few permutations, aren't there?'

'That's what Simon and I were saying. We haven't said anything to Stella yet.'

'Very wise, or you'd be pestered to death! "When's the baby coming, Mummy?" Bless her!' Joan smiled lovingly at Stella, who had nodded off for a catnap as she tended to do after a ride in her pushchair; she was always up with the lark, raring to start the day.

'I'll take your advice and not make any more baby clothes,' said Fiona, 'but I thought I'd try my hand at a cot blanket. In thick wool, so that it'll grow faster,' she laughed. 'I'm not the most patient person when I'm knitting. I like to see quick results. What do you suggest?'

'Bright colours for a start,' said Joan, 'as a change from the baby pastel shades. What about this?' She showed Fiona some chunky wool in variegated colours, changing from bright blue, to mauve, to yellow, to green as you knitted, and a lacy pattern that was quite easy to follow.

Stella woke up as they were ready to go. 'Hello, Aunty Joan,' she said sleepily.

'It's goodbye now, darling,' said Joan, kissing her cheek. Then she hugged Fiona. 'Take care, love. I'm so thrilled at your news.'

–

The tea party for the church group from Bradford on the following Saturday was just as successful as the previous one had been. Fiona took Stella round to the church hall towards the end of the proceedings. She didn't want to partake of the tea as she and Simon would be dining later, but she liked to be there for part of the time, as the rector's wife, to chat with the ladies – they were mostly ladies, with just a few men – from the visiting church and make them feel welcome.

They were coming to the end of their meal. Once again it had been a salad meal, with cold chicken this time, and potato salad, followed by luscious cream cakes from the local bakery instead of trifle. In the centre of each table there was a small arrangement of autumn flowers – miniature chrysanthemums, dahlias, late flowering roses and Michaelmas daisies – which added a festive touch.

Fiona popped into the kitchen to say hello to the band of willing helpers there. Possibly rather too many? she wondered, milling about and getting into one another's way; but presumably they knew what they were doing. Josh, the curate, was there too. For some reason he liked to help out in the kitchen, especially when it was time to clear away and wash up. At the moment they seemed to be making extra tea for those who wanted a second cup.

She went back to join Stella, who was in Simon's charge, and being fussed over by ladies she hadn't met before. 'What a delightful child, Mrs Norwood,' said one of the women. 'My goodness, you'll have your hands full soon, though, won't you?' Simon hadn't been able to keep their news to himself for even a day.

Fiona didn't have time to answer. There was a shout and a shriek from the kitchen, and she dashed back there as quickly as she could. Mrs Bayliss was doubled up, clearly in some pain, and at the side of her was an upturned metal jug in which there must have been boiling water.

It was Josh who took control of everything. He ran out and grabbed a chair from the hall and, between them, he and Fiona helped Mrs Bayliss to sit down. Simon appeared in the kitchen, but Fiona told him that everything was under control, so he must keep the party going in the hall, and look after Stella.

'Now, Mrs Bayliss,' said Josh, putting a comforting arm round her shoulders, 'first of all you'd better get your stocking off before it starts to stick to your leg. It's all right,' he smiled, at her look of horror. 'I won't watch. Fiona will help you, but I do know a bit about first aid. I used to be a Scout; "Be Prepared" and all that.'

'Where's the first aid box?' asked one of the ladies. 'Oh dear! We don't often need it, do we? I think it's in this cupboard.'

'What about some vaseline, or some TCP?' said another person. 'And there's some bandages in the box.'

'No, nothing like that.' Josh shook his head. 'We need to pour lukewarm water over the scald, no ointment. Obviously you can't hold your leg under the tap, can you, Mrs Bayliss?' He smiled a little mischievously at her.

'No, I doubt it, young man,' she said with a touch of her usual asperity. 'I'm not quite as agile as I used to be.'

'So we'll get a bowl of water and bathe it. Come along, ladies; a washing-up bowl, please, and a jug and a clean cloth.'

Mrs Fowler filled a bowl and Josh tested it with his hand. 'Yes; that seems OK. Now, Mrs Bayliss, you pop your foot in there.'

'And take these aspirin tablets, Ethel,' said Blanche Fowler, handing her two tablets and a glass of water. 'They'll help take the pain away, and I'll make you a nice cup of tea.'

Ethel looked very shaken and embarrassed, too, with her skirt held high above her plump knee and calf. The skin was red and blistering, and she was obviously in pain. She took hold of Fiona's hand. 'Thank you, dear,' she said, 'and you too... Mr Bellamy. You're very kind.'

Josh started to pour the water on the affected area, over and over again. 'Is that easing it?' he asked gently. 'Feeling a bit better now, Mrs Bayliss?'

'I think so,' she said. 'But it's smarting and tingling. Oh dear! I'm a silly fool, aren't I? I don't know what happened. I just filled the jug up from the boiler, then perhaps I turned round too quickly and slipped… I don't know.'

'Accidents just happen, don't they?' said Josh, carrying on with the bathing, '…in a split second. You'll be fine, Mrs Bayliss, I'm sure, but it might be as well to let a doctor take a look at you. I'm only a novice… But maybe I'm capable of doing a bit more than clowning around, do you think?' He grinned at her roguishly.

Ethel smiled back, a shade diffidently. 'Oh, I think so… Joshua,' she replied. 'I'm getting older, you know; rather more set in my ways. Although I've never taken readily to change… But I reckon you'll do very well.'

'Thank you for that,' said the curate, humbly. 'It means a lot to me.' He sounded as though he really meant it. 'Not so much of the getting old, though,' he whispered. 'You're just a spring chicken compared with some of 'em, isn't she, Fiona?'

'Yes, I'll second that,' agreed Fiona. 'You have far more energy than I have at the moment, Mrs Bayliss.'

'But then I'm not expecting twins, am I?' smiled the lady. 'Arthur and I were so pleased to hear about it.'

'News travels fast, doesn't it?' said Fiona. She turned to Josh. 'What do you think we should do next, for Mrs Bayliss?'

'No bandaging,' said Josh. 'What about some poly-thene bags wrapped loosely round the area? Would you see if you can find some, please, Fiona?'

'I'll be trussed up like a turkey,' said Ethel. 'I tell you what, Fiona. It's a good job I don't wear these newfangled tights that all you lasses are wearing. It must be quite a pantomime getting them on and off.'

'You get used to them,' smiled Fiona, 'and they're very comfortable. This is women's talk,' she said, at an enquiring look from Josh. 'Not for your ears, Joshua!'

'Now, what have you been doing to yerself, lass?' said a familiar voice. Arthur Bayliss appeared in the kitchen, hurrying over to his wife. 'My goodness! That looks a bit of a mess, doesn't it?'

'It would have been worse if these kind people hadn't taken care of me,' said Ethel. 'They've been wonderful. What are you doing here anyway, Arthur?'

'Simon rang me up, and I came straight away,' he said. 'Now, I reckon we'd best let a doctor have a look at you. Come on, lass, we'll get up to the hospital. I've got the car outside. See, I've brought your slippers, both of 'em. I didn't know which leg it was.'

Ethel managed to slip her foot into the slipper. 'Now, can you manage to walk? Hold on to my arm.'

With her husband and Josh on either side of her she managed to hobble out of the kitchen and through the hall. She was greeted by calls from the visitors.

'Good luck, Mrs Bayliss...'

'Hope you go on all right...'

'Thank you ever so much for a lovely tea...'

'Take care now, dear...'

Fiona and Simon, with Stella holding on to his hand, walked with them to Arthur's car and settled her in the front seat. Ethel seemed very touched by the good wishes from the folk from Bradford.

'What a nice lot of people,' she said. 'They seem a jolly crowd. And everybody's been very kind. Thanks again... Joshua, and all of you, of course.' Fiona thought she could see an incipient tear in the corner of one eye, something she had never thought would be possible.

'Come on then, let's be having you,' said Arthur. He started up the engine. 'Thanks from me an' all. I'll let you know how Ethel goes on.'

'Poor old Ethel!' said Simon, although he would never dream of using her Christian name to her face. 'She seems... almost subdued, doesn't she? And that's something I never thought we'd see.'

'And she's made a new friend as well,' said Fiona, smiling mischievously at the curate. 'Hasn't she, Josh?'

'Wonders never cease!' said Simon. 'Thank you, Josh, for performing a miracle.'

The curate laughed. 'Let's hope she's OK. It was rather a nasty scald. She won't be able to dash around quite as much. She'll be forced to take a back seat for a while, I shouldn't wonder.'

Fiona laughed. 'Then let's be thankful for small mercies! No... I don't suppose I really mean that. Joking apart, the ladies will feel lost without Ethel at the helm.'

Nineteen

There was one more church visit booked by a group from the Durham area for mid-October. Mrs Bayliss hoped, by then, to be fit enough to take some part in the event. It had been a pretty bad scald, but the good lady was always quick to say that it might have been much worse if Joshua – she usually gave him his full name – had not given her first aid treatment so speedily. The use of his Christian name did, indeed, show that he was now regarded much more favourably. She had formerly referred to him as 'that curate'.

Everyone had to admit that she was a plucky old girl. She was clearly in a good deal of pain, but she limped into church each Sunday with the aid of a stick. And, to everyone's surprise, as the day for the next high tea drew near, she suggested that she would be willing to let Mrs Catchpole take charge of the proceedings on that day.

'But you must be there to help,' Florence Catchpole told her most diplomatically. 'I shall feel happier if you are there, Ethel, to see that we are doing things properly.' Did she have her tongue in her cheek? some of the women asked one another on the quiet. But whatever their true feelings were, Florence and Ethel now appeared to be the best of friends, which made for a much more congenial atmosphere among the ladies of the catering committee.

All went well on that occasion. The group from Durham spent some time in Richmond, viewing the castle and visiting the market, then, after a tour around the picturesque dales, ended up at St Peter's for tea. At the suggestion of Henry Tweedale, the organist and choir leader, the choir gave a short recital of popular songs, mainly songs from shows, and some 'golden oldies' with which the audience could join in.

'And that's the end of the visits for this year,' Simon told the members at the next church council meeting. 'I'm pleased to say they have been most successful, thanks to our team of willing workers. I'm sure that we now have a good reputation, and the word will spread that you can get a jolly good meal at St Peter's, with entertainment thrown in as well! Thanks to Henry and the choir for their contribution. So we'll start again with the adverts in the church newspapers, shall we, Graham?' he asked Graham Heap, the treasurer.

'Yes, and the advert has already gone in the local paper about the concert in November,' said Graham.

The suggestion that guest artistes should be invited to perform at St Peter's had been approved and acted upon. After a good deal of discussion it had been decided that the first such concert should be by a brass band. Yorkshire was renowned for its brass bands; such famous ones as the Grimethorpe Colliery band, the Brighouse and Rastrick, and the Black Dyke Mills were household names. There was, however, a brass band in their area, in the neighbouring village of Abercombe. It was not as large or as famous as some of the others, but those who had heard it declared that it was equally as good.

The conductor of the band had been approached and had said that they would be pleased to come; moreover, he had offered their services at a much reduced rate as it was for such a worthy cause as the rebuilding of the church roof, and because Aberthwaite and Abercombe were near neighbours.

There was also discussion as to how much the members of the audience should be charged for tickets. The charge for church concerts with their own choir and members of the congregation taking part was in the region of half a crown. It was decided, therefore, that five shillings would be an appropriate price to listen to a brass band. And that, of course, always included a cup of tea and a biscuit at the interval.

'It might be a good idea to invite Greg to come for that weekend,' Simon suggested to Fiona. 'He's due for a visit, isn't he? That is if you feel you can cope with him, darling? D'you think he'd be interested in a brass band?'

'I should imagine so,' replied Fiona. 'Most people like to listen to a good brass band, no matter what their musical taste is. He may be more of a Rolling Stones fan, though. You should know better than me about that. Yes, let's invite him; it'll be good to see him again. And don't worry about me; of course I can cope. Greg's no trouble at all, and just because I'm expecting twins it doesn't mean that I'm not able to have visitors.'

'That's OK then,' said Simon. 'I shall make sure you don't overdo things… I'm not doing too badly with my efforts in the kitchen, am I, darling?'

'You're doing splendidly,' she told him. Simon was, indeed, pulling his weight in every way that he could, and had even managed to cook some very tasty meals. That evening they had enjoyed sausage and mash with onion gravy, and Fiona had declared that she couldn't have done any better herself.

It had been his idea that he should help more around the house, and she had agreed, knowing how much he was concerned about her well-being. She was, in fact, keeping very well; watching her weight and having her blood pressure checked. The doctor assured her that she was doing fine and that, so far, there were no complications.

–

Fiona had kept in touch with Debbie, as she had promised she would do. They had exchanged a couple of letters, and it was hoped that Debbie would be able to visit Aberthwaite for a weekend quite soon.

One evening in early October the rectory phone rang, and because Simon was out at a meeting, Fiona answered it. She heard Debbie's excited voice.

'Hi, Fiona. It's me, Debbie. And guess what? We're on the phone! They came yesterday and put it in, so I had to let you know. I'll be able to ring you now, instead of writing.'

Debbie heard Fiona laugh. 'Just spare a thought for your parent's phone bill, won't you, love? It's so easy to use the phone, but not so pleasant when a massive bill arrives. Anyway, that's lovely, Debbie. It'll be useful for all of you.'

'Yes, my mum said that I haven't to keep ringing up all my friends. But she said it was all right to phone you. How are you, Fiona, and… the baby?'

'Very well, thank you.' She heard Fiona's merry chuckle again. 'And I have some news for you, too. Guess what? No, I know you'll never guess. I'm expecting twins!'

'Oh! Oh, how lovely! That's great news… Are you pleased?'

'Yes, and so is Simon. We haven't told Stella yet, not even about one baby, so two will be an even bigger surprise. Now, what about your visit to Aberthwaite? We'd be very pleased to see you, and so would Stella. She hasn't forgotten you, you know. Only the other day she said, 'Where's Debbie?''

'Aah... did she? How nice! I'm dying to see her again.'

'Well, let's not leave it too long then. The twins are due early December, then I should imagine that life will be very hectic for all of us.'

'I could come at half-term. I'm not sure when it is, but I'll let you know. I should be able to find my way this time.' Debbie laughed. 'I'll make sure I don't miss the bus!'

'Don't worry about that. If you get as far as Northallerton, then Simon can meet you there with the car. Is that OK?'

'Ooh yes, thanks! That'd be great. I'll let you know when I'll be coming as soon as I can. I'm really looking forward to it...'

'We'd better say cheerio now, Debbie. Time just slips away when you're on the phone, as I know to my cost. Bye for now, love. Nice to hear from you. Love to your mum and dad.'

'Yes, bye, Fiona... Love to Simon and Stella. And take care, won't you, Fiona? Bye for now...'

—

'Guess what?' Debbie dashed into the living room where her parents were sitting. 'Fiona's expecting twins!'

'Good gracious!' exclaimed Vera. 'That's exciting news, isn't it, pet? So long as she's keeping well... Is she?'

'Yes, as far as I know. She sounds OK, and she says they're very pleased about it, her and Simon. Stella doesn't know yet.'

'Happen she'll have two little lads then this time,' said Stanley, putting his newspaper down to join in the conversation. 'That'd be a change for her, and it would be nice for Simon to have a lad.'

'There's no telling what the good Lord in his wisdom decides to send,' said Vera, 'and you have to be thankful whichever it is. We were able to choose, though, weren't we? We so badly wanted a little girl... and we've never regretted it, have we?'

Debbie was not sure to whom her mother was addressing the remark, to her or to her father. Probably to both of them. She was glad to hear them say again that they had no regrets.

'No, I don't suppose we have,' Stanley answered, grinning at Debbie. 'She's turned out all right, has our lass... But Simon's already got a son, hasn't he? I dunno! Talk about complicated families! Did you ever hear the like?'

'I think it's rather nice,' said Vera quietly. She turned back to her knitting with a satisfied smile.

–

Things had settled down well in the Hargreaves home following Debbie's quest to trace her birth mother. Far better than she deserved; Debbie knew that only too well. It could have all gone so badly wrong and caused a lot of trouble, if it hadn't been for the understanding of everyone concerned.

Debbie was happy at home now in Whitesands Bay, more contented than she had been for a long time. Her little adventure had led, in fact, to a better relationship with her parents, most especially with her mother.

'I'm glad you've found out about Fiona,' Vera had said to her the day after her return. 'If you hadn't done it would have been niggling away at you for now and evermore, knowing you, Debbie, and your enquiring mind. I must admit that we were upset, though, your daddy and me, when we knew what you had done. And frantic when you were missing, you naughty girl!'

'I know, Mum. I'm sorry...'

'But it's all ended happily, thank God. Fiona's a lovely young woman, isn't she? I've wondered about her too, you know, over the years. All I knew was that she was a young lass who had got into trouble, as they say, and had to part with her lovely baby. I knew how sad she must have been – you were such a beautiful baby – and I used to pray that she'd be happy again one day. I don't mean all the time; just when it came into my mind. And she is happy, isn't she, with Simon? She has a lovely little girl of her own, and now another baby on the way. And such a good husband as well.'

'Yes... She told me all about the little teddy bear, Mum. Her boyfriend gave it to her; he won it at a stall at the fairground. They'd gone to London – on a church trip, it was – to see the Festival of Britain. And that's when... it happened. Her parents were furious and so ashamed of her, and they sent her away. And she never saw the boy again. He doesn't even know about it. So... well, he doesn't come into it at all. Except that I've got dark hair, like he had, I suppose... She was only seventeen, Mum. And she did love him...'

'Yes, times and attitudes are changing, Debbie. When we were courting, your dad and me, that sort of thing just didn't go on. Well, there were always girls who "had to get married" as they say, but it was frowned upon, that sort of carry-on. Most couples waited until they were married before they... well, you know what I mean.' Vera looked somewhat ill at ease. She very rarely talked about such intimate matters.

'When you were born it was looked upon as being something shameful,' she went on. 'I suppose I can understand Fiona's parents being so shocked. It was always a question of "Whatever will people think?", and trying to hide it away.' She smiled at her daughter. 'I hope, though, that I might have shown a little more Christian charity than Fiona's parents did. Poor lass! I'm sure she was a very nice girl – she still is, isn't she? – and that they just got carried away because they were on holiday: more freedom, being away from home and all that.'

'Yes, that's how she said it happened.'

'Things are different now,' said Vera, 'but whether it's for better or for worse, I'm not sure. They're calling it the "swinging sixties", aren't they? And young folk are behaving... well, very differently than they did in our young days. And I guess it'll get even worse as time goes on. That's why I worried about you, pet, when you started going out with Kevin. It wasn't that I didn't trust you, but mothers can't help worrying about what might happen.'

'You didn't need to worry about me,' said Debbie. 'There was never anything like that with Kevin and me. Well, he was my boyfriend for a while, but we didn't... and I don't think any of my friends do, either.'

'He's a nice lad,' said Vera. 'I know you must have been upset when it came to an end. I can understand why you didn't want to tell us. Is that why you don't want to go back to work at Sunnyhill?'

'Yes I suppose it is, really,' Debbie admitted. 'But I think I'm going to change my mind. Mr Hill asked me if I'd carry on working the weekends, and I think I will, if they still want me. It'll be a bit of extra money, and it'll help with all the stuff I need for the sixth form.'

'I think it's a very good idea,' smiled Vera. 'You must keep your hand in with the gardening, if that's what you're planning to do... for a career, like you said.'

Debbie knew that her mother still thought that her choice of a career was an unusual one. She had said very little about it, though, seeming content that Debbie was back home after her little escapade, and that the outcome had been a happy one.

She had returned to work at Sunnyhill, just for the weekends. She went there a little shamefacedly at first, wondering how Mr Hill would react to her asking if she could have her job back. She guessed, too, that news of her little adventure would have reached the ears of those at the garden centre.

To her relief Mr Hill had taken her back unreservedly. 'Of course you can come back, Debbie,' he assured her. 'We've missed you. We've been busy at the weekends, and Muriel will be glad of an extra pair of hands to help with the floral arrangements. She's doing autumn ones at the moment, and then before we have time to turn round it'll be Christmas. Muriel has all sorts of ideas for the festive season. She'll tell you about them...'

Debbie had felt more apprehensive about meeting Kevin again. She decided she would behave as though they were just good mates. She would try not to think about them having been rather more than that for a time, or bear him any ill will for having dumped her. If she was honest, she wasn't all that bothered any more. She was enjoying school now she was in the sixth form. As Fiona had told her, it wasn't like ordinary school. They were allowed a lot more freedom, and being able to drop subjects that she was not too keen on, and at which she didn't excel – History and French, in Debbie's case – made studying more pleasant.

Several of the girls she had been with since the age of eleven were still at school, although some were studying different subjects. There were some new students, too; both boys and girls as the sixth form had a good reputation. As Debbie was studying science subjects rather than the arts, then boys outnumbered the girls in her groups. There was a lad called Mike whom she rather liked the look of, and on further acquaintance he was easy to talk to. She and Ryan Gregson were often in the same groups because he had decided that science was his forte, and he had an idea he would like to work in a laboratory. He was still friendly with Shirley, who had decided – for the moment at least – to go ahead with her idea of becoming an infant teacher.

There was very little pairing off so far with the boys and girls. A crowd of them sometimes went out together on a Saturday night, to a coffee bar or the cinema, or to a 'hop' at a local church Youth Club.

When Debbie first returned to Sunnyhill, Kevin was not there. His father told her that he had gone camping up in Scotland for a fortnight, with two of his mates, travelling from one campsite to another in the car that belonged, jointly, to his mates, Rick and Pete, who were brothers.

So she didn't see him again until the end of September. He greeted her in a friendly way, making a joke of her little escapade. 'Hi there, Debbie,' he said. 'Good to see you again. You got back safe and sound then?' Of course he had known about it. She had found out that her mother had rung Kevin before contacting anyone else, to see if he knew of her whereabouts.

'Yes…' She smiled at him. 'It was all rather traumatic, but it worked out well in the end.'

'Your mum was in a real old tizzy,' he told her. 'I sort of guessed where you might have gone, but I didn't know for sure, did I? That's why I told her to ask Shirley. Anyway… did you find out what you wanted to know?' He sounded quite sympathetic and interested.

'Yes… I did. I found my birth mother; she's a really nice person. I'm satisfied, now that I know, Kevin. I was a bit of a chump, but nobody seems to be thinking too badly of me for what I did; my mum and dad I mean, most of all. I didn't really stop to think what it might do to them, how hurt they might be. But they seemed to understand. And I'm getting on much better with my mum now.' She wasn't sure why she was telling Kevin all this, but he seemed genuinely concerned. She smiled at him. 'So it's all OK again now.'

'Good; I'm pleased about that,' he answered. 'I know how much it had been on your mind.' To her surprise he added, 'Perhaps we could go out sometime, Debbie, and have a good chat?' He felt that she had changed quite a lot, and it was for the better. She seemed to be a much nicer person now. He wasn't sure that he wanted to take up with her again, as a regular girlfriend… but time would tell.

'Yes, why not?' she replied. 'That would be nice…' But she didn't, in truth, feel like getting too friendly with any one person at that moment. She knew that there would be lots of challenges and interesting times ahead.

Twenty

Debbie found out that the half-term holiday was at the very end of October. She hoped it would be possible for her to visit Fiona and Simon at the end of the second weekend, from the Friday till the Sunday.

She phoned Fiona to tell her the dates, and she answered that of course it would be all right; they would love to see her again. Debbie, however, thought she heard just a little hesitation in Fiona's voice. 'Are you sure?' she asked. 'Do say if it's not convenient.'

'Yes it is,' said Fiona. 'We have a concert at church, though, that weekend. We've got a brass band from the next village performing on the Saturday night. It'll be quite a big occasion for us. I was wondering if it would be... your cup of tea?'

'Ooh yes, it would, actually,' replied Debbie. 'My dad loves brass bands. He's got a lot of records, and I listen to them with him. Yes, that'll be great. I shall love it!'

'That's settled then. We'll sort out details nearer the time. As I said before, Simon will pick you up at Northallerton.'

They chatted for a little while, then Fiona sent her regards to Vera and Stanley, and put the phone down, thoughtfully...

She hadn't wanted to say no to Debbie, but that was the weekend that Greg was coming to stay. She knew what Simon would say: that it would be too much for her, she had to take care and not overdo things. Sure enough, that was what he said when she told him, but she made little of his objections. She knew though he wasn't really objecting; he was just concerned about her well-being.

'I'll be fine, darling,' she assured him. 'Greg's no trouble, and Debbie won't be, either. And we have two spare bedrooms.'

'Not for much longer,' he reminded her.

'No, but we have at the moment, and it's rather a nice idea, when you come to think of it. Debbie and Greg will be able to meet. They've heard of one another, and they would have to get to know one another sometime. If we waited any longer before seeing Debbie I might be feeling too tired. I'm keeping very well, Simon, as you know. It'll be a busy weekend, but you'll be there to help me. And Josh is preaching that Sunday, isn't he? There's just one slight problem, though… I said you'd meet Debbie on the Friday, but what about the return journey on the Sunday; driving her to catch the train at Northallerton?'

'Mmm, yes, I see. Never mind, we'll think of something. I'm sure we'll be able to find somebody to help out with a lift for Debbie.'

The week before the concert another problem arose. Greg rang up to see if he could bring his brother Graham with him. He was quite a devotee of brass band music, much more so than Greg. He played the French horn, having learnt at school and performed in school concerts, and Greg knew it would be a real treat for him.

Once again, Fiona didn't see it as a problem. 'By all means, Greg,' she answered. 'It'll be good to meet your brother. So long as you're not thinking of bringing your sister along as well,' she said with a laugh. 'That might be rather more tricky, but we'd love to meet her sometime.'

'No; Grace has other plans that weekend. It really is very good of you, Fiona. I promise we won't be any trouble.'

'By heck! You're a glutton for punishment!' Simon told her. 'Three visitors now! Are you quite sure you'll be able to manage?'

'Of course,' she replied. 'Casserole dishes; that's the answer. Easy to prepare, and a lot to go round. And you must let Josh take some of the workload from you at church.'

'He already does,' said Simon. 'That young man has been an answer to a prayer, sure enough.'

–

Yet another complication arose when Simon was asked to conduct a funeral on the first of November, the Friday that Debbie was due to arrive. Bill Heathcote was a long-standing member of St Peter's who had been ill for some time, so his death was not unexpected. The service was to be held at two o'clock on Friday afternoon, followed by the burial at the cemetery just outside the town.

'I shall have to be there,' Simon told his wife. 'This is one task that I can't allocate to Josh. Bill has been a stalwart member of the church, and his wife is a keen member of the Mothers' Union.' He couldn't help but comment, 'It never rains but it pours! Never mind, though, we'll think of something.'

Josh expressed a wish to help at the funeral service, too. He had visited the elderly man both at home and in hospital, and had become friendly with him, and with his wife. The liking was reciprocated. Mary Heathcote had said how much her husband looked forward to the young curate's visits. Josh was proving to be an excellent sick visitor, always ready with a cheery word as well as sympathy and understanding.

Fiona had had an idea that Josh might be prevailed upon to meet Debbie, but she hadn't voiced it, and she soon saw that it was impractical. Many of the members of the congregation would want to be at the service as well... so what were they going to do about Debbie?

Simon was preoccupied, his head full of church matters, which was only as it should be. Then she thought about Greg. It depended on what time he and his brother intended to arrive in Aberthwaite. If they came in the morning she could provide them with lunch and then, perhaps, they could make the journey to Northallerton to meet Debbie from the train? It wasn't all that far, and she knew that Greg loved driving around in his new mini car. Would it be an awful cheek to ask him? she wondered.

She mentioned it to Simon, and he said he thought that Greg would agree, but that it was up to her to make the arrangements. She must be the one to ring Greg and ask him. They had not had one wrong word about the situation that had arisen – the three visitors, the work involved with the concert, then, on top of it all, the funeral. She knew, though, that Simon felt she was partly responsible for the confusion, because she had agreed to entertain three guests at the same time, therefore she must be the one to sort it out.

She rang Greg at his flat and, as she had guessed, he had agreed at once, and eagerly, too, to do as she requested.

'Great!' he exclaimed. 'Of course I'll go and meet Debbie. I've been looking forward to it ever since you told me about her turning up. Let's see… what is she? My stepsister?'

Fiona laughed. 'Yes, I think so. I haven't really worked it out.'

'I've already got a half-brother, and two half-sisters, haven't I? Curiouser and curiouser!'

'And two more on the way,' Fiona reminded him. 'Half-brothers or half-sisters, or one of each! We don't know.'

'And how are you, Fiona?' he asked. 'Are you sure you will be able to cope with such an influx of visitors. You didn't tell me that Debbie would be there when I asked if I could invite Graham, did you?'

'No, that's true. I just liked the idea of both sides of the family getting together. To be honest, I think Simon's just the teeniest bit cross with me, although he hasn't said so.'

'Oh dear! We can't have that. You two never fall out, do you?'

'No, not really. We don't always see eye to eye about everything, but we manage to sort it out in the end.'

'I can understand how he feels,' said Greg. 'You've taken a lot on, but Graham and I will help, I promise.'

'I'm thinking of some nice, easy-to-prepare meals,' Fiona went on, before Greg interrupted.

'I've just thought of something. Could you get a babysitter for Friday evening?'

'Er… yes, I think so. There are some girls in the Youth Club. We've asked one of them on the rare occasions that we want to go out…'

'And do you know of a good restaurant in Aberthwaite, or nearby?'

'I'm sure we could find one…'

'Well then, we'll all have a meal out on the Friday night; you and Simon, Graham and me, and Debbie. My treat, of course. What do you think?'

'I think that would be lovely,' said Fiona. She knew that Greg meant it wholeheartedly. It would be his way of saying thank you. And how nice it would be to dress up and go out for a change, even if she did feel the size of a whale. 'Thank you very much, Greg. It will be a great treat for us. Simon has that funeral in the afternoon, so it's just what he needs. Funerals always make him feel sad.'

'Will you make the booking then? Wherever you and Simon would like to go?'

Fiona agreed that she would, then they went on to talk about Debbie's arrival. Greg said that Graham was staying with him on Thursday night, and they would set off from Manchester early on the Friday morning. Then, after lunch, Greg, with his brother, would drive to Northallerton and wait for Debbie in the station car park.

'I'd better ask her what she will be wearing,' said Fiona, 'then you'll be able to spot her.'

'No need,' answered Greg. 'Just tell her to look out for a red mini car and two handsome young men!'

'Of course!' laughed Fiona. 'Why didn't I think of that? OK, I'll ring Debbie and tell her what we've sorted out. She'll be delighted, I'm sure. And I know you'll like her. Thanks for your help, Greg. We'll look forward to seeing you and Graham on Friday... Bye for now.'

–

'Wow! It's all go, isn't it?' Simon remarked when Fiona told him of the plans she had made. 'I'm sorry if I've been a bit irritable with you just lately, darling.'

'You haven't, Simon,' she assured him.

'Well, rather preoccupied and offhand, maybe. It all seems to be happening at once, and it's you that I'm worried about, of course. Most of the work involved — at home, at any rate — will fall on you.'

'I'm OK, honestly,' she answered him. 'I got a good report at the clinic last time. There's nothing to worry about. Anyway, it'll be lovely — for all of us — to see Debbie again and to meet Graham for the first time. Families and friendships such as these are so important, aren't they?'

'Yes, and the family's spreading wider and wider,' agreed Simon. 'It's very good of Greg to suggest an evening out. Have you any idea as to a venue?'

'I've heard good reports of that new Italian place — Giovanni's — in the market square,' said Fiona. 'Joan and Henry have been and she was very impressed. They serve more traditional food — you know; steak and fish and chicken — as well as a wide variety of Italian food.'

'Good, then it should suit us all,' said Simon. 'I'll make the booking, so you don't have to worry about that. Five of us, aren't there? It'll help me to forget the sadness of the afternoon. Well, not exactly forget, but you know what I mean, don't you. Funerals always make me sad. I've never really got over the feeling. I know we talk about eternal life — and I believe it — but it's not much consolation to the grieving friends and family at the time.'

Fiona reflected that it was what made Simon such a good parish priest, to give him his full title. He cared so much about all his parishioners.

–

Greg and his brother arrived at mid-morning on the Friday. It was Fiona, holding Stella by the hand, who greeted them; she had heard the car pull up and stop on the driveway. Simon was in his study, preparing for the afternoon with a period of calm reflection, as she knew he did before a funeral.

Greg jumped from the driving seat and gave her a hug and a kiss on the cheek. By no means a tight hug because of her size. She was well aware of that, although Greg made no comment. She knew, though, that she was much larger than the last time he had seen her. He stooped down then to give Stella a hug. She said, 'Hello, Greg,' in a quiet voice, appearing shy at the sight of a stranger with him.

'And this is my little brother, Graham,' he joked. Graham was not little at all, being taller than Greg by a few inches. He had a look of his brother, but not all that much. He couldn't, of course, look anything like Simon, as Greg did. Greg resembled his birth father with regard to features, but he had brown eyes and dark hair, whereas Simon was fairish. Graham, too, had brown eyes and dark hair with no hint of a wave, but his face was less rounded than his brother's, with a more pronounced nose. He was, though, a good-looking lad, in a different way.

Fiona realized at once that he was quieter, however, than his somewhat extrovert brother, unless he was just overawed by the situation. He shook hands with Fiona, smiling pleasantly; a smile that lit up his eyes and quite transformed his face. He said he was pleased to meet her and how kind she was to let him come with Greg.

Simon appeared then and greeted them both, helping to take their travel bags out of the small boot.

'Gosh!' said Graham, though a little diffidently. 'I can see the resemblance. So that's where you get your handsome looks from, bro!'

'You're not so bad yourself,' Greg told him, giving him a playful shove. 'Fiona has told Debbie to look out for two handsome young men, haven't you, Fiona? She won't be able to believe her luck!'

'I might have said something of the sort,' laughed Fiona. 'Come along in, and you can help Graham to make himself at home, like you always do.'

Greg had, indeed, become very much part of the family since the day he had first arrived on their doorstep. And, of course, he and Stella had become firm friends.

They had an early lunch, an easily prepared meal of cottage pie, so that the two young men would have ample time to drive north to meet another member of the family. Debbie was due to arrive at the station at half past two. They set off soon after one o'clock to give them time to spare.

'And so that you don't need to drive like Stirling Moss!' Graham told his brother.

'No, I won't, I promise,' Greg assured Fiona. 'I'll drive very steadily, and I'll take great care of my stepsister!'

–

Debbie was excited about her forthcoming visit to Aberthwaite, especially so, since she had been told she would meet Greg. And not only Greg but his brother Graham as well. She felt rather nervous, though. It had started by her wanting to find out about her birth mother, and then going to find her. Now, though, it was leading to a whole new wealth of experiences. She had a delightful little half-sister, and there were two more babies on the way. Now she was to meet a young man who was… a stepbrother? And another young man who was linked to this family whose tentacles seemed to be spreading even wider.

'You don't mind me going to see Fiona again, do you, Mum?' she had asked Vera.

'No, of course not, pet,' Vera had answered. 'I think it's rather exciting, all these folk that we never knew about, popping up out of the blue. I knew you were rather restless before... before you found out. You feel much more settled in your mind now, don't you, love?'

'Yes... yes, I do. And it doesn't alter the way that I feel about you and Dad, honestly, it doesn't.'

'I know that, love,' said Vera. They had smiled at one another with a quiet understanding. They were not inclined, as a family, to be over demonstrative. There had been rather more hugging and shows of affection than usual when Debbie had returned from her little escapade, but they had settled down now to a tacit acceptance of the situation.

Stanley had asked his wife how she felt about it all. 'Don't you feel a bit... well, jealous, like, of this Fiona? Nobody could blame you, lass, if you did.'

'No, funnily enough, I don't,' she answered. 'If I'd known what our Debbie was up to I'd have been upset. She'd started asking questions... oh, ages ago, and I remember being a bit crabby with her then. I thought she'd decided to let it drop, but obviously it had still been worrying her. No, it's best it's all out in the open, Stanley. And she's changed, hasn't she? We're all getting along much better now, don't you think?'

'Aye; I have to admit she's not as nowty as she used to be. And you got your own way about her staying on at school, didn't you, Vera?'

'Yes, I suppose I did. But I still don't understand what it is she wants to do. Sorting out folks' gardens for 'em?

Doesn't sound like much of a job to me. You've always sorted ours out without any help, haven't you, Stanley?'

'Well, it's what I do for a living, isn't it? So I do have a bit more idea than some folk have,' said Stanley, feeling a little peeved. 'There's more to gardening than meets the eye. And our Debbie wants to do it on a much larger scale. She'll surprise us one day, this lass of ours, you mark my words.'

Debbie set out on her journey this time with a much lighter heart. She knew where she was going; it was no longer a step into the unknown. She started off a little earlier than before to make sure that she caught the connection from Darlington, the one that she had missed the previous time.

She had dressed with care, in the cherry red coat she had chosen from C and A on the shopping expedition with her mother. With it she wore knee-high black patent leather boots, and carried a matching shoulder bag, a recent purchase that she had saved up to buy with the money she earned at the garden centre.

The journey was uneventful and she coped with the change of trains at Newcastle and Darlington without any problems. She knew where she was bound this time, and the landmarks and the change of scenery from industrial to a more rural vista was pleasantly familiar.

She had told Fiona that she would be wearing a red coat, but it wasn't likely that she and the brothers would fail to find one another. The lads would be in a red mini car. 'Two very nice young men,' Fiona had told her. 'Aren't you a lucky girl?'

Debbie, in fact, felt very apprehensive when she alighted from the train at Northallerton. Her stomach was tied up in knots, although she wasn't sure why she should feel so anxious. She picked up her travel bag and made her way to the adjacent car park. She spotted them at once: two dark-haired young men leaning against the bonnet of a red mini. The shorter of the two, whom she guessed was Greg, gave a cheery wave and hurried towards her.

'Hello there. You must be Debbie?'

'Yes, that's right; I am. And you are... Greg?'

'That's me!' he grinned. 'Here, let me take your bag.' He opened the boot and put her travel bag inside, whilst she looked at him more closely without him being aware of it. He was so much like Simon, apart from his colouring.

'You look like Simon,' she told him a little shyly, as he turned round.

'Guilty as charged!' he laughed. 'And you look like Fiona, apart from the hair. "Aye, it's a rum do!", to quote my grandad... And this is my little brother, Graham.'

The other young man stepped forward, holding out his hand. 'Hi, pleased to meet you, Debbie,' he said. He was a few inches taller than Greg although three or four years younger. He seemed, at least on a first acquaintance, to be rather more reserved than his brother. He, also, was a good-looking young man, but in a different way; leaner in features and with a more prominent nose, which didn't alter the fact that he was a pleasantly handsome lad. Debbie did a quick calculation in her head. She knew he was at Leeds uni, just into his second year. So he must be... nineteen, going on twenty?

'Hello,' she said, taking his outstretched hand. 'I'm pleased to meet you as well, Graham.'

'OK then, let's get on our way,' said Greg. 'Where do you want to sit, you two? Would you like to sit in the front with me, Debbie?'

'No, we'll both sit in the back,' said Graham, 'then you can concentrate on your driving, Greg. I'll keep Debbie amused.' He smiled, rather shyly, at her, and his brown eyes lit up with warmth and a sort of unspoken question.

'OK by me,' she said, climbing into the back seat. 'Smashing little car you've got, Greg. Just the sort I would like… some day. I'm not old enough to drive though yet, not till next May.'

'I'm old enough, but I can't afford it,' said Graham, sitting at the side of her. 'Greg's let me take the wheel now and again, well away from the town, of course; but I shall need some proper lessons, from an expert, I mean.'

'Are you casting aspersions on my driving?' joked Greg as he started up the engine.

'Not at all, but you know what I mean. Come on, put your foot down. But remember what you promised Fiona. No whizzing round the corners on two wheels!'

'That sounds exciting,' said Debbie. 'He doesn't really, does he?'

'No, rest assured. I'm as safe as houses,' said Greg. 'I'll drive like Grandad does, when they're out for a Sunday afternoon jaunt. I've got precious cargo on board.'

Debbie's anxiety had flown away as she had been put at her ease by these two nice young men. As Fiona had said, she was a lucky girl! She found herself looking forward immensely to the weekend ahead, with all its new experiences. Graham was a newcomer to Aberthwaite and to St Peter's church, just as she was. She guessed that he might be feeling apprehensive as well, but they would be able to face it together.

She learnt more about him as they travelled along the country roads to Aberthwaite. He was, as she had thought, in his second year at Leeds uni, studying for a degree in architecture with the aim of becoming a draughtsman.

'Clever stuff!' she commented. 'I'm impressed. Do you mean you want to design houses for people? Or offices and places of work, that sort of thing?'

'I'm not absolutely sure yet. I shall wait and see where it leads to when I'm getting near the end of my course.' He was, as she had thought, a quiet and modest sort of young man, not bumptious in any way. 'What about you, Debbie?' he asked. 'Which A level subjects are you taking?'

'Well, funnily enough, I'm into design as well,' she told him. 'But I want to design gardens; you know – landscaping, water features, rockeries and all that. My parents think it's a funny sort of thing to want to do. At least my mum does, although I think Dad understands a bit more. He works as a gardener for the council – that's how I got interested – and I work part-time at a garden centre. So I'm doing an art course, and biology and chemistry as well. An odd mixture, but I suppose it covers all the aspects of gardening. I don't know what I'll take a degree in… if I get that far.'

'They keep coming up with more and more new courses,' said Graham. 'You'll have to wait and see which is most relevant. Anyway, that's enough about studying. Are you looking forward to the brass band concert? That was why I wanted to come, actually, apart from meeting… everybody.'

He told her that his love of that type of music had started when he was in the fifth form, and he had been persuaded to learn to play the French horn and join the school band. He still played, and was now a member of a college band. 'So my taste in music is pretty wide,' he said. 'We play all sorts in a brass band: classical, pop, marches, opera, ballet, Gilbert and Sullivan… you name it, we play it.'

Debbie said that she wasn't knowledgeable about music, but she knew what she liked and that, above all, was something tuneful. And she still had a fondness for the Beatles.

'We play that as well,' said Graham.

It seemed that in no time at all they were there, pulling up at the rectory door. Debbie was surprised when she saw Fiona, and tried not to look too closely at her. She was, of course, expecting twins, but she had never seen anyone look so large as Fiona did. Poor thing! she thought. However was she coping? But Fiona seemed very cheerful and agile, too, in the very best of spirits as she welcomed everyone. She kissed Debbie on the cheek and said how lovely it was to see her again.

'Debbie, Debbie!' called a little voice at her side, and there was Stella tugging at her coat. To Debbie's delight the child had remembered her.

She stooped down to hug her. 'Hello, Stella. Haven't you grown? What a big girl you are! Not a baby any more.' She seemed to be a few inches taller, more of a little girl now, than a baby.

'I be two soon,' she said. 'And we're going to have two babies!'

'We thought it was better to tell her before someone else did,' said Fiona. 'It's been quite a talking point in the parish, as you can imagine! Anyway, come on in, all of you. I can see you've got acquainted, and I'm sure we're going to have an exciting weekend.'

Twenty-One

Giovanni's was a surprisingly upmarket place for a little town like Aberthwaite. It had been opened about a year ago, and was now a popular venue for eating out, a pastime that more and more people were enjoying. The owners, Giovanni and Maria Verdi, were genuine Italians.

Giovanni admitted, unashamedly, that he had been a prisoner of war, working at a farm not far from Aberthwaite. He had fallen in love with the Yorkshire countryside, and the people, too, and had had no desire to return to Milan, the city of his birth, as both his parents had died. He had persuaded his sweetheart, back home, to join him, and they had both found employment in cafes and restaurants in Leeds. They worked hard. Giovanni rose from a lowly position in the kitchens to become a first-class chef. They saved hard, too, and eventually realized their dream, a restaurant of their own in the town that Giovanni had always loved. Maria did the bookkeeping, their pretty daughter, Tessa, waited at the tables, and their son, Marco, was the second-in-command to his father.

Debbie was thrilled to be dining out as it was something that she and her parents – and most of their acquaintances – did very rarely. She was wearing for the occasion a new dress that she had bought from Marks and Spencer in Newcastle. A mini dress – but not so mini as to 'show yer next week's washing!' as her father put it – in woollen rayon with horizontal stripes of red and black running across the bodice, and vertical stripes below the dropped waistline. Her black patent leather boots and her shoulder bag went very well with it, and the finishing touch was her pair of large black earrings – Woolworth's best – in the shape of a daisy.

Debbie and the two young men walked to the restaurant as it was only a short distance away, whilst Simon and Fiona drove there in the car. Fiona had told Debbie that she was very self-conscious about her size. 'Only another month to go now, and I can't wait, believe me!'

'You look fine,' Debbie had assured her, and it was true. She looked radiant and happy, despite her obvious discomfort. Her blue eyes were as bright as ever and her hair shone like a feathery golden halo. She wore a loose pinafore dress in her favourite blue, with a floral blouse beneath it. She could not disguise her pregnancy, nor did she want to, but she managed to look elegant.

Tessa, in a black dress and a red frilly apron handed them the giant-sized menus.

'Remember, it's my treat,' said Greg. 'Choose whatever you like.'

The choice was vast, ranging from pizzas and pasta dishes to fish, pork, beef steak; even sausage and mash or ham and eggs for the less adventurous diners. They all decided to forgo the starters, apart from a large platter of garlic bread with a cheesy topping which they ate whilst they waited for the main course.

They all decided to 'go Italian', the younger ones choosing giant-sized pizzas, and Simon and Fiona opting for lasagne and the chef's speciality, spaghetti bolognese. Simon insisted that he must pay for the wine, a rich red

Cabernet Sauvignon which, he was assured, would be the perfect accompaniment to the meals. And what could they finish with but ice cream in a myriad of flavours, made as only the Italians could do.

Debbie looked round at the stylish surroundings; an Italian setting, inevitably, but not overdone. Wrought iron candle holders and wall brackets, colourful jugs and plates in the chunky Majolica style, lamps fashioned from Chianti bottles, and sepia photos of old Milan, Rome and Verona on the walls. She felt as though she was in another world, a dream from which she would soon awake. But it was all real enough. She sat between the two brothers, wishing that her friends from school could see her now. She gave a contented smile, one that Simon noticed.

'Enjoying yourself, are you, Debbie?' he asked, grinning at her in a friendly way.

'Ooh yes! Ever so much,' she replied. 'It's been a lovely evening. Thank you, Greg, and Simon… and everybody.' She knew that the wine had affected her just a little bit, making her feel even happier than she was already. But Fiona had made sure that she drank only one glass. Debbie knew why; she remembered how Fiona had told her about what happened to her at Battersea Park. Fiona, too, had drunk very little that night, no doubt because of the babies.

'Well, unwilling as I am to break up the party, we'd better get back to our babysitter,' said Simon. He helped Fiona and Debbie with their coats whilst Greg paid the bill.

'Ciao!' Greg said to Maria. 'We've had a great time. You can be sure we'll come again.'

Maria, and Giovanni, too, portly in his black suit, and with a well-groomed moustache, both stood at the door to say goodbye, as they all stepped out into the cold evening air. The three young ones linked arms, Debbie in the middle, as they strode along the High Street and then up the lane that led to the rectory. She felt at ease with both of them; she hoped she would see them again… sometime.

–

Debbie insisted on helping Fiona as much as she could the next day. Simon and the two lads had gone hiking, taking sandwiches for their lunch.

'We'll have a sandwich lunch, too,' said Fiona, 'then this afternoon we'll go to the market.'

It was good helping Fiona in the kitchen, preparing the vegetables and potatoes for the casserole she would be making for their early evening meal, then keeping Stella amused, playing with her building bricks and her large family of dolls and animals. She felt that Fiona was like a friend or a big sister, and she didn't feel awkward now at using her first name.

Debbie loved the market, as Fiona had said she would. They had only a market hall at home, not an outdoor country market. It seemed so much more exciting out of doors. She loved the smell of the fruit and vegetable stalls, and the stalls with farmers' produce – cheese, eggs, butter, and home-made jams and pickles. And on the other side of the market cross, the stall with knitting wool and material, the ironmongery, and the china and crockery. Fiona did some shopping, storing it in the bag attached to Stella's pushchair, and Debbie bought a box of assorted fudge for her parents.

'Now, there's someone I want you to meet,' said Fiona when they had seen all that the market had to offer.

They walked a little way along the High Street to a shop with a colourful window display. Knitting wool, material, ribbons, lace… everything that one might need for sewing and handicrafts.

The doorbell pinged as Fiona entered, followed by Debbie who was now pushing the pram. There were no customers in the shop, only a ginger-haired lady with a pleasant face and a friendly smile behind the counter. Debbie thought she looked familiar, then she gave a little gasp of surprise. It was the kind lady who had given her a lift when she missed the bus.

'I think you two have met before,' said Fiona. 'Debbie, this is my good friend, Joan.'

The woman stepped from behind the counter and gave her a quick hug. 'Good to see you again, Debbie,' she said. 'I've heard a lot about you.'

'Oh…' Debbie was taken aback for a moment. 'Hello… yes, nice to see you again… I'm sorry I told you a fib; Fiona's not my aunty. But thank you for rescuing me.'

'No, I guessed that at the time,' said Joan, with a twinkle in her eye. 'I already knew Fiona's story. And I'm really pleased it's turned out so well for all of you. You've come to listen to the band, have you?'

'Yes, but I was coming anyway to see Fiona and Simon, and Stella of course. The concert's an extra treat, and meeting Greg and Graham as well.'

'Goodness! You're having a busy weekend, Fiona,' said Joan. 'Mind you don't overdo it.'

'Debbie is being a great help, and the lads as well,' replied Fiona. 'So don't worry about me, I'm fine.'

They chatted for a while whilst Stella had a nap as she usually did after a ride in her pushchair. 'Cheerio for now,' said Joan as they departed. 'See you tonight. We shall go nice and early; we're expecting a good crowd.'

–

The church hall was already more than half full when Simon and his family arrived at just turned seven o'clock. Simon had left the organization and the catering to the team of helpers. He would be in charge of the proceedings, as the rector, but apart from that he had little to do but socialize and make everyone welcome.

Fiona had come along, as the babysitter was available again. Debbie sensed, though, that she was a little tired and uncomfortable, despite her insistence that she was fine. Fiona didn't introduce her to anyone but Debbie felt, from the looks she was receiving – curious but not unfriendly – and the knowing little smiles, that people had realized who she could be. It was the same with Greg, of course, but they had met him before. No doubt they would be wondering who Graham might be!

The room soon filled up, and extra chairs were brought in for the latecomers. Then, on the dot of seven thirty, the members of the band marched down the centre aisle, resplendent in their maroon uniforms, with gold braid and brass buttons. Their brass instruments gleamed brightly, and the smiles of the musicians were bright as well as they were greeted by the anticipatory applause of the audience. Simon made a short speech of welcome to the Abercombe and District Brass Band, then the concert began.

It was a feast of the very best in brass band music from beginning to end. They started with 'Strike Up the Band', which was their signature tune, followed by the Radetsky march, then 'The Carnival of Venice' with a splendid cornet solo. The young man blushed as he received an extra round of applause.

The majority of the band members were men, both young and not so young, although there were a few women as well, two young and two rather older, playing the clarinet and the French horn. There was music for all tastes; haunting tunes such as 'Greensleeves' and 'Finlandia' as well as the more traditional marches.

Tea and biscuits were served at the interval, for which everyone queued up at the serving hatch. Debbie offered to bring a cup for Fiona, but she insisted on getting up as she was stiff with sitting for so long. She introduced Debbie to a group of young – well, youngish – women who stopped to speak to her and ask her how she was feeling.

'These are my friends from the Young Wives group,' she said. 'Ruth, Heather, Gillian, Sandra… and you've met Joan, of course. Ladies, this is Debbie, my long-lost daughter!'

Debbie smiled and said, 'Hello…' a little shyly.

'It's alright; they all know the story,' said Fiona.

'Yes, we do, and we were so pleased to hear that you had found one another,' said one.

'Such a happy ending!' said another.

'Yes it is,' said Debbie, smiling at Fiona. 'It's lovely, because I've got my mum and dad at home, and now I've got Fiona and Simon, and little Stella.'

'And two more on the way,' laughed another of the ladies.

'As if I could forget!' said Fiona, with a grimace.

There was another lady, too, behind the serving hatch, pouring out the tea. She was much older and plumper and she wore a felt hat. She smiled at Debbie in a questioning sort of way, so Debbie smiled back at her.

'Oh, Mrs Bayliss...' said Fiona, and Debbie could hear a touch of amusement in her voice. 'This is Debbie. She's my daughter, in case you were wondering. You remember the story, of course? She came to find me. You may have heard about it?'

'Well, yes, actually I did hear something about it,' said the woman. 'How nice to meet you, Debbie. And where do you live, my dear?'

'In Whitesands Bay, in Northumberland,' said Debbie, 'with my mum and dad. I've just come for a visit, to see Fiona and everybody.'

'I see... That's nice... You're a pretty girl,' she added. 'Just like Fiona. Well, enjoy the rest of the concert, dear.'

'Thank you; I'm sure I will,' said Debbie.

The woman turned round, and as Debbie walked away, carrying the cups of tea, she was aware of Fiona smiling to herself.

'Who was that?' she asked. 'Do I sense a sort of... what? Rivalry... disapproval?'

'Mrs Bayliss is an old adversary of mine. She was rather critical of me when I first married Simon,' Fiona told Debbie in a quiet voice. 'She was the big noise in the Mothers' Union, and she didn't like the idea of the rector's wife taking over. Not that I tried to; I started the Young Wives group instead. And she was horrified when she found out about my first pregnancy.' She smiled at Debbie. 'But I'm forgiven now – though it's not completely forgotten – and Ethel and I get along quite well.'

They sat down to drink their tea. 'You have to try to get on with everyone, I suppose,' said Debbie, 'with you being the rector's wife. It can't always be easy.'

'No, it isn't,' said Fiona. 'I didn't realize, until I married Simon, about all the inner politics of the church, and the arguing and backbiting that can go on beneath the surface. It only takes one or two to upset the apple cart!'

'I'm sure it's a happy church, though, isn't it, with Simon in charge?' said Debbie. 'He has all the right qualities. He's dynamic, and friendly, and understanding… I'm glad that everything has worked out so well for you, Fiona.'

'Thank you, Debbie,' said Fiona quietly. 'Yes; you've had splendid parents, and I found a good husband. I've come to realize, since I met Simon, that God does have a hand in our worldly affairs. Anyway, no sermonizing, eh? Would you take these cups back, please, there's a good girl? Then we'll enjoy the rest of the concert.'

The band started the second half with the 'Grand March' from *Aida* followed by the overture to *Iolanthe*. There followed music from opera and ballet, a French horn soloist playing 'The Swan' by Saint Saens, which was of particular interest to Graham, and even a Beatles' medley.

After the concert Simon gave a well-deserved vote of thanks, and there was rapturous applause as the members of the band marched out.

'A huge success,' he told the helpers, 'and I'm sure we'll have made a good amount towards our roofing fund.'

Simon was urged not to stay behind and help with the clearing away – the ever helpful Josh was on hand to do that – but to go home with Fiona who was looking pleased and happy, but very tired. She admitted as much when they arrived back at the rectory. The babysitter, Jennifer, assured them that Stella had been no trouble at all.

'I'll go and take a peep at her,' said Fiona. 'Then, if no one minds, I'll go straight to bed.'

'Yes, off you go, darling,' said Simon. 'Would you like me to bring you a drink?'

'No thanks,' she said. 'I'm ready to go straight to sleep.'

Debbie, who was quite at home in the kitchen now, made tea for all of them. Simon retired to bed after a little while, leaving the younger ones to stay up chatting till midnight.

Twenty-Two

Fiona fell asleep almost at once, physically and mentally tired by the events of the day but happy, too, at the thought of her extended family around her. She woke a couple of hours later, as was usual, for her trip to the bathroom, one of the more annoying symptoms of pregnancy in the later stages.

She woke up again after a few more hours with a very different sort of sensation in her abdomen. She glanced at the luminous dial on the clock; it was quarter past five. It would not be fair to wake Simon until she was sure, so she lay still and waited. The babies were not due for another month or so, but babies were not aware of the date they were supposed to arrive. She waited… and five minutes later the pain came again, a stronger one this time.

Simon was sleeping peacefully, snoring gently; a sound she had come to accept, knowing that he needed his sleep. It never disturbed her or stopped her from dropping off to sleep again. But not this time. A few minutes later she knew that she was definitely in labour, and that she must waken him.

'Simon… Simon…' She nudged him gently, and he stirred at once.

'What? What is it? Are you all right, darling?'

'Well, yes… I'm all right, but I think I've started. In fact I'm sure I have.'

'What? Started with the baby… I mean, babies? But you can't have. They're not due for another four weeks.'

She laughed. 'I don't think they know that! Oh… oh, help!' A sudden pain made her cry out. Instantly Simon was wide awake. He leapt out of bed.

'We'd better get moving; get you to hospital. Have you packed your bag, like they told you to?'

'Fortunately, yes. They advise you to get ready early, just in case…'

They scurried around, washing and dressing at speed. 'We'll have to wake the others,' said Simon. 'Our visitors. What a blessing it is that they're here. Do you think Debbie will be able to cope with Stella?'

'I'm sure she will,' said Fiona. 'And we must let Josh know what's happening.'

Simon knocked on the lads' bedroom door, and Fiona knocked and entered Debbie's room.

'Debbie, love. I'm sorry to disturb you…' The girl sleepily opened her eyes. 'I've started… in labour, so Simon's taking me to hospital. We don't know how long he'll stay there. Could you see to Stella's breakfast please, love?'

Debbie was sitting up now and listening intently.

'And see to her getting washed and dressed? She'll show you what to do!' Fiona laughed before she doubled up with another pain.

'Fiona!' Debbie jumped out of bed. 'Oh dear!' She put an arm round her. 'Are you all right?'

'Of course I am. It's quite normal, but we'd better get moving. You go back to bed. Stella won't wake till half past seven or so. Thank you, Debbie love. See you later…'

Simon alerted the young men and told them what was happening. 'Here's the curate's phone number,' he told

Greg. 'Ring him, about nine o'clock if I'm not back, and tell him to take charge. He's preaching today, so that's one less worry. I must dash now. Fiona's ready and waiting.'

They drove at speed to the hospital. At six o'clock in the morning there was nothing else on the road. Fiona's waters had broken as she got into the car so there was no time to lose.

It was all go when they arrived. Fiona was wheeled off to the maternity ward with Simon walking anxiously at the side of her. He was told, very politely, that he could wait in a side room whilst they attended to his wife. He gave her a quick kiss, then watched in a daze as she was wheeled away. It had all happened so quickly, and in a little while – not too long, he hoped – he would be the father of twins. He did not want to go back home. He knew that Debbie and the lads were quite capable of managing, and Stella was not likely to make a fuss because her mummy was not there. Simon wanted to be near his wife. Something, or somebody, was telling him that he must stay.

–

Fiona was soon in the second stage of labour. She had known what to expect as she had been through it all before. But this time it was happening very quickly. She was given an injection which eased the pain a little, and the gas and air helped.

'Push, Fiona, push, there's a good girl,' she was exhorted. A moment later there was the sensation that she remembered so well, of being torn apart. Then she heard the voice of the midwife.

'Well done, Fiona. It's a boy! A tiny one, but he's all right.' There was a feeble cry from the infant.

'Can I see him?' asked Fiona.

'Not just now, dear. We've not quite finished yet, have we?'

Fiona was exhausted by the first effort but there was no time to relax. A little while later – she could not tell how long; five, ten minutes? – she was told to push again. It seemed just a fraction easier this time as she felt the second baby slip out of her.

'Another boy!' said the midwife. 'Well done, Fiona; you've got twin sons. Isn't that great?'

Fiona smiled weakly. 'Are they both alright?'

'Yes... small, as we expected. But their lungs are working well,' said the doctor who was in attendance, as well as the midwife and an auxiliary nurse. 'Now, just the afterbirth, Fiona. You're doing splendidly.'

There was silence in the delivery room as the midwife and nurse looked after the babies. The doctor was staying close to Fiona. She lay still, exhausted but very contented. Twin boys! Simon would be pleased, she knew that. She heard the doctor's voice. 'Just a little push, dear, then it will all be over...' He hesitated, then he said, 'Here, nurse, if you please... I do believe... Yes, there's another one! Fiona, another big push, there's a good girl.'

She tried to do as she was asked, but she was unbelievably tired and felt that she had no strength left. She gave a shout. 'Oh... oh! What's happening?' as she felt another pain. Despite her weariness she had to push down again, and she felt something... slide out of her body.

'It's a little girl,' said the midwife in a hushed voice. 'Heavens above! Who'd have believed it?'

Fiona lay back, scarcely aware of what was happening. Then she heard the doctor's voice. 'Fiona, my dear, you've just given birth to a baby girl. You've had triplets! We had no idea… Just lie still whilst we see to everything.'

Fiona was feeling too drained and exhausted to think coherently. 'A little girl as well?' she whispered. 'Three babies…' Her eyes closed and she drifted off into unconsciousness.

'She's losing too much blood,' said the doctor. The afterbirth was released, but the haemorrhaging did not stop. 'She needs a blood transfusion. Quickly, nurse. Have you got her blood group?'

'Yes… it's group B.'

'Damn! That could prove tricky… We had that emergency yesterday, you know – the road accident – and I know we're running low. But you must go and tell the husband that he's got triplets. And… try not to scare him, but tell him his wife needs a blood transfusion… and that we're looking after her.'

'Triplets! I don't believe it!' exclaimed Simon, 'Three of them? Two boys and a girl? That's wonderful! May I see her now?'

'No, not just yet, Mr Norwood,' the nurse told him. 'Your wife lost quite a lot of blood – only to be expected, of course – and she's having a blood transfusion. Don't worry, she'll be fine, but it was necessary.'

'But Fiona has a rare blood group; well, quite uncommon, I believe. She's group B… Are you quite sure she'll be alright?' Simon knew that the doctors and nurses would do their best and that he should not interfere, but he suddenly felt extremely anxious about Fiona. It was something in the nurse's facial expression. She was smiling and trying to reassure him, but he had the sense that she might be keeping something back from him.

He knew he had to ask; if she thought he was out of order, then so be it. It was his beloved wife whom he feared might be in danger. 'Do you have enough... of group B blood?' he asked.

'Yes, of course,' she answered hurriedly, 'but it is, as you say, Mr Norwood, rather uncommon.' Then, of her own volition, the midwife asked, 'Does your wife have any relatives who might have the same blood group? It does run in families. It's not likely that yours is the same, I suppose?'

'No, I'm group O,' he replied. 'Fiona has no sister or brothers and her parents are dead.' A thought struck him. Could it be possible? He said a silent prayer that it might be so. He had a feeling that Fiona might need all the help she could get. 'She has a daughter,' he said. 'Debbie... she's not my daughter. She's sixteen. She's staying with us at the moment; but I don't know her blood group.'

He thought the midwife looked relieved. 'It's worth a try, Mr Norwood,' she said. She was smiling. He knew she was trying to reassure him. 'We are not worried, you understand, but it might be as well to find out. Could you contact Fiona's daughter... just in case?'

'Right away,' he said. 'She's at my home now, waiting for news, with... the rest of my family. I'll bring her back with me... if it is so... just in case, as you say. Please take care of Fiona, won't you? She means all the world to me.'

He drove home, not quite as speedily, although time was of the essence now. The two lads and Debbie looked up anxiously as he entered the kitchen. 'Daddy!' said Stella, holding out her arms to him. 'Where's Mummy?'

'I've told her she's gone to hospital,' said Debbie. 'She's been quite happy, but she doesn't understand.'

'Mummy's in hospital, darling,' he said. 'Like we told you, to get the babies.' He put her down again. 'Great news!' he said. The good news first, he decided. 'You'll never guess! Fiona's had... triplets! Two boys and a girl!'

There was an outcry of joy and excitement before they enquired about Fiona.

'I've not seen any of them yet,' said Simon. 'I'm afraid Fiona has lost quite a lot of blood. Only to be expected, but she was being given a blood transfusion when I left. Debbie... do you happen to know your blood group?'

'Of course,' she replied. 'I'm group B. I've given blood a few times, when there was an appeal. My mum persuaded me that it was something I could do, with it being rare. Why? Do you mean...? Fiona's not in any danger, is she?'

'No, I don't think so. But I got the impression that they weren't entirely happy. The nurse asked me about Fiona's relations, and their blood groups. Just in case, she said. But... Debbie, I think you had better come back with me, that is, if you're willing?'

'To give blood? For Fiona?' Simon saw tears forming in her eyes. 'Of course I will. Come on; let's go now!'

'I was just about to phone your curate,' said Greg. 'You said nine o'clock, didn't you?' It was just about nine now, and the table was strewn with the remnants of a hastily prepared breakfast.

'Don't tell him anything yet,' said Simon, 'except that Fiona's in hospital and I want him to hold the fort. Could you take Stella to the crèche, please... and ask Josh to say prayers for Fiona, although I know that he will. We'll save the news about the triplets for later.'

–

Simon could tell by the worried look on the nurse's face when they arrived back at the hospital that they had been waiting anxiously for Debbie.

'It's OK, she's group B,' said Simon.

'Well, that's good news,' said the nurse. 'Come along, my dear. If you could oblige us with a little of your blood we'd be most grateful.'

Debbie returned to where Simon was waiting about half an hour later. She didn't tell him, but she felt that they had taken rather more than a little. The nurse brought her a cup of hot sweet tea, which she sipped gratefully. She felt weak and wobbly, but it was partly because she was concerned about Fiona.

They waited together for what seemed ages. 'So I inherited Fiona's blood group,' said Debbie. 'I often wondered...'

'And thank God you did,' said Simon. 'I think you helped to save her life, Debbie. I don't know for sure, and they probably won't admit that there was a shortage of blood, but that is what I believe. I'm so glad you are a part of our family, Debbie. I know now that there was a purpose to it all. It was meant to be − "All things work together for good". I've always believed that to be true.'

The doctor appeared eventually. 'Your wife has come round, Mr Norwood,' he said. 'You may come and see her, only for a moment, you understand. She is still very tired. And you, of course, Debbie. We're very grateful to you for what you've been able to do. Fiona doesn't know yet. We'll tell her when she's a little stronger.'

Fiona opened her eyes as they entered the room. She gave a weak smile but her eyes shone with happiness. Simon bent to kiss her gently whilst Debbie hung back. This was a time for husband and wife.

'We have three babies, Simon,' said Fiona. 'I can hardly believe it.'

'It's true, my darling,' he said. 'But you are all right, and that's the main thing. And here is Debbie to see you...'

Debbie kissed Fiona's cheek. 'Congratulations!' she said. 'Two boys and a girl! It couldn't be better. Stella's got a sister and two brothers.'

'You mean two sisters and three brothers,' said Fiona. She sounded tired, but her mind was as alert as ever.

'We must go now,' said Simon. 'Doctor's orders, but I'll be back later. God bless you, my darling... I love you,' he added.

'Would you like to come and see the babies, Mr Norwood?' said the midwife.

He and Debbie followed her to the special unit for premature babies. They were in three separate cots, tiny little infants, like small baby dolls, their heads no larger than a tennis ball, with a fine covering of downy hair. There were tubes attached to them, but the nurse assured them that it was normal procedure. They were doing well and there was no cause for alarm, but they would need to stay in the hospital for a few weeks until they were stronger and had gained sufficient weight to be allowed home.

'It's a miracle,' whispered Simon. 'Birth is always a miracle... but three of them! It's an unbelievable blessing. Come along, Debbie. Let's go and spread the good news!'

Epilogue

There was great rejoicing at the service on that Sunday evening when the congregation heard that their rector's wife had given birth to triplets. They were told that mother and the babies were all going well, but it would be several days before Fiona was home again, and several weeks before the babies could leave hospital.

–

Simon and Fiona decided to wait until the spring for the christening – or baptism, as some preferred to call it – of the three babies. It took place at the end of April when spring had really arrived. The trees around the church were almost in full leaf, the pale green of springtime, when they were at their loveliest. The gardens were bright with daffodils, narcissi and tulips, and vases of these flowers adorned the communion table and the window ledges of the church. There was no fear of rain coming in as the work on the church roof was now completed. As it happened, though, it was a gloriously sunny day.

The church was packed for the triplets' christening service, even more so than it had been for that of little Stella. There was to be a family gathering at the rectory afterwards for the immediate friends and family, but the baptism itself was for the wider family of the church.

Simon had asked Joshua, the curate, to officiate as he wanted to be a godparent to his infants, along with Fiona.

It was really only a formality as to how many godparents each child should have. Simon and Fiona had been in perfect agreement about who they should choose as godmother and godfathers. Each of them, before consulting the other, had decided upon Debbie, Greg and Graham. Who else could they choose who would be as fitting? They had all been there on that weekend when the triplets had been born, and Debbie had played her own special part.

It was a real family occasion – their extended family, as Fiona called it – with Vera and Stanley, Debbie's parents, in the congregation. They were delighted to have been invited; and so was Grace, the sister of Greg and Graham. Yvonne was not there, as she was on honeymoon with her new husband.

Debbie, Greg and Graham each held a baby in their arms, the young men rather gingerly, though Debbie was proud and confident. She looked down lovingly at the child she was holding. She had a definite look of Fiona now that her features were forming, and of herself, too, Debbie reflected. They stood forward in turn handing the babies to Joshua. He made the sign of the cross on each tiny forehead with the water from the baptismal font. They were given their names, Matthew, Mark, and Michelle.

What lovely names, thought Debbie; and how touched she had been when Fiona had asked her to be a godmother to the babies. She turned to smile at Fiona, and at Stella, holding on to her mummy's hand. Fiona smiled back. The two of them knew that they now had a very special bond. Then she smiled at her parents who were sitting in the front pew. Vera and Stanley looked proud and happy. They smiled back lovingly, both of them nodding contentedly. How well they understood her...